Flame of Mercy

ELEANOR BERTIN

Author photo by Hayley Leschert, Out of the Barrel Photography

Cover art by Roseanna M. White, www.RoseannaWhiteDesigns.com

Published by Leaf & Blade Publishing, Big Valley, Canada

Library and Archives Canada
Cataloguing in Publication

Bertin, Eleanor, author

Flame of Mercy / Eleanor Bertin.

Issued in print and electronic formats.

ISBN 978-1-7771825-3-3 (paperback)

Welcome to The Mosaic Collection

We are sisters, a beautiful mosaic united by
the love of God through the blood of Christ.

Each month The Mosaic Collection releases one
faith-based novel or anthology exploring our theme, Family by His
Design, and
sharing stories that feature diverse, God-designed families. All are
contemporary stories ranging from mystery and women's fiction to
comedic and
literary fiction. We hope you'll join our Mosaic family as we explore
together
what truly defines a family.

If you're like us, loneliness and suffering
have touched your life in ways you never imagined; but Dear One,

while you may
feel alone in your suffering—whatever it is—you are never alone!

Subscribe to *Grace & Glory*, the
official newsletter of The Mosaic Collection, to receive monthly
encouragement
from Mosaic authors, as well as timely updates about events, new
releases, and
giveaways.

Learn more about The Mosaic Collection at
www.mosaiccollectionbooks.com

Join our Reader Community, too!
www.facebook.com/groups/TheMosaicCollection

Books in The Mosaic Collection

Tethered by Eleanor Bertin
Calm Before the Storm by Janice L. Dick
Heart Restoration by Regina Rudd Merrick
Pieces of Granite by Brenda S. Anderson
Watercolors by Lorna Seilstad
A
Star Will Rise: A Mosaic Christmas Anthology II
Eye of the Storm by Janice L. Dick
Totally Booked: A Book Lover's Companion
Lifelines by Eleanor Bertin
The Third Grace by Deb Elkink
Crazy About Maisie by Janice L. Dick
Rebuilding Joy by Regina Rudd Merrick
Song of Grace: Stories to Amaze the Soul
Written in Ink by Sara Davison
Open Circle by Stacy Monson
Where Hope Starts by Angela D. Meyer
Flame of Mercy by Eleanor Bertin
Through the Lettered Veil by Candace West
Broken Together by Brenda S. Anderson

Learn more at www.mosaiccollectionbooks.com/mosaic-books

To my daughter Becky,
who, like her namesake, my sister,
had a heart for God from a young age
and inspired the character, Lynnie.

Ihsan adjusted his hat against the powerful glare of the Nigerian sun and sank to a crouch beneath the closest tree. A slight movement caught his eye. Below the plateau, on the road coming from the village, a vehicle inched along. Ihsan's nerves tingled a warning. Farther north on the road, a puff of powdery dun-coloured dirt rose and he could hear the distant sound of shouts.

"Fulani," someone hissed. "Look."

Like watching a child run into the path of an oncoming truck, a collision was inevitable.

This did not bode well.

Amid the clouds of dust, the notorious herdsmen appeared, storming the lone vehicle. Their shouts were louder now, angry. Rocks popped against the metal of the vehicle. A faint tinkle of glass breaking. From the heights where Ihsan and his fellow villagers crouched, they held in a collective breath, and they watched.

Chapter 1

I went out full, but the Lord has brought me back empty.
~Ruth 1:21

Potholed tarmac slid by in the shadow of our Lufthansa plane as it gained speed and taxied for takeoff from Lagos Murtala Muhammed airport. A giant lump in my throat matched the rock in my belly, a rock of remembrance that had been weighing me down for the past twenty-four days.

How could it be a mere four years since the Lynnie I used to be had arrived here in Nigeria, the land of overwhelming contrasts? The cacophony of sounds and smells and colours in its close and crowded bustle clashed in every way with my upbringing and personality. How had a home-loving, introverted, Canadian prairie girl like me ever come to such a place? And more astonishing still, how had a girl like me ever found her cozy niche and fit in so well?

I put it down to the books my Grandma Hardy gave me for Christmas when I was eleven. Earlier, my mom's mother, Nanny Roundell, had picked up on my love for reading and presented me with a bunch of fantasy novels. Not being literary, Nanny bought books with titles that appealed to her. My sister Lissa and I devoured them at a ferocious rate in those days, and Nanny kept up an ample supply. But in the subtle Battle of the Grandmothers that we kids were all too familiar with, when Grandma H. caught a glimpse of the "sensuous" fairy on one of the covers, her customary sober expression deepened into a disapproving glare.

"'Whatsoever things are true, whatsoever things are pure,' Evelyn." As always, she used my full name. Being the first grandchild, I was named after her and she took it as a personal affront that a perfectly classic name should be submitted to the indignity of what she considered a cutesy diminutive.

"'If there be any virtue, think on these things,'" she stated firmly, and just as firmly confiscated the fantasy novels. Most of the time, Grandma let our parents do the heavy rowing of parenting, but on occasions when she thought our souls were in mortal danger, she had no qualms about sticking in her oar. So that day, she gathered the paperbacks, carried them to the kitchen garbage, and dumped them in. She even scanned the counter tops for a suitably disgusting substance with which to smother them. Finding a bowl of solidified bacon grease, she scraped that onto the offending volumes.

Lissa was furious. She gave off waves of resentment like a kettle emits steam as she stormed out of the room. I, too, was stunned at Grandma's extreme reaction, though not angry. Perhaps that was because deep down I knew those books consumed my entire thought life, even making the Bible uninteresting. I had ignored my pangs of conscience and idled instead of doing anything about it, telling myself the novels were harmless fun. Trust Grandma to do something about it for me. And come Christmas, she did something else about it. A complete series of hardcover missionary biographies appeared under the Christmas tree for me and Lissa that year. They were lovely books and looked distinguished on our bookshelf.

"Thank you, Grandma," I dutifully said after unwrapping the package. But though my parents had trained me to tell her how I would use the gift, my words stalled. Lissa shot me one of her looks, but I turned away before she could either remind me to be mad or worse, make me laugh.

The covers of these books didn't feature the airbrushed fairies and mystical forests that drew me in without fail. They weren't even fiction. But only a rural kid who's run out of library books before the end of Christmas vacation can understand the book-desperation it took to get me to crack open a missionary biography. Knowing Grandma, it wouldn't be long before she asked for a full report, too. Grandma had been a schoolteacher before marrying my grandpa, so she tended to be rigorous in having us think about what we read.

I hadn't expected to find the biographies interesting, let alone enjoy them. Lissa never cared for them and read only two under duress, at Mom's insistence. But after reading the first one, I was hooked. There was something about the drive of these men and women, many of whom had devoted themselves at a young age to spreading the gospel in Asia, central America, Africa, and around the world. They were gifted young people who could have achieved any number of amazing accomplishments but chose to spend their lives with the poor, the illiterate, and the often ungrateful. They gave up wealth and comfort, fame and families to live in mud huts, struggle to learn new languages, treat the sick, and translate the Bible. Many of them left home never to see their families again. They suffered disease and the loss of children or spouses, and even gave their own lives because of their work. Their selfless sacrifice lit in me a fire of admiration and longing.

Grandma let me have an old map of the world I found rolled up in the closet of her guest room. I tacked it to the wall next to my bed and, lying there on bright summer nights, I studied it. I cut *National Geographic* pictures of faces from different people groups around the world and stuck them on the countries where they belonged. I looked up things like the weather and the geography of whichever was my favourite country that week and found out what languages they spoke. Grandma had lots of magazines and missionary newsletters that told about the progress of Bible translation all over the globe and I ate them up. As I got older, the wall above my bunk became a stark contrast to Lissa's wall, plastered with photos from teen magazines and the latest music and movie stars. Maybe that pinpoints where our paths separated. Grandma's approving nod at my interests and her frown at Lissa's likely didn't help.

One of the things this new obsession gave me was legitimacy. When I was in middle school, my teacher had gone around the classroom asking us what we wanted to be when we grew up. Mrs. Gillis added her encouraging comments to each one. When my turn came, I naively told the truth. I wanted to be a mom. After a split-second silence, the whole class burst out laughing. The heat shot up my neck in acute embarrassment. Even Mrs. Gillis smiled. She said nothing but simply went on to the next kid. I was crushed. It didn't change my dream, but it did drive it underground.

My fascination with missions gave a new focus to my life. Now I wanted to be a missionary wife and mother. And though I left off the wife and mother part when anyone asked, and the term missionary at times brought blank stares, at least no one laughed. All my extracurricular studying of geography, linguistics and history didn't hurt my grades, either.

Something staggered me though. For all my fervent enthusiasm for foreign parts, how was I ever to overcome what I hadn't been able to conquer in the normal rites of childhood? I was a homebody in the extreme. I loved my family and felt safe and comfortable with them. I had become so ill in the first few weeks of kindergarten that my parents had given up and kept me out of school. After three years of homeschooling, I did attend the small local public school, though stomachaches plagued me, and I often had to stay home because of them. Over the years, I got used to the brief separation of the school day, but while Lissa eagerly anticipated overnights with cousins, I stayed home. I never did attend summer camp, though each of my siblings regaled me with the fun they'd had there. None of this extreme dependence had disappeared in my teens. More and more, it worried me. I felt called to a helping vocation, but I was paralyzed by a fear of leaving my family. It didn't make sense that God would have put two such conflicting motivations inside me.

Then a seismic shock caused a shift in my family. The day after she turned eighteen, Lissa eloped with her boyfriend Mark. Overnight, Mom and Dad lost confidence. They became tentative in their treatment of my brother, kid sister, and me. My mother's eyes were often shadowed when she spoke to us. As if she feared offending us, though I can't imagine she ever did.

My sister's running away had a different effect on me. It left me with a strange restlessness. I didn't like to admit I was jealous, but I had always thought I would be the first to be married, something that would happen in the distant future. After all, neither of us was even out of our teens yet. But more than that, her leaving home had suddenly dropped the question of my future into my lap, hot and pressing. I had worked at Velvet's Tea Room part-time since high school and nannied for a couple of local families and had been content with that. But now I felt a vague shame at my resume, though I had no idea how to proceed. The logical step would have been short-term missions but leaving home—that was the rub.

I wasn't alone in thinking about my future. Soon after the elopement, following a Sunday dinner at Nanny's, she asked me to join my parents and her in the living room while the younger kids went downstairs. She looked from one to the other of us and smiled her apple-cheeked smile.

"I believe it's time Lyn got out and met some young people. We don't want the same thing happening to her as happened with Lissa." She looked at me next. "Such a smart girl. You should go to university and find a career." Nanny wasn't what you'd call a die-hard feminist. She wasn't a die-hard anything. But she'd been abandoned by her husband when my mom was a newborn, and the bitterness she tried to hide surfaced at times. That day's advice was candy coated and accompanied by a loving pat on the cheek with her soft hand, but her message was unmistakable. Don't be dependent on a man, look out for yourself first. In the next year, her urgings grew to insistence. I didn't bother to explain to her my goals. Having no interest in religious matters, she wouldn't have understood.

When Grandma Hardy began making the same suggestions, though, my parents and I took notice. She insisted I fill out an online application to a well-known local Christian college that had a Missions program. She even offered to fund half the tuition. I agreed to do it but a war still raged inside me that I needed to win.

And look where that got me.

Chapter 2

Rise up, O men of God!
Have done with lesser things;
Give heart and soul and mind and
strength
To serve the King of Kings.
~Rise Up, O Men of God! by William P. Merrill, 1867-1954

I took a fortifying breath and forced myself to take firm steps into summer school class the May after my second year of college. I wanted the extra credit and found out the school offered a summer linguistics program. Being a day student during the school year, I was at a slight disadvantage getting to know people, but I'd found a small set of friends through a couple of student groups I was active in. Now everything would be new again. At least I had more confidence than I'd felt as a freshman. Still, I arrived early, a self-protective habit I'd developed to allow time for choosing the perfect seat—not too near the front so as not to be called on by the prof but near enough to hear and see the lecture notes.

That spring day, only one other student had arrived ahead of me. I found a seat on the opposite side of the classroom from him and opened my binder to the syllabus. From the corner of my eye, I sensed movement. He hoisted his laptop and shoulder bag and moved to my side of the room. The seat beside me, in fact. I shifted away and scrutinized the course outline as though it were the most riveting document ever. I felt him watching me.

He cleared his throat.

I blushed and wiped the dampness from my hand in my hoodie pocket.

"What's the hobbitses got in its pocketses?" he asked.

The Tolkien line made me burst forth with an unladylike laugh. I covered my mouth with my hand and turned toward him at last. Anyone quoting Tolkien was an instant friend.

"You're a fan, I take it?" He lifted one eyebrow.

Nodding and still giggling, I scanned my classmate. I didn't recognize him from previous years and wondered why a freshman would be taking a third-year course. His wiry black hair was long in the front but trimmed tight above the ears and when he smiled, a pair of endearing divots appeared in his cheeks. Also, he had a cleft chin. I thought of the silly "dream guy" lists Lissa and I used to make. Mine had always included "cleft chin."

His black eyes held mine with an intensity that made me blush. Could he see what I was thinking?

"James Min," he said, sticking out his hand.

I pulled mine out of my pocket and shook his. "Lyn Hardy."

His hand was wide and strong. "I assume you're in this class for the same reason I am?" he asked, shifting in the desk to face me.

"Uh, what?" I stammered. *Real clever, Lyn.* "I mean, probably to understand language, right?" *Better still, girl.*

"You mean this isn't Elvish 201?" With a worried frown, he rifled through papers in his leather bag, then looked up at me again and chuckled.

I laughed, liking him, and relaxed a notch.

I discovered he was an IT student but was taking this course at the insistence of his mother.

"I was a problem child and gave my mom a lot of grief when I was a teen," he told me. "I figure since I wore out her knees praying for me all these years, taking this course is the least I can do."

This was heartening news. "So you're here to please your mom. Do you have any personal interest in it?"

"I do indeed. There was a presentation at my church last fall about Bible translation and that's all it took. I mean, the looks on the faces of those people in the video, getting the word of God in their own language for the first time ever, crying and hugging the books to themselves." He shook his head. "Almost made me want to switch majors and start over again. I'd like to see if there's some way I could combine my tech skills with translation work. So what brought you to linguistics?"

"It's been an interest of mine since I was about eleven." I hesitated. The warm openness on his face invited me to trust him. "I've always wanted to be a missionary..."

He nodded, so I took an even greater risk.

"...and a wife and mother." I watched his face for reaction, surprised by my own boldness. It was a test, of sorts, and would tell me something important about him.

His eyes narrowed and he half smiled. I took this as contempt and my heart sank, wishing I hadn't added the personal part.

After what seemed a long pause, he said, "That's a noble calling. I've never met a girl who would admit it, even though my mom says all women want that, deep down inside."

I let out a relieved breath and grinned. "I'm starting to like your mom, although I don't know whether that's true of *all* women."

His smile faded. "I was beginning to believe there weren't any at all who thought that way. I can't imagine any of the girls in my university tech courses wanting to get married and have children."

"Maybe there's more to them than meets the eye. I learned a long time ago that it was social suicide to mention it out loud."

"Pitiful, isn't it? No one should ever have to be embarrassed about doing what's right."

From then on, we sat together every class and like everything, he made them an adventure. He asked thoughtful questions of the prof and loosened everyone up, making them laugh. I was a moth to his flame. We ate our lunches together and began taking long walks around the spring-blooming campus talking about our love for God and hopes for the future. He challenged me to memorize scripture, and I started to use my commute time to recite small portions that were precious to me.

"My mom said that if she was going to help pay for my education, I had to memorize a book of the Bible for every year of my degree." He gave a sheepish smile. "I started with the shortest book I could find, Second John. But after a while, it got easier and became a habit. I think it's the reason I got through university with my faith intact. Right now, I'm on chapter twelve of Romans."

"Meaning you've memorized all the way through from chapter one?" I thought I had done well by committing lists of topical verses and several psalms to memory.

"Yup. You wanna hear it?"

I thought he was joking but he wasn't. Often on our walks he would hand me a Bible and ask me to check his progress as he recited to me. James brought up theological matters that he was wrestling through, questioning me with such an intensity that I was sometimes near tears. In fact, one afternoon as we headed down the bike path, I joked, "I wonder what I'm going to cry about today."

He stopped and stared at me. "What do you mean? I thought you enjoyed talking about the Bible as much as I do."

"I do." Now I felt silly. "It's just that, I haven't always thought about things as deeply as you have. And I can't articulate what I believe as well as you can. Sometimes I think, can't we just love Jesus without going into all these issues?"

"But it's important to know why you believe." His eyes glowed as he launched into a discussion of predestination and free will.

I cried during that one because his ideas were different from what I had grown up hearing, especially from Grandma who had strong views on such matters. Yet his points were so well supported by the scriptures he showed me that I couldn't argue.

All the same, I looked forward to our talks and, as the end of June and our last linguistics class loomed ahead, I dreaded not seeing James anymore. I found myself hoping he felt the same way. He never held my hand or put his arm around me, which I appreciated since I had set some parameters for myself years earlier. But it left me without any hint about his feelings for me. I noticed he was careful never to talk about a mutual future together, except for one passing comment about the importance of being like-minded for the purpose of ministry. I held onto that as a clue that he was thinking of a ministry the two of us might go into together.

I had told my parents about James early on but had kept the relationship close to my heart, not sharing with my siblings or grandmothers. I wanted time to consider whether James might in fact be the one God had for me. Yet it was growing harder to keep secret something that was filling my heart to bursting.

"I've met someone," I told Lissa one Sunday when she and Mark and their babies had come over for dinner.

She gave me a wry look. "Well, it's about time. Does this guy check off all the boxes from your impossibly long and ridiculously unrealistic dream guy list?"

I scrutinized her face to see if she was patronizing me as she sometimes did. But she wore a smile that softened her words.

"Mostly," I said, excitement bubbling up inside me. I could hardly contain myself.

"So, out with it already. What's he like?"

"Well," I began, not knowing where to start in recounting all James's great qualities, yet not wanting to gush, "he's not all that tall, and he doesn't have the auburn hair I used to think was a must.

And he's from Toronto, so he doesn't farm next door to us like I hoped for, but—"

"Girl!" Lissa laughed. "This better not be one of your charity cases. Always bringing home the nerdiest friends, like bedraggled stray kittens. You're such an empath you used to feel sorry for the number four because the number five seemed mean. Haven't I warned you about falling for the first guy that comes along just 'cause you feel sorry for him?"

"I do not feel sorry for him." Heat rose up my neck. "There's nothing to feel sorry for. He's super smart. He just graduated summa cum laude in computer engineering. And he's witty and outgoing and everybody loves him. He even has a cleft chin. The best part is that he loves Jesus and wants to use his tech skills to serve God."

That last bit sobered Lissa as I expected it would. When I was baptized at age twelve, Lissa had refused Grandma's urging to do the same and my sister had shown no interest in God or the Bible for a long time.

"Great then. I'm happy for you." She picked up baby Dylan from his car seat though he hadn't started to fuss.

I hoped she meant it. I wanted everyone to like James the way I did.

Chapter 3

I'll go where You want me to go, dear Lord,
O'er mountain or plain or sea;
I'll say what You want me to say, dear Lord,
I'll be what You want me to be.

~I'll Go Where You Want Me to Go, by Mary Brown, 19th century

So there I was, nine years later on a plane that rattled my teeth as it sped along the rutted runway.

"Bumpy-wumpy," my three-year-old, Josie, would have said.

The memory caught in my throat. At last, we lifted off, and I was cut from the continent to which I was irrevocably bound, barred from my Eden by a sword of flame. I leaned back in the seat, reached up to switch off the overhead cabin light, and shut my eyes, knowing I wouldn't sleep. My thoughts roamed back to those treasured days of falling in love.

I had feared that my friendship with James might end along with the last linguistics class. But while I was washing breakfast dishes at home one summer day shortly after the final exam, my dad beckoned to me to take a ride with him in the tractor. This was standard procedure for Dad when he had something important to discuss with us. Lissa had dreaded the rides, but since I rarely got reprimanded, I had nothing to fear. Though I was curious. I was now twenty-two years old with a clear path through the next two years of college. I couldn't imagine what my dad had to talk to me about.

"Beautiful day for haying," Dad commented as we pulled out of the yard in the tractor, me in the small jump-seat at his side.

I waited for him to get to the point, enjoying the faint smell of diesel, the rumble of the machine beneath us, and the view ahead where the green and purple haze of the alfalfa field met the clear blue of summer sky.

He pointed to the field's edge on the left as we chugged past a stand of young bushes covered in red berries. "Should be a good crop of saskatoons in a couple weeks."

I peeked at him and caught him peering back at me.

"What?" I asked with a growing curiosity. I figured I was out here with him for a reason. Why wasn't he getting to the point?

Dad appeared to be focused on the bluff of poplars at the far end of the field, chewing on his lower lip. At last he blurted, "What do you think of James Min?"

I cranked my head to face him. "Why?" The way he asked the question set my heart thudding.

He only smiled, which sent my mind racing in every direction.

I clutched his arm, staring at him. "Why do you ask?"

"I got a call from him about a week ago."

"Oh no, oh no, oh no." I moaned, tipping back in my cramped seat. Nervous excitement tied my insides in knots. I could only think of one reason James might have called my father. Could James have called Dad to ask ... what? *To marry me? Whoa, girl. Don't get ahead of yourself!*

"So you don't like him much."

"What?" I cried, thrills of anticipation battling inside me against a cowering fear of the unknown. "Yes. I mean, no. I mean, I do. I like him a lot."

"Hmm."

"Dad! Just tell me already! What are you talking about?"

Dad chuckled. "Seems you have a suitor."

I rolled my eyes at the medieval term but the butterflies in my belly went wild. I shook his arm.

"My Lynnie-girl." He put his arm around me and squeezed my shoulder. "Your James seems like a fine young man. It's just that I find I'm not ready to let you go."

"Let me go?" My words came out as a squeak. Now I had to know what was said in that phone call. I pulled away to fix Dad with an expectant stare.

He sighed. "James called last Friday morning. He gave me some background on himself, his upbringing, his values and beliefs. Then he asked my permission to get to know you better. I believe his exact words were 'with a view to the possibility of a future together.'"

"He said that? A future together?"

Dad nodded. "I must say, he's a confident and well-spoken young fellow. I'd have been stammering all over myself if I'd made a call like that back in the day." His eyes twinkled. "But if you're not interested, I'll just tell him to be on his way..."

"Don't you dare!"

My dad smiled silently again.

That was how it began for James and me. We soon fell into a pattern of evening phone calls when James was home from work. And he drove up on weekends. He helped with harvest, eager to learn to operate the combine or grain cart. Dad and my brother Lance were impressed with how quickly he caught on. His tech skills even came in handy once when the combine GPS acted up.

He played games with my niece and nephew even when the rest of us were too tired after a day of working in the field. Mom appreciated his good manners and Nanny was impressed with his job at an oil company in Calgary, which she was certain must be "worth a pot-full."

At Thanksgiving, he brought his violin, but I asked my younger sister, Katie, to accompany him on the piano as he played. I was proficient but not talented the way Katie was, even as a young teen. Our whole family was enthralled by the music he drew out of those strings, and I saw Grandma's face soften as she closed her eyes to listen.

"You're really good," Mom said when he finished the piece. "Why didn't you pursue music at university?"

James relaxed his grip on the violin, grinning. "I talked to a few musicians struggling to find work." He tucked the instrument under his chin again, nodding to Katie to choose another song.

"Is there anything he isn't good at?" Lissa whispered to me while we listened.

I blushed with the pleasure of how this man had won over my family. I knew long before he proposed that I would follow him to the ends of the earth.

What I didn't know was how far those ends of the earth would turn out to be.

One Wednesday morning during fall reading week, I felt a presence behind me as I tried to focus on my Early Childhood Psych text. I dropped the book and snapped my head around, coming face to face with James's welcome grin. I gasped in surprise, trying to cover my tattered sweatpants with the large book.

"I don't know anyone else who actually reads during reading week," he said, straightening up.

"What are you doing here? Why aren't you at work?"

"Uh, your dad waves to me from the tractor and your mom welcomes me into the house. But all I get from you is, 'Why aren't you at work?'" He laughed. "I have the day off so I figured I'd come up and see you. Wanna go for a drive?"

I glanced at Mom and caught her smiling strangely before she snatched opened a cupboard door, apparently transfixed by a stack of dinner plates.

"Okay. Let me get changed first though."

Filled with confusion, I dashed up the stairs. Something was up and I was sure it wasn't only my heart rate.

Over giant cinnamon rolls at Velvet's Tea Room in town, I brought up an ethical question discussed in one of my courses, but James seemed distracted. From there, we set off for a drive up to the lake.

James glanced at me. "You're quiet."

"I'm always quiet."

"More so today."

I wanted to ask what was up, yet I didn't want to presume, in case it was nothing. So I smiled at him and remained silent.

We walked out to the end of the dock where the wind was lashing the water into whitecaps. I couldn't help shivering and would have welcomed his arm around me, but when James noticed, he simply suggested we hurry back to the car. Soon we were on the road again and I was still shivering, not from cold but from nerves. What was all this about, James's sudden visit in the middle of the week, the odd look from Mom? Twilight was encroaching, and we were nearly back at my home.

Abruptly, James eased the car off the highway into the treed lane of an abandoned farm site and parked. Before us, the western sky glowed in a golden panorama.

"Lyn." James pulled up his knee, angling toward me.

My chest started hammering as I stared at the horizon. He cupped my chin in his hand, pulling my gaze to meet his. It was the first intentional physical contact he had ever made, and it sent a tingle through my body.

He took both my hands in his. "When I saw you sitting across the room from me last spring, I had the strangest sense that you were the girl meant for me. You know by now I don't hold to a lot of mystical experience stuff. But it was unmistakable. And as I've gotten to know you, and to love you—"

A flush of heat flooded my cheeks.

"—I was beyond grateful to God for His good idea. You are everything I've ever hoped for in a woman and I... His grip on my hands grew tighter as he searched my face. "Would you marry me?"

I have always had trouble making decisions. My family used to tease me that if some guy ever proposed to me, I would dither so long he'd grow old and die before I answered. But I had not even a smidgen of hesitation now. "With all my heart, yes!"

I never had any doubts that I had given the right answer.

By February, Mom had to prod me into planning the wedding, scheduled for May when I would be finished my third year of college. I made no secret to them or to James that I was nervous about leaving home for good. I also didn't relish being the centre of attention or making extra work for my parents, so I envisioned the simplest of ceremonies. But with Lissa's elopement, my parents had missed out hosting a wedding for the whole church and community, and it seemed they wanted to make up for it with ours. I wasn't ungrateful, but there were a few things I dug in my heels over. I mean, more than my two sisters as bridesmaids was unnecessary. So was a lot of the frou-frou that can produce enough stress to transform nice girl into Bridezilla. Somehow, we ended up with a simple but special celebration that pleased everyone.

I think my family was amazed at how I adjusted to married life. We rented a condo in a town halfway between the city where James worked and my college. James wasn't ready to purchase a home because now his mind was on foreign missions, and he wanted to have the flexibility to go when the opportunity arose. I finished the final year of my degree, having trouble at times in keeping up my previous grade-point average because my heart was thrown into homemaking and being a wife to James. I loved furnishing our cozy space and finding new recipes to try on my husband. It almost edged out my homesickness for my family, though we saw them every weekend.

When James found out about a Bible translation project going on in Nigeria he was captivated. I understood, perhaps even before he did, that from that moment, we were destined for Africa.

The program had started when a group of Nigerian pastors, representing hundreds of different language groups, found out other nationals in Africa were translating scripture for themselves. The Nigerians called for special Bible translation technology so they could translate scripture into their own languages. It was a huge boost in speeding up the work of translating the three-hundred-some Nigerian languages that still didn't have even a line of the Bible. For months, James talked about nothing else after he came home from work or on weekends. I was genuinely excited for him. But in quiet moments, I found myself perplexed by my wariness.

I had always pictured myself as a missionary in some Asian country, which might have been one of the reasons I was drawn to James and his Korean heritage. I had never been all that flexible when it came to new experiences and having to switch my sights to Africa caught me off guard.

While he was eager to press ahead and plan, I was conflicted with what my vocation was to be there. It was clear he was uniquely suited to the role of tech support for the project. But what was I called to do? Then I came across words by Martin Luther that answered my questions. "How is it possible that you have not been called? You are already a wife, a child, a daughter... Nobody is without command and calling ... God's eyes look not upon the works, but on the obedience in the work." Eventually, I found contentment in my behind-the-scenes role as helper to James, communicator to our supporters at home, and, before long, mama to the sweetest baby ever.

Chapter 4

When for my deep grief I find no relief
Though my tears flow all the night long...
~Does Jesus Care? by Frank E. Graeff, 1860-1919

When we were descending on Lagos, Nigeria for the first time, four years ago, eager for an African adventure, James had leaned across me to drink in the panoramic view of the exotic land below the clouds. My overly exuberant husband. Even after sixteen hours of flights and layovers, and the baggage confusion in Addis Ababa, he couldn't wait to take in every detail of his new assignment. I, on the other hand, was beyond exhausted. We were still unaware of the third member of our family, though she was beginning to make her presence felt in tiredness. And we still had a day's drive north in a jouncy Jeep before we would arrive at our new home at the center for translation in Jos.

Our term was for five years. We were that close to finishing and going home. Like I used to do as a girl the day before Christmas, I had begun in advance to grieve the ending of something special. I dreaded the prospect of goodbyes to precious friends, favourite foods, and the vibrancy of life there. Because it hadn't taken long to be welcomed into Nigerian culture. Our church and neighbourhood enfolded us into a snug hug of life together so quickly it was as though I had grown up there. This ever-present embrace of community was something I had known sporadically while growing up in rural central Alberta. At funerals, or when someone's house had burned down, and the like. It wasn't that my Canadian family and friends were cold and distant, far from it. But Africa was different. For one thing, in Nigeria, Africa's fastest growing nation, people were everywhere. A cynic might have doubted their effusive ways, their lavish use of endearments. I was always Lynnie Darling as though that were my middle name. And I couldn't help reciprocating.

Now I was returning from Africa alone.

Somewhere above the Atlantic on the trip back to Canada, I was suspended between two worlds, no longer belonging to either one. Beside me, our mission director, Dr. Lachlan, had fallen into an open-mouthed snore. But for me, sleepless in my first-class seat, I had hours to ruminate and remember.

The anguished, wet faces of my beautiful, brown friends crowding the doorway of my house await my response. I can't look at them, as they stand there suffering in swollen-hearted sympathy. Instead, I hold back the shriek that wants to force its way up my throat, and I flee through the back door. When that scream finally blasts out of my mouth it is followed by another and more. The shrill sound streams out behind me as I stumble through the rutted alleys of Jos. If it were visible, it would look like a pillar of dark cloud. It vents from my mouth like the steam from the street vendors' chicken-plucking vats in the marketplace. I storm through, heedless of the sharp or sympathetic words and outstretched arms of the strangers I pass. Like an actress in a movie, I race crazily, directionless. But this is no movie. I wish it were.

Later, when Pastor Sam catches up with me, I follow him, meek and misty as a spent raincloud, back to his and Judith's home. All through the evening, Judith and their daughter Ebos and my friend Damaris soothe and stroke me like they did both times I was in labour.

"Lynnie," they urged me then, *"let your body do its work. Sink into the pain."*

And obediently I sank into that peaking ring of fire that would yield my greatest joy.

Now they say, "Let it out. Let the tears fall." And I whimper and wail, sinking into this new, fruitless pain. This unrelenting contraction of soul and spirit that has no peak and no end and can yield nothing other than more of its kind.

But the Nigerian way is a marvel. That night I sleep the slumber of the exhausted.

What happens in Africa stays in Africa. But did I want it to? Did I want to leave my friends, my life, my belonging to this place that at first, I had found foreign and inscrutable? Because now to leave Africa meant I must leave behind my home, my identity, my very lifeblood.

On my way out of the bright continent, the trip south to the international airport in Lagos was a quiet one. Dr. Lachlan, the mission's Canadian director, paid our driver, then guided me through the negotiation of tickets, luggage, and customs. His hand steering my elbow at times was a comfort, even as I steeled myself against the memories of the last time I had been to the terminal. Back then, I had been filled with weary but curious anticipation. Now I was full of the knowledge of good and evil and the sword of flame that lay behind me. It seemed almost unendurable.

After we boarded, the mission director let me into the seat next to the window, then settled his bony frame beside me. I was grateful for the extra comfort of first class, an extravagance insisted upon and provided for by my home church congregation. "It's the least we can do," they told Dr. Lachlan and he repeated to me, "with all she has to bear."

Out of respect, or perhaps uncertainty, he hadn't said much since the day he arrived at my house in Jos. By then, the electrifying news that sent me ranting through the streets had run its course. I was calm, drained for the moment but bracing for the next gush of hot tears. But more than anything, I felt rushed. I craved time, unhurried by the urgent, to examine this gaping hole that had opened in my life.

The day Dr. Lachlan knocked at my door, I had been folding twenty-month-old Anya's onesie. It had pink raccoons on it, one of a set printed with Canadian wildlife that I'd received in the mail from my sister, Katie. According to its postmark, it had taken three months to arrive. It was a good thing Katie had sent eighteen-month and not newborn size.

After Pastor Sam answered the door and ushered the director in, I returned to my careful task, smoothing the tiny garment. When I found a lump between the folds, I shook it out and refolded it. The stubborn bulge of seam refused to cooperate. I tried again and again, concentrating on this vital task as though my baby's life depended on it. I folded it fifteen times as though *my* life depended on it, and perhaps in that moment it did. But I simply could not get it smooth.

I had to accept the bump.

"Evelyn, I'm so very sorry," Dr. Lachlan had begun, once Sam had offered the rumpled man a chair. I pulled my reluctant attention from the baby clothes to the director. He must have come to my home straight from the airport. Dark bags slouched under his eyes. Bravely, he picked his way through the landmine of emotions he must have seen on my face, and those of Sam and his wife Judith in the room with me. "When word reached us at mission headquarters in Calgary, we were all in shock. I cleared my schedule, and we went to prayer immediately while I waited for the first available flight. I wish I had been able to get here sooner and that I could have brought June with me. She sends her love, as do our entire staff."

He looked as though he might reach out one of his long arms and give me an awkward embrace on his wife's behalf but seemed to decide against it. He took a deep breath. "You must recall that the position James held here was for a five-year term and that monthly support was raised for that position only." He watched me, perhaps hoping he wouldn't have to say the part that came next.

But my sluggish brain couldn't comprehend where he was going with this talk, and he was forced to spell it out.

"I'm told James has done an exceptional job here. You can be sure that his efforts on the current translation project have been a tremendous boost in making the New Testament in that language a reality. We are grateful the work is so close to completion. The translation team assures me they are confident they can manage the rest." He leaned forward as though to make his meaning clearer. "I'm afraid, my dear, that it is time for you to return home to Canada."

I sat stunned at the news. Yet what did I expect? We had come here with the full understanding that we were supported on the donors' dime to do a specific job for a designated length of time.

I swallowed and licked my lips. "How long do I still have here?"

I didn't ask, "When can I go home?" I asked, "How long can I stay?" There's a difference. It was the difference between a foreigner and family. Finding myself at home with these dear ones had happened rapidly, though it was temporary. But the words branded into my brain by the men from the language project ten days ago had sentenced my life to change forever and sunk deep roots here in an instant. Blood roots.

Chapter 5

From every stormy wind that blows,
From every swelling tide of woes,
There is a calm, a sure retreat—
'Tis found beneath the mercy seat.
-*Every Stormy Wind That Blows, by Hugh Stowell 1799-1865*

Only Mom and Dad showed up at the airport to meet me, which was a great relief. Surprisingly enough, I had slept through much of the trip after all. Sheer escapism, I guess, fighting off a rehashing of all the trauma of the past weeks. But I had been wide awake for the last half hour, anxious about my homecoming. Drawing from memories of past returning missionaries, I had envisioned a crowd of our supporters from church thronging the airport arrivals area, some with Welcome Home signs, others with funny hats and noisemakers, all culminating in a watered-down-juice-and-brownies reception at the church. But that was a child's memory. They wouldn't inflict such overwhelming activities on a poor, jet-lagged traveller like me, would they? One who had been through a personal cataclysm of epic proportions? Whatever the case, I was grateful to find my parents had the sensitivity to know I wasn't up to a group reunion.

Dad took me in his hard-sinewed arms, Mom sandwiched me softly from behind, and I cried yet again, washed over by their heartbroken compassion.

"More tears!" I pulled away, trying to keep a light tone. "Doesn't seem to be any end to how much salt water the human body can produce."

Mom dabbed at my cheeks with a Kleenex, folded it over, and sopped up her own tears.

"Dr. Lachlan," Dad pumped the older man's hand. "Thank you for seeing our Lynnie home. We appreciate all you've done for her."

"It was my privilege." The doctor turned to me and laid a hand on my shoulder, fixing his eyes on me. "I'll keep you up to date with anything we hear from the Nigerian authorities on the matter. And now I want you to promise me you'll call on me or June for anything you might need or that you might want to discuss, yes?"

I nodded. "Thank you for everything."

Dr. Lachlan headed toward the baggage claim.

"You two find a spot to sit while I go get your bags," Dad said to Mom and me, turning to follow the doctor.

"Wait," Mom said. "You won't know which ones are hers."

Dad swiveled with a chagrined look on his face. "Right. Well, come on along then."

My parents were both quiet while we waited arm in arm. I couldn't help noticing other travelers around us now uniting with their families. Across the carousel from us, a pair of seniors were making much of young grandchildren they mustn't have seen in a long time, perhaps had never even met. Their effusive joy caused a sharp edge of the stone inside me to twist and gouge. My parents had never made the trip to Nigeria together, although Mom had come to help me after each of my babies were born. Dad had never met either of them in person. The leaden lump of loss threatened to weigh me down again.

At last, my two suitcases appeared on the carousel. Dad picked up the ones I pointed to, and I made a move to leave.

"That's all?" Mom asked, puzzled. "Just these two?"

"Uh-huh."

"But all that packing when you were going out, and trying to fit everything into the size and weight restrictions, and all the packages we sent you..." Her face had the look of someone who had just stepped in muck.

"I know, Mom. But I gave everything away to the women of my church. You saw what they needed. How could I bring it all back with me when I wouldn't need any of it again?"

Mom's face twisted in doubt. "Well, I just hope—"

"It's okay. Really. I won't regret it."

Dad led the way through the air terminal to the parking garage. When the sliding doors opened and the blast of frigid March air hit me, I gasped, then coughed.

Both my parents looked at me with concern. Mom hurriedly pulled the jacket from her own shoulders and offered it to me. She buttoned the thick sweater she had on underneath.

"Just a bit of a shock, is all," I said, slipping into the warm coat.

"For us it's a reprieve," Dad said with a crooked smile. "We've just suffered through the coldest February on record."

Prodded by the biting air, we picked up the pace and soon arrived at the car. I climbed in the back, shivering until I was stiff. The cold should have been welcome after what had happened. But like a fly to the sunny side of the house, Africa's heat still attracted me. Had I ever once been cold there, even in the coolest month of August? I doubted it.

"Could you use a bite to eat?" Mom asked as we settled inside the vehicle.

Hearing her predictable question took me back to college days. It was as if I were still a dependent twenty-year-old student, eager to tell Momsie and Daddy about my last tough exam, about my classmates' exploits, about campus events. As if I had never been a wife, never traveled to the other side of the world, learned pidgin, given birth, been a mother.

When I failed to respond, Dad filled the silence with a hearty voice. "Well, I, for one, could sure stand some sustenance." He maneuvered the car onto the main road and pointed to an all-day breakfast restaurant up ahead. "This one look alright?"

"Yeah, sure," I said, finding my voice again. If there was one thing I'd already determined I wouldn't be, it was someone folks had to tiptoe around. Poor Mom and Dad. They were doing their best.

The burger platter the waitress brought me was enough to feed a family of four. I'd forgotten what North American portions were like. I managed half the burger and the small bowl of coleslaw before pushing my plate away. The wasted food prompted a brief memory of the Jos market beggars, giving me a momentary pang of guilt. At least in the restaurant clatter I was spared having to talk.

On the road again, Dad drove and Mom faced forward, leaving me to rest in the back seat. It took at least an hour before heat seeped back into my shoes to warm my chilled toes. As I thawed, I began to get drowsy. Beyond the edge of the city lay the great dormancy of Alberta's farmland, its blue twilight shadows lengthened by the sinking sun. After the teeming city of Jos that had been my home for more than four years, or even the busy villages of the surrounding Nigerian countryside, the emptiness here was a shock. When I grew up here, I had never thought about how few people and homes there were.

"Where is everybody?" I murmured, imagining that's what my friends Judith or Ebos might say if they were with me now, riding past field after field of flat, snow-skiffed stubble, with only a sparse dotting of farmyard lights here and there.

Mom turned to me. "A lot of people wanted to come. Grandma and Nanny. Katie, people from church. But we didn't think you'd be up to a big welcoming committee. After such a long flight, I mean."

"No, that's not what I meant. Don't mind me, you did the right thing. Just you and Dad coming was perfect."

After what seemed like hours, Mom's voice sounded in the darkened car, rousing me. "Lynnie?"

I straightened my head to ease the kink in my neck. "Yeah?"

"We've been working on a bit of a surprise for you." Her voice held a suppressed excitement.

"What's that?" I asked, not sure I was up to any more surprises. I had discovered they came in many flavours, not all of them sweet.

"You'll see when we get you home." The blue-green of the vehicle dash lit Mom's warm smile. "I'll just give you a hint: You won't have to share a room with your sister."

How many times had Lissa and I complained about sharing a room? Sometimes, with the addition of the youngest sister, Katie, it had been all three of us girls in one cramped space while Dad worked on the upstairs bedrooms. "I was pretty selfish and ungrateful back then, wasn't I? But seriously, I wouldn't mind rooming with Katie."

"No, we have just the spot for you. Katie helped me get the last bit of it ready this morning. All you have to do is flop into your bed."

"Okay, thanks," I said, trying to sound enthusiastic. I hoped my reaction wouldn't disappoint her. Expectations had always stressed me out. I had never been one to gush and I always felt as if my thank-yous were a letdown to the giver. The prospect of a freshly made bed was appealing, though.

I was so weary I took no notice of the building Mom led me to when we got home but that night, for the first time since the disaster, I dreamed.

A baby is crying. I know it is Anya. She is crying and crying, but I am helpless to reach her. The door to the room where the sound comes from is white-hot.

Chapter 6

Northern Nigeria, late February

A powerful pity for his wife filled Ihsan bin Ibrahim's heart. She lay limp on the tousled bedding in their small house, with uncovered head, weeping again into the already dampened sheet. It was the third such loss in a year and a half. And as much as he too, longed for a child, he could see that each disappointment had taken something from her, and not just physically. Daniya, the feisty girl he had married whose sass had always amused and even aroused him, though it was generally frowned on in a wife, had become an empty shell of a woman. Even her skin had lost its dark, rich luster and gone ashy.

He patted her shoulder with his callused hand, then turned to leave, helpless in the face of her grief. The Quran gave him the right to take another wife, but he was not a Big Man. His small herd of goats and the sparser and sparser grasslands in the region made such a luxury an impossibility. Yet he often reminded Daniya that she was young, with many years ahead for childbearing. It had happened to his mother, after all. Fruitfulness had come to her in her late thirties when it had eluded her in her youth. He would stop in on his sister on his way out to grazing. Perhaps she would take time once again to sit with Daniya today.

His eyes adjusted to the white light of the morning as he exited their darkened home and opened the stick enclosure where his goats awaited milking. Fresh milk would invigorate his wife. He would fill her cup before he took the rest to the marketplace.

After leaving the morning's production of milk with the seller, Ihsan pushed his handcart in the direction of home. The now-empty milk canisters rattled when he turned to make a short detour to his sister's place.

Uma crouched in the shade of the west side of her home, mixing *puff-puff* dough in a turquoise plastic basin.

Ihsan determined to come back later and enjoy some of the deep-fried fritters.

Uma's *khimar* stuck to her damp neck and shoulders in the heat as she made the rhythmic motions.

"*Assalamu alaikim*, sister."

She jumped and her hand made a reflexive move to her head covering lest it had fallen away from her hair. Then she looked up at him and smiled. "*Wa-Alaikim Assalaam!* Always up to your old trick of startling me?" One of her toddling twins appeared at her doorway and reached his plump arms toward her. She stood, covered the dough bowl with a cloth, and set it inside the door on a bench. Then she scooped up her small son to ride on her broad hip. She turned to Ihsan. "You're here to ask me to sit with Daniya again, yes?"

He nodded. "Tell her about Mother."

Uma gave a short laugh. "You say that every time you ask, brother. And at times when I think she will receive it, I have told her. But Daniya...She thinks she is the only one this has ever happened to. She is all alone and God is punishing her for something. Who knows what?"

"Tell her how joyful our mother was, how thankful she was for the three of us born later in life."

Uma rolled her eyes and shook her head. "You men! Perhaps you don't know what Mother endured in the years of her barrenness. No doubt she was as heartbroken as Daniya. These things take time. Only time." She flicked his arm as she bumped passed him, moving toward the house. "But I will stop by and see her, never fear." She looked him over thoughtfully. "You live up to your name. She is lucky to have a kind husband such as you. And now be patient with her. It is a great sorrow she bears."

He nodded, satisfied that Uma would do what she could, then returned to his home for the goats. He paused to listen at the window for sounds of movement. Yes, he heard shuffling, which meant Daniya had risen from her bed. It was a good sign.

This morning, Ihsan was determined to join the other farmers of the community, mainly Christians. He had heard talk last night of a sizable stand of grass and even some shrubbery that lay to the east of the village. He poured water into his own canteen, then into the goats' trough, impatient for them to drink their fill before leading the flock in that direction. By his neighbour's description, the pasture was farther away than he was in the habit of taking his animals. It was a hopeful piece of news in a difficult time. But it meant taking a risk, entering an unknown area reputed to be Fulani territory.

In recent years, the desert encroaching from the north of Nigeria had pressed the nomadic Fulani farther south with their hungry herds of cattle, onto pastureland and watering points that were owned by farmers. What their cattle didn't devour, they ruined with their churning hooves. But the farmers could do little to defend their land. The Fulani were fierce in their demands and well armed, with backing from powerful Islamists in the north. And the threat to the land was not the only thing that concerned Ihsan.

For years since his father had bought land in this Christian community and though his family's religion put them in the minority, they had lived in harmony with their neighbours. But recent Fulani attacks on Christians and their villages had increased. Ihsan was as horrified at these reports as anyone, yet he couldn't help noticing the sidelong glances and distrustful looks from his neighbours. The nomadic, now militant group's terror attacks were making life more difficult for peaceable Muslims.

He adjusted his hat against the powerful glare of the sun, tapped his lead doe's flank with his staff to nudge her eastward, and joined the other farmers from the village. By now the dusty track out of the village was searing hot and he could smell the softening rubber of his sandals mingling with the animal odours.

The sun was high overhead when they stopped in the shade of a tree. Up ahead, one of his neighbour pointed to the plateau rising above the savannah. Taking a swig from his canteen, Ihsan capped it and pushed on with the others, all of them now keeping alert both for animal predators as well as the human kind. They avoided the steep cliff straight ahead and took a zigzag route to the top allowing their goats to find their own nimble way. Atop the tableland, Ihsan paused to catch his breath, pleased to see shrubs and tall grass as well as some welcome shade. The men separated from one another, each staking out about a day's graze for his animals. The goats began tearing and munching immediately.

Joining the others, Ihsan sank to a crouch beneath the closest tree and unwrapped the groundnuts and cold rice he had scrounged for himself from a kitchen ill-supplied with prepared foods. He envied Uma's bread, no doubt baked by now and being devoured by her noisy children. It had been a long time since Daniya had made such an effort. Washing down the last of his lunch with more of the tepid water, he listened to the desultory conversation of the others. For him, talk was too much effort in the heat. He half-drowsed, keeping his eyes slitted just in case.

When it was his turn, he rose to circle the flock for a headcount. All present and accounted for. At the edge of the embankment, he stopped to view the expansive panorama below, the horizon so flat a carpenter's level might have achieved it. A slight movement caught his eye. Without a word, he beckoned to his mates. Below, on the road from the village, a vehicle inched along northward. Rutted and gouged by the rainy season, it wasn't the best road and was little traveled. At the same time, one of his mates pointed toward the northwest. Ihsan felt his nerves tingle a warning. A puff of dust rose along with the distant sound of shouts. When the source of the movement emerged from behind a copse of trees, they saw a vast herd of cattle and the distinctive wide-brimmed hats of the nomadic group.

"Fulani," someone hissed.

Ihsan shivered, despite the heat.

"Time to head home," Ihsan's neighbour spoke in a low tone. No need to alert the cattlemen below with loud talking or sudden movement.

"But they're moving south on our road. We're safer up here."

"Look." The man next to Ihsan pointed down at the road. Inexorably, like watching a distant child run into the path of a truck, a collision of a different kind was in the making. The Jeep moving northward was about to be cut off by the milling herd of cattle driven by Fulani herdsmen.

This did not bode well.

Not only was the vehicle cut off in front but now a second stream of the bony, horned cattle was surging behind it, fencing in the Jeep. Amid the clouds of dust, herdsmen appeared, storming the lone vehicle. Their shouts were louder now, angry. In momentary clear glimpses, Ihsan could see them yelling at the driver. The sound of rocks popping against the metal of the vehicle. A faint tinkle of glass breaking. Obscured by cattle, still the merciless Fulani plan was plain. The herdsmen drove the last of their cattle past to a safe distance.

From the heights where Ihsan and the villagers crouched, they held in a collective breath, and they watched. A rag was jammed into the petrol tank of the vehicle. One of the Fulani approached it, unmistakably intending to light it.

No! No! No!

As one, the watchers on the plateau hit the ground, instinctively flattening themselves. Ihsan's chest thundered in horror at the scene below, yet he could not tear his gaze away. Like the prophet Musa in the Quran who had witnessed the burning bush, Ihsan felt compelled by this moment. A terrific explosion roared, and a blaze of flame engulfed the Jeep.

Chapter 7

When peace, like a river, attendeth my way
When sorrows like sea-billows roll
Whatever my lot Thou has taught me to say
It is well, it is well with my soul.
~It Is Well With My Soul, by Horatio Spafford,
1828-1888

One urgent task compelled me the morning after arriving at my parents' home. It had intruded itself all through the ragged tasks I'd had to step through during the previous three weeks. The day I went with Dr. Lachlan to the Jos police station pursuing answers about how my husband had died, I had longed for nothing more than to turn back the clock. I only wanted to live our charmed courtship again, the brief and happy marriage, and the joyful chaotic years of motherhood. Entering the police station, I was wishing myself somewhere far away, alone, where I could process the ripping and tearing that was even then happening inside me.

Frowning at the inattention of the officers, Dr. Lachlan slams his palm on the counter. Not having lived in Africa for any length of time, he's unused to the local lackadaisical pace of government service. The nearest uniform slowly raises his head from his cell phone, but his feet remain on his desk.

Pastor Sam picks up on the director's disapproval and speaks sharply to the cop. "Can we get some action here?" Sam asks, knocking on the dusty counter for emphasis.

The officer swings his legs down and with a broad grin at us, approaches the counter. No doubt he is expecting cash, or at least a gift of food. The black name tag on his wrinkled white shirt reads Akinde.

"We want to know the details about what has happened to this lady's husband and daughters. They were ambushed and murdered on the road to Kano. We want to know what you've discovered in your investigation." Sam emphasizes the last word. He's already told us he's sure the police have done nothing. And he has made it clear he doesn't expect they will do anything. With all the killings of Christians in the country's Middle Belt by Islamist groups, the government has dragged its feet on taking action, perhaps not wanting to take sides. But inaction is taking a side, I protested. Pastor Sam had given a sad nod.

"You must help this lady," Sam says, pointing to me. "We would like to know who reported the crime to you so that we could talk to that person."

"I need to find out why there are only two bodies," I tell the cop, using my news reporter voice. Nigerian women speak at a low pitch and I'm well aware my regular voice seems odd to them. "I need to know what has become of my youngest daughter. Where is she?" I finish on a shrill note, unable to hide my panic.

Akinde winces but starts to make his leisurely way through a stack of paperwork on his desk. He shuffles through pages, turns some over to read, opens files, leafing through their contents. If James were here, he would mutter some wisecrack about bureaucrats perfecting the art of looking busy. But James is not here and the sudden thought of him makes me gasp in almost physical pain. Dr. Lachlan sets his hand on my shoulder in support, and I try to firm up my resolve.

The cop shuffles papers, smiling his dazzling white smile at us every so often in apology. I feel like shaking him or yelling into his generous-

sized ear, anything to speed him up. It wouldn't make any difference. Sam has already given us the gloomy warning. "They never arrest anyone when Christians are killed." Churches burned, women and girls kidnapped, and thousands of believers murdered—yet still there is no justice.

Officer Akinde finally saunters toward us, spreading his hands with a shrug. "No word yet. We will let you know whatever we find out." He lays his hands, palm up, on the counter in a not-so-subtle hint that next time we should fill them.

Three more visits to the station in the next two weeks failed to produce any action from the cops. And we couldn't spend all our time nagging at them. There were arrangements and decisions to be made. Without any experience or precedent, I, the most indecisive creature on the planet, had to make choices about burial in Africa or shipping the bodies back home and a multitude of other details.

Through it all, I'd felt hurried and pressured. I had itched for a buffer of solitude to examine my life up to that point. And not just mine, but James's life. I wanted to step back, to view his time on this earth, from the earliest days before I knew him, to the fateful day of his death, piecing together a chronology, some sort of flow. Was it to find some overarching theme that characterized him? To search for a key that would unlock the hidden purpose in it all? I didn't know. But I knew I had to do it and for that I needed time and seclusion.

Waking in the cottage my parents had prepared for me, I gazed around in wonder. Had Mom somehow known I would need a retreat like this? I craned my neck in the brand-new bed with the black iron headboard, taking in the place. Light streamed in through three pairs of French doors set into the curving walls of the grain bin. Years ago, Mom had clipped an article from a farm magazine about making a cottage out of a round metal granary. She'd even suggested we should move one of the old ones on our farm over to the edge of a slough west of the house. Lissa and I had rolled our eyes at each other and giggled over this familiar impasse between our parents—another entry on the endless and futile Honey Do list. Tears blurred my eyes at the thought of Mom and Dad's long marriage. Thirty-three years, wasn't it? I opened my eyes wide, to keep the tears from spilling over and forced myself to take in the details planned by my mom.

A white, beamed and boarded ceiling, eight-sided like a spider's web, spread in every direction from the vaulted center of the conical structure to the paneled walls. Incredibly, something on Mom's historic list had been completed. Even in my lethargy, I could see Dad had done a nice job. Everything was compact, but well planned. The bed was enclosed by walls that rose to about eight feet, allowing the ceiling in all its glory to soar to its central peak.

I looked around for a washroom and glimpsed it through a door to the right. Rising with a heavy feeling, I padded through and used the facilities, enjoying the feel of cold water on my swollen eyelids. Cold water from the tap, instead of the lukewarm liquid that came from Nigerian faucets. It was something, but it wasn't much. A mere grain of pleasure easily dissolved by an ocean of pain. Small mercies. *Look for them, collect them. They'll be useful for those times when life feels like nothing but sorrow.* That sounded like Damaris giving advice. How I missed her!

I dried my hands on the plush blue towel and searched through my carry-on bag. Mom must have placed it in the bathroom. I had little recollection of our arrival here last night. Only that they had led me to the lovely turned-back covers of the freshly made bed where I had slept a long time. I dragged a brush through my waist-length hair, longer now than it had ever been in my life, thanks to the African humidity. I bound it up in my habitual messy bun, rummaged for my robe and took a stroll around the cabin.

A cherry-red wood stove and a neat stack of pine firewood stood against the wall to the left of the glass doors.

One thing I knew for certain—I wouldn't be using that.

It was surrounded by a pair of chairs and a small sofa plumped with fat cushions and fuzzy throws. On the other side of the bedroom wall, a small kitchen was equipped with bar sink, microwave, toaster oven, and mini fridge. It had everything. I could live here for years, and maybe I would.

Through the wall of glass, I stared at the tall brown grass surrounding the silver slush of melting ice on a large slough. There were still patches of snowbank under the trees on the opposite shore. No doubt Mom had plans for Dad to build a pier, with maybe a canoe or two. I suspected this space was planned for use by farm vacationers or as a bed and breakfast. Given the shaky financial picture I had grown up with, I would have to limit my time here. But even that vague deadline made me anxious. Where would I go from here? What would I do next or for that matter, with the rest of my life?

A muffled knock sounded, and I hurried to let Mom in. Her arms were full, carrying a large plastic tote. She eased out of her shoes, set the tote on the kitchen bar, and began pulling out muffins and fruit. "I hope you found what I stocked the fridge with. There's milk, eggs, cheese. Bread and cereal are in the cupboard." She paused, uncertainty and sympathy competing on her face.

The warmth of the muffins was fogging the plastic bag they were in. "These look good," I said, wishing I could thank her, reassure her. But my brain was as foggy as the muffin bag. "Blueberry?"

"Two kinds, blueberry-lemon, and cranberry-orange. Take your choice." She found a plate in the cupboard and opened a drawer for a knife. "Can I make you some coffee?"

I opened the bag for a blueberry muffin. Mom handed me the plate and knife, then hurried to the fridge for butter.

"Mom." I laughed. "You're hovering."

"I'm sorry." She didn't laugh but slid the butter dish across the counter to me. "It's just that..." When I looked up, her eyes had filled with tears.

She came around to my side of the island and wrapped her arms around me. Her shuddering sob made me feel deficient for my dry eyes. But tears were not something I could conjure up at will.

She pulled back and stroked my cheek. "I don't know how to act with you, honey, or what to say. I feel terrible that I've never experienced anything like what you're going through because I want to help you, to take away your pain, but I have no idea how."

I gave her a quick squeeze in return. "I know. There's nothing anyone can say or do. But it helps to know you care. It really does." I pulled up the barstool and sat, cutting my muffin in half.

Mom settled onto the other stool, watching me eat. After a while, she started twisting her hands together the way she did when she was nervous.

"Something you need to say?"

"I hate to hit you with this the minute you get home, but so many people have been asking when they can come see you. I've put them off because I know you've always been such a private person, but lots of them care and want to express their love." Mom's hands were getting put through the wringer. "Have you thought about whether to have a memorial service? Or maybe we could set up a day to have folks in one at a time? It's up to you."

Facing a crowd was the absolute last thing I wanted to do. "Our church in Jos already had a three-day funeral, Mom."

"I know," she said, and her shoulders dropped.

Chapter 8

Must I be carried to the skies
on flow'ry beds of ease
While others fought to win the prize
and sailed through bloody seas?
~ *Am I A Soldier of the Cross, by Isaac Watts, 1674-1748*

I watched Grandma Hardy picking her way across the yard around the last few dirty snowbanks between her small house and my cabin. The sight of her made my hands clammy despite the dry air.

When I was little, we moved from the city to the farm when Grandpa's lifelong depression worsened so Dad could help with the work. It was supposed to have been temporary, but when Grandpa died a couple of years later, everyone in the family agreed to Dad taking over the farm altogether. By the time there were three of us kids, Grandma decided we should trade houses; she would move to the two-bedroom house on the property, and we to the old two-storey. So we grew up with Grandma on the same yard, which had advantages and disadvantages. Her presence made a firm and far-reaching imprint on our family and my upbringing.

It was nice for my parents to have someone to look after the four of us kids when they had to be somewhere else. Being the hard worker she was, Grandma was a big help with the huge garden we grew, and with all the canning and freezing of produce. She and Mom got along strangely well, working quietly while they sang hymns together. Dad, however, had a low tolerance for his mother. Somehow, she brought out the worst in him, though I'm sure she meant well. We kids could tell by his face when he came in the door whenever she'd had "a talk" with him. Or more likely, at him. He didn't say much about these talks, and my mom was careful never to ask him about them in front of us. But from things I overheard now and again, I figured out the talks most often had to do with his not going into full-time ministry.

By the time we kids were teenagers, we knew firsthand what such talks were like. Lissa, especially, endured a lot of them. She used to tease me about being Grandma's favourite, but that was by contrast to her. My sister was what Grandma, frowning, called "frivolous." And Lissa was mischievous enough to do things on purpose that would get Grandma's goat. I mean, cavorting through the sprinkler in a bikini directly in front of Grandma's kitchen window was outright asking for a lecture. You couldn't call it a scolding since Grandma never raised her voice, but it was always a one-way communication generously salted with Bible verses. Lissa told me Grandma even referred to hand-written notes a couple of times while talking to her. And Grandma's tone carried the expectation that we would change our ways accordingly. We had been taught to respect our elders so there was no answering back. We only meekly listened.

I'd come in for a different kind of Grandma's speeches myself, the last one occurring a week before James and I were to leave for Africa. It was a brief one.

I had been sitting on the floor of my room next to a bathroom scale for weighing my baggage, surrounded by half-packed boxes and suitcases, with a checklist a mile long in my hand when Grandma marched through my door.

"Evelyn, I wonder if you've counted the cost of going to Africa?" she asked, bending to peer into my eyes.

I knew she didn't mean the financial cost. Rather she wanted to know if I had considered the risks and sacrifices, the potential for danger in the venture. Yet her question perplexed me. Hadn't she been the one to sigh and lament that not one of her children or grandchildren were "serving the Lord" full-time? Hadn't she been the one to ply me with clippings and tidbits of news from the periodicals she subscribed to, ever since she discovered my interest in world missions from the time I was in middle school?

"I think so, Grandma."

"There have been churches burned in Nigeria and thousands of Christians have lost their lives in recent years," she warned, still commanding my attention with her fixed gaze.

I stood up. "I know. It's scary, but James and I have prayed about it for a long time and we're trusting in God's protection."

She straightened and exhaled, then patted my arm. I must have given the right answer. "That's good then," she said. "I'll be praying for you every day."

When she had gone, Mom came to my door. She raised her eyebrows in question.

I grinned. "Just Grandma being Grandma, wanting to be sure I knew what I was getting into."

Had I known what I was getting into? It was hard to know, hard to think back to the before. Before my life had been turned upside down, shaken, and emptied of everything and everyone in it right down to the final crumb.

I braced myself now as Grandma tramped up the wooden steps of the deck. I knew the first thing she would want to know: Was there sin in my life for which God was chastening me? My parents had never gone in much for that line of reasoning, but I'd been around Grandma enough that I knew what to expect. And it wasn't as though the question hadn't occurred to me, too, in the aftermath.

But James had drilled into me the biblical truth about suffering and God's purpose in it so that I didn't entertain that unfounded guilt for long.

Grandma gave three sharp raps on the glass door and opened it before I could get there. She looked thinner, if that were possible, than I remembered. I gave her the obligatory hug, a practice Mom had required of us since childhood. Lissa had always described it as "hugging a fencepost." But Mom knew we readily gave and received hugs from her own mother, our Nanny, and wanted to keep things fair.

To my amazement, this time Grandma squeezed back. When she pulled away to look at me, there was moisture in her eyes. She blinked and made a brisk swipe at them with a gloved hand, then passed me the Tupperware container she carried. "Good nourishing soup," she announced.

I took the bowl to the fridge and, when I turned back, she had removed her coat, laid it neatly on the back of a chair and sat down by the wood stove. This was to be a proper visit, then. I turned on the burner under the bright red kettle and opened a cupboard door to search for cups and tea.

"Come sit, Evelyn."

I rounded the back of the loveseat and obediently sat across from her.

"Tell me all about it," she said. "Spare me no details. I must hear it all." She closed her eyes as if fortifying herself for a lurid tale.

My stomach clenched. I wasn't sure I was up to reliving the whole ordeal. I got up from the couch to attend to the whistling tea kettle, giving myself time to think. "There's still so much we don't know."

She opened her eyes. "Then simply tell me what you know for certain."

Years of training in honouring Grandma kicked in. I sketched out the news I had received that terrible day, leaving out my crazed tantrum through the Jos marketplace. It embarrassed me now, and

Grandma would not have approved. A Christian lady did not give vent to unseemly outbursts.

When I finished, she sat upright and opened her eyes. "I had read what goes on in that country and time and again I dreamed you and your little family were attacked. But I did nothing to stop you."

Grandma and her dreams. As though imagining the worst-case scenario could somehow prevent it. "You're not that powerful, Grandma. None of us are."

"None of us *is*," she corrected.

It almost made me smile. The teacher in her couldn't help it.

"I feel this deeply, Evelyn." Her eyes began to water again. This time she didn't bother to wipe them.

I nodded, dry eyed. Yet how could she possibly feel it as deeply as I did? A weak flag of doubt waved inside me, then sank as I remembered she too, had lost a child and later a husband. But that was long ago, and it didn't happen all at once, self-pity protested inside me. Even as I thought it, I knew the futility of playing that game. Why would I think an old wound was any less painful than a recent one? Maybe Grandma's years of silent hurt had accumulated to an unbearable weight.

"I prayed for years that my children would give their lives to the Lord's service," she went on, "and none of them ever did. But when you showed an interest, and at such a young age, I prayed that you would go." Grandma paused and fished a tissue out of her pocket to blot up the rivulets on her wrinkled cheeks.

"I still remember you getting me to memorize the hymn, 'Untold Millions are Still Untold.'" I did owe a lot to Grandma's encouragement, not to mention her substantial contribution to our monthly support for the past few years.

Grandma leaned forward with a fervour in her eyes. "Did you tell people about Jesus? How many Nigerians were saved under your ministry?"

I sighed, feeling the pressure rising in me to satisfy her hunger for results. How to explain that there were churches on nearly every street corner in Nigeria? That an irreligious Nigerian was far rarer than a Christian Canadian. That the faithful people of our church in Nigeria like Pastor Sam and Judith, and their daughter Ebos, had nourished and challenged my faith far beyond anything I had offered them. And that friends like Damaris and Rose had modelled for me how to endure suffering with grace and godly power. Damaris's son had been murdered, and Rose's two daughters had been kidnapped by Boko Haram, the Islamist terrorist sect, not long before we had arrived in Jos. Yet my friends' hope and trust in God never dimmed. So many dear ones there had lived through unimaginable sorrows that I knew I could never play the grief card, a sort of you-don't know-what-I've-been-through superiority.

"You remember that we went there because of James's tech skills, right?" I answered instead. "That the work of Bible translation is being carried out by nationals and he was only there for tech support?"

"Of course I know. I read every one of the newsletters your mother printed off for me." She fixed me with another intense stare. "But ever since your father brought me the tragic news I've been fasting and praying that God would get some mileage out of this tragedy. He must plan to bring many souls to Christ through it."

I gulped, unable to imagine any good that could come of my loss. Wasn't that what a proper Christian should want? I'd heard my Nigerian friends pray it and long ago I'd read *Foxe's Book of Martyrs*. The blood of the martyrs is the seed of the church. I was ashamed of how little I had prayed for that. Why had I been so negligent?

Chapter 9

"Pack up your troubles in your old kit bag
And smile, smile, smile."
~lyrics by George Henry Powell, 1916

I would have stayed in my grain bin cottage and never come out if Mom hadn't brought me my bundle of redirected mail. There shouldn't have been much in the stack since we had authorized her to open any correspondence while we were away and deal with it as needed.

The only piece of business was my driver's licence, up for renewal, and that required me to be there in person, so we drove to town to get it done. I needed my car out of storage so I could feel less like a dependent girl and more like the woman I was.

Pulling onto the highway, Mom said, "We've been getting mail from all over the country for you. By the looks of them, I'd say sympathy cards and letters."

"I can't, Mom."

"I know. Maybe later. They'll keep." She focused on the road, then added, "I even got a call from CBC radio yesterday."

At this, I turned to her in surprise. "Yeah?"

"Mm. Somehow, they'd heard the story of what happened to you."

Panic rose inside me. "No way do I want to face the media, Mom. You didn't—"

"Absolutely not. I knew you wouldn't be up to speaking about it publicly. The reporter didn't seem all that persistent. It's likely too distant for people here to relate to. I don't think they'll pursue the story."

I calmed down but, contrarily, felt offended that my life-altering tragedy was unworthy of news coverage. "OK." We rode in silence the rest of the way to town while I tried to sort out my conflicting emotions.

Naturally, sitting for my picture at the registry office triggered memories of having our passport photos taken prior to flying out. There was no need for the woman behind the camera to warn me not to smile. I had nothing to smile about. The picture came out looking like I was too ill to travel.

Before heading out of town, Mom swung by Nanny's house. She'd had her hip replaced a month earlier and was still cautious about going out anywhere, but she was up and about, using her ribbon-decorated cane when we arrived. She met us at the door of her tiny house and engulfed me in one of her soft, tight, lilac-scented embraces. Her cheeks, lightly rouged, balled up in a merry smile like apples.

"Lynnie, love! You're home at last. How we've missed you." She backed up to make room for us in the cramped entry hall. "Come in, come in!"

Mom and I hung our jackets on hooks and made our way to the living room couch.

The colourful house smelled of Nanny's talcum powder and coffee. Its usual cheerful state of disarray filled me with fun and nostalgic memories. Through the wide opening into the small kitchen, I spied Nanny's junk cart and smiled to myself. As when I was growing up, it was now pulled out of the pantry and sat visitor-ready with an array of sweet and salty treats.

Nanny limped ahead of us, then turned, looking me up and down. "You're wasting away to nothing, girl. We need to fatten you up." She bustled over to the kitchen and wheeled the cart next to me. "Let's see if we can't cheer you up, lovey. Nothing has calories today. I just declared it so," she said, smiling and patting my arm, then sitting in the floral armchair next to me.

I wasn't at all hungry but I chose a mini chocolate bar to please her and took my time opening it.

"Now, tell me, dear. Aren't you glad to be back in the motherland after all that muggy heat? We've had such a cold winter, but spring is on its way. And won't I be the gladdest to see it? Last year I couldn't work in my garden much, what with the pain in my hip. But this year, let me tell you, I'm itching to get back at it. I am sharp as a tack and raring to go." She leaned to the side to pat her thickly padded hip. "Did your mom tell you about my replacement part?"

"She did," I answered between nibbles of my chocolate. "You seem to be getting around pretty well."

Nanny's eyes twinkled. "Better every day. It's given me my life back. Why, with my dentures and glasses, a new knee and a stainless steel hip, I'm eighty percent fake." She cackled her infectious laugh and we joined in, exchanging glances. Being in Nanny's presence never failed to lift my spirits.

The contrast between my two grandmothers couldn't be more extreme, and we kids had always had our clear preference. We knew better, however, than to say anything about that in the presence of either of them. Even at home, we tried to low-key our enthusiasm for going to town to see Nanny. Mom was a stickler for equal treatment.

"Now then, dearie. What do you think that young nephew of yours said last time he was over here for lunch?"

School-day lunch at Nanny's. Thinking about a second generation enjoying that thrill made me smile. No doubt she served them deep-fried cherry fritters until they were full to bursting like she did us. We used to love being invited to Nanny's instead of eating a bag lunch at school. I once won the fritter-eating contest against Lissa and my brother, Lance. Fourteen fritters were enough to make my after-lunch Phys. Ed class that day an extreme agony. But as I recalled, it had been worth it. Now Lissa's kids, Jade and Dylan, had the fun of walking to Nanny's at noon like the town kids and having a fritter lunch here. I crumpled the candy wrapper in my fist, squelching a sudden pang when I thought about Josie and Anya never growing up to carry on the tradition.

Mom took a peek at me and must have seen I was choking up. "What did Dylan say?" she filled in for me.

Nanny giggled. "He and Jade were looking at my old photo albums when Jade looks up and says to me, 'Nanny, I just realized you've known people from three different centuries.' So then Dylan gets this hard-thinking look on his face and says all serious-like, 'Are you three hundred years old'?" She trilled her high-pitched laugh. "That boy! Isn't he just a scream?"

I laughed as naturally as I could manage.

"The kiddies have taken to paging through my old magazines here whenever they come by. Sue, why don't you grab a couple of those and show them to Lynnie?" She pointed to a basket next to the fireplace.

My mom got up to fetch some of the ripply-paged periodicals and laid one in my lap.

"We dug these up," Nanny explained, "when your mom was helping me sort through the basement after Christmas."

"Life magazine, 1945." I flipped the crispy pages. "'In your Victory Kitchen, choose a Kelvinator,'" I read. "'Every second pair of Florsheim shoes goes to the war effort.'" The headline of one ad for motor oil stopped me cold. 'How to Keep a Jeep in Shape for the Japs.' James was Korean Canadian, not Japanese, but the harsh wording came as a shock.

"Oh, those kids had their laughs about some of those pictures. Like the old-fashioned telephone. 'Did you have one of these phones when you were a kid, Nanny?' Like I'm as old as dirt." She clapped a hand to one knee. "It puts me in mind of the time you were just a little tyke, Lynnie, sitting on my lap. You stroked my cheek so lovingly. And then you said, 'Nanny, your neck is kind of squishy.'" She threw back her head in a fit of giggles. When she settled, she pulled a tissue from her sweater pocket and dabbed at her eyes.

"Yeah, sorry about that, Nan. Tact wasn't my strong suit back in the day."

"Never you mind, dearie. I thought it was hilarious." Her eyes strayed to the mantel clock. "Gosh, it's time I was stirring my stumps. The Handibus is coming to get me at eleven. Mustn't miss my euchre game at the seniors' centre." She winked at me. "Never know when some handsome silver-haired rooster will join us old biddies." She struggled to rise from her armchair until Mom and I hoisted her out by the arms.

"There now," the old dear said, straightening her blouse, "how do I look?"

"Gorgeous as always, Nanny." I kissed her cheek. "Thanks for the treat."

"Now listen, there's plenty more. Why don't you take a bunch home?" She started for the kitchen, but I stopped her, explaining I didn't have much appetite these days.

She patted my cheek. "Well, get your mother to cook something that'll stick to those ribs of yours. You need plumping up. And you be sure to keep on filling your mind with happy things too, Lynnie. Okay? Don't let those negative thoughts take over." Nanny pressed something into my coat pocket and squeezed me around the shoulders again. She said to Mom, "Drive carefully, Susie dear."

In the car on the way home, I fished out the bill Nanny had given me. A fifty. Mom glanced away from the road when I lifted it to show her.

"That's Nanny for you." Mom shook her head with a smile, then sobered. Her eyes searched my face. "Was it helpful? What she said?"

"You mean, the 'think positive' message?"

Mom nodded in a way that made me think she doubted its benefits.

I considered for a bit. Nanny was so loving, so dear, I didn't usually stop to think about whether what she said was helpful. "I mean, it wasn't profound or anything, but she means well." Only thinking about our visit later did I realize Nanny hadn't expressed condolences or even asked me anything about the tragedy.

Chapter 10

"You were a firebrand plucked from the burning."

~Amos 4:11

Ihsan kept still in utter horror at the smoky scene below him. The other herders from his village began a hasty retreat from the plateau where they had been grazing their flocks, their movements guarded and wary. Did they look at him with suspicion? Was their silence now due to resentment against him for his belief in the religion of those who had set aflame the vehicle of innocent travelers? Or did they merely wish to avoid drawing the attention of the Fulani? By this time the clouds of dust raised by the nomadic herdsmen and their cattle had subsided as they disappeared steadily eastward on the flat savanna.

He couldn't look into his neighbours' eyes, both shamed at what his fellow Muslims had done and fearful of his fellow villagers' reaction. Yet surely his grandfather, his father, and now Ihsan himself had proved over the decades that they could live in peace with the Christians. These atrocities had become more frequent and reports of the Fulani bands storming the north country in the past few years had been rampant, making Ihsan cringe. But had he not grown up playing side by side with his Christian neighbours? He would never hurt them. Did they not know him and accept him as different from these perpetrators? He hoped so, and he was determined to keep the peace his grandfather had forged in their community.

He rose to a crouch from his position on his belly at the edge of the embankment, cracking his neck joints to release their stiffness. Pulling away from the precipice, he scanned the grassy area for his own goats, clucking and whistling for them. The entire mass of animals gradually separated into groups, each knowing their own herder and flocking after him. The other villagers had already begun the roundabout descent to the roadway. With a last shuddering glance down at the scene of the wreck, Ihsan took his position at the rear. For a time, he focused on keeping his footing on the steep and loose-stoned way. The goats, of course, took no such caution but surged ahead to the road below. By the time he reached the bottom, the gap between him and the other men was widening. Everyone was in a hurry to put such a dreadful memory behind him. Even Ihsan's animals had moved after them, but without the occasional warning touch of his staff on their flanks. they now paused and scattered to forage for what little grew at the bottom of the embankment.

With the noise of his neighbours' flocks diminishing in the distance, a silence descended on the savanna. Ihsan took a moment to relieve his full bladder, scanning in every direction for beasts of prey, which in recent years were more likely to be human than animal. Farmers of his village grazed their flocks in the safety of numbers for good reason. In the quiet, his attention was jerked again by a sound from the direction of the smoldering car down the road. The sound didn't belong in this wild outback where nothing with a human voice would ever utter. It came from the direction of the smoking vehicle. Impossible. He strained to listen. Another sound. Like the bleating of a kid. Now he was certain it came from the wreckage.

He straightened his clothing, already rushing down the road to the spot. His sandals pounded the hard ground. He ignored the jaw-jarring impact, fixed on reaching the blackened vehicle. The acrid odor of burning paint and plastic gave way to another, more sickening smell—charred flesh. He came to a stop a short distance from what was left of the Jeep, clamping his sleeve against his mouth and nose to staunch the odour.

I am a fool. What I heard must have been the cry of some bird. Nothing could survive this. No one! Yet he stood and stared. A grim fascination impelled him to bear witness to this calamity. On this forsaken road only minutes ago, some unfortunate driver had met his maker. To Ihsan, it seemed almost like holy ground.

Blackened fragments of paint curled away from the metal skeleton of the vehicle, metal that must still be scorching to the touch. Perhaps there would be some useful tool or even some coins remaining. He glanced back at his flock where he'd left them wondering if he dared linger.

He gave the Jeep a wide berth, staring into its darkened interior through the gaping rear window. Its frame was littered with shattered glass. He could feel the heat as he drew nearer. His gaze roamed the charred wreck, fearful of what grisly sights he might find. There could be no signs of life. But there were remains of what so recently had been life. A human being like him, with intentions and hopes, faith and fear.

Inside the vehicle, a shape slumped forward against the steering column. Once the body of a man. He peered into the passenger seat. Another man, now an immobile mound of corpse hunched sideways across the width of the seat.

Ihsan's innards roiled at the sight. With effort he forced his gut to stay put. He was about to turn away when he noticed a small foot protruding from under the body in the passenger seat. A child's foot, the glossy black of a sandal melted onto the crusty skin. Now he was sick, unable to control his body's heaving revulsion at the carnage. He bent down to empty himself of his recent meal.

Then he heard the sound again, this time to his right, at the side of the road. A scrubby bush clung to the rocky ground there, barely eking moisture out of the cracked earth to produce stunted gray-green leaves. Behind it he glimpsed movement. Life? Something small and dun-coloured like the surrounding dirt. In a moment, his pulse stopped in alarm. He rushed toward the small creature, again scanning the surrounding area for danger.

Hunkered against the base of the bush was a child. Yet how could this be? A light-skinned child, but for the smudges of dust coating its wispy, straight hair and its face and arms. The child caught sight of him coming toward it and uttered a long, pitiful wail.

He stopped short of the bush and crouched on one knee. The child appeared to be a girl if the grimy lace on her shirt was any indication. A scratch on her forehead dripped a thin line of blood. From the thorn bush or from the Fulani? No, they would have done worse to the child. Had her father put her out of the car before the Fulani approached? But then, what of the other child beneath him? Had this little one climbed out through the window broken by rocks before the explosion? Ihsan shook his head in shock and wonder. By whatever miraculous means, Allah had been merciful to this one. The child's dark eyes, tilted upward at the corners, were filled with tears spilling over into muddy tracks on her cheeks.

"Little one, little one." He spoke in the soft voice he used for his newborn animals, holding out his hand, fearing he might scare her off. "How have you escaped the flames? How has Allah spared you?"

She stared at him, snuffling and whimpering.

He inched closer, reaching for her. "Come to me, little girl. Come to me now. Do not be afraid." He waited, holding his breath.

She sat motionless, watching him. What must she be thinking, feeling? How much had she seen of her father's last moments? The child could not be much past the age of weaning. Did she not have a family somewhere, a mother? They would hear of this atrocity, wondering what became of her. And yet, the bodies in the Jeep were those of two men. Perhaps these were kidnappers who had snatched the children to sell them. Perhaps this child had been spared a life worse than death by burning. The urge to protect and shield the child welled up in Ihsan.

With the heat of the fire added to that of the baking sun, the child must surely be thirsty. Ihsan reached for the canteen slung behind him and opened it. He held it out to her, dribbling a few drops onto his other hand to demonstrate his meaning. She stretched out her hands and he saw with alarm that they were bleeding. He recalled the broken glass. Advancing toward her, he put the opening of the canteen to her mouth. She tipped her head eagerly as he poured the thin, life-giving stream out for her. At last, she held slender arms up to him, a look of utter dependence in her eyes.

Something inside him shifted. What if he, Ihsan bin Ibrahim, was meant to find this child, to rescue her from flames, or slavery, or whatever else the forces of evil had intended for her? In the moment, that moment of decision and destiny, Ihsan's heart constricted in pity. Then it expanded in compassion. He swept the child into his arms.

She clung to him, gripping his ribs with her knees and burying her head into the space under his jaw. A space that had been made for just such a person, though he had never known it. Making his choice, he turned back along the road with his precious cargo, determined to protect her. He would carry her home with him. The feel of the child, her arms clinging about his neck, her helpless need and vulnerability, tugged at his heart. "My child." His voice cracked with emotion.

He caught up to his flock and gathered them together to prod them with his staff toward home.

Chapter 11

Some through the fire,
but all through the blood
God leads His dear children along.
~God Leads Us Along, by G. A. Young, 19th century

My little girl's soft arms reach up to me, her eyes brimming with tears. My heart melts with overwhelming love for her. I bend to take Anya in my arms, to kiss her boo-boo, soothe her fears, feed her, bathe her, and rock her to sleep in my arms. But when I touch her, she flakes away in blackened leaves of ash like the pages of a burnt book.

My eyes opened as I jerked awake, heart hammering in my chest. Panting in panic, I told myself it was a dream I tried to steer my thoughts to safe ground. I forced myself to exhale long and slow, focusing on the in and out, until gradually my pulse returned to normal. The luminescent hands of the bedside clock read five twenty. Shaky still, I sank back onto my pillow and covered myself with the quilt Mom and Grandma had made. In the twilight of my cottage, the moon lit up a patch of the wall beside my bed to a silver sheen.

Don't think about it, don't think about it. Part of me warned that if I thought through what happened to James and the girls in all its lurid detail, I would never recover, never be able to face living again.

Another part of my brain strained to recapture their every word and movement of the morning they left on their trip. I wanted to save the memories of that day and all the time before, grasping hold of time so I could preserve my beloved ones. I smiled to think how James had suggested he take both girls with him and Chuk, the other IT guy, on their daytrip north.

The night before, he had pulled me away from dinner-making and into his arms. "You deserve a day to yourself for a change."

This captured the attention of the girls from the front room, as it never failed to do. I could sense them watching, big-eyed, as he kissed me lingeringly. "We'll be driving right through the Lame Burra and Yankari game reserves," he murmured. "Could be the last opportunity the kids ever have to see big game before we go back to Canada."

I was touched. James was an intense kind of guy, immersed in work he loved and in which he believed fervently. He became so engrossed in it that I'd often teased him about his unconsciousness of anything going on around him. I had grown used to his way and, because I believed in the work too, I was convinced my home-keeping was my contribution to it. The idea that he had paused long enough to think about my need as an introvert for some alone-time made me tender toward him. As out of sync with modern life as it was, I loved my role in the home, with the girls. Still, the very dailyness of life with littles wore even on someone like me who loved children. Besides, I knew the girls would love going on a trip with Daddy, and even the long drive would be an adventure to them, since we rarely drove anywhere. A day to catch up on emails or maybe do a bit of shopping with my friend Ebos? Sounded marvelous. I didn't need much persuading. "Okay. I'll make a lunch for the four of you tonight."

James leaped over the back of the couch with a raucous trumpeting, swinging one arm for a makeshift elephant trunk. Josie and Anya dropped the toys they held and flung themselves at his legs for an elephant ride. They clung, each to a leg, while he stomped around our living room, screeching for peanuts.

"Give him peanuts, Mommy!" Josie piped, her eyes shining.

"Nut-nut, Mama!" Anya shrilled, her pink mouth wide open in laughing excitement.

At bedtime that night, James read the next chapter in our Bible story book. Now I wondered which one. Suddenly, my heart lurched to a stop in scrolling through the memory of that evening. *Could I be mistaken?* But no. I recalled it clearly. It was the story of God speaking to Moses through the burning bush. *Why that one?* I caught my breath in turmoil, balling my hands into fists. Was there some meaning to this? I released a long slow breath, letting my hands fall limp into my lap. If it was more than coincidence, I didn't understand what it could mean. I set my confusion aside and forged on with my reminiscence of that night.

I had swayed with Anya in my arms while we sang, "Going on a Lion Hunt." Draped over my shoulder, Anya chimed in with a word or two that she knew. In the previous month she had begun repeating quite a few of the last syllables of words she heard her sister say. We chuckled about her late-to-the-party echo, but her vocabulary was coming along.

James had made the girls recite the list of animals they would go a-hunting for. "Lions and tigers and bears, oh my!"

"But no tigers here. And no bears," Josie said. "Bears are in Candada." We exulted over our not-quite three-year-old's clear and near-perfect enunciation, but she always struggled with Canada.

"Beah," Anya squealed. I rubbed her back in the circular motion she loved.

"That's right," James said. "In Canada there are bears. But in Nigeria what do we have?"

"Elephants. And hippos. And giraffes." Josie's confident answers made us smile.

"'Raff," Anya said. James and I exchanged impressed glances. Our little girl was growing up.

Josie raised her finger to her lips, her forehead wrinkled in thought. "And gorillas?"

"I don't think we'll see gorillas this time. They like the mountains where they can hide better." James kissed her brow. "Let's pray and then we'll get a good sleep so we can be ready to go a-hunting tomorrow, okay?"

After prayer, we tucked them into their bed and crib, kissing them and stroking their hair in turn, then returned to the kitchen. While I packaged food for a lunch for two men and two children, James told me what he planned to discuss with some of the tech guys at Kano State University of Technology.

"I'm hoping Chuk and I can set up a liaison between them and our translators so that once I leave, they can do any troubleshooting and fixing of glitches that might come up. But I hope those will be few and far between." As usual, he was full of enthusiastic ideas, even after a long day of work, even if he had been out in the heat. He never seemed tired or down.

And that's about where I always had to end my reliving of last things. The last kisses of downy baby cheeks, the last sensation of a soft, fresh-from-the-bath child in my arms, the final time in my husband's impassioned embrace. I had to keep those precious memories from moving forward into the next morning. If I drifted into recollections of my carefree, leisurely waking to the empty house that I thought was a delightful treat...If I remembered that day with nothing but time on my hands, of my cheerful and humorous online messages to family and supporters about our wonderful life in Jos, funny things the girls had said, adventures in the marketplace, quirky accounts of the neighbours or our occasionally deaf-at-will house help, well, I couldn't let myself go there. Too often I would tumble into a dark imagining, over and over, of what must have taken place on that terrible day. While I was enjoying myself at home, the ones I loved most in this world were enduring unspeakable—No! I refused to allow my mind to go there.

Yet now, not for the first time, a dream had brought me face to face with the horrible reality I had fought so hard to escape. It had seemed so real; Anya had seemed so alive. I could almost hear her cry, feel her skin, smell her lovely baby smell. And why were the dreams only of Anya? Why not Josie, too? At sixteen months apart, I couldn't even remember us as a couple with one child. They were my two babies, both in diapers for a while, back and forth with clothing and colds, songs and stories, toys and tantrums. What I did for one, I made sure I did for the other. I had often held them both in my arms, soothing them at the same time. There had been moments when their overwhelming demands had all three of us crying at once. So why did I now dream of Anya alone?

Officer Akinde had said, "No word yet. We will let you know whatever we find out." And no further word had ever come.

When Damaris's husband Kelechi and Pastor Sam had been forced by police inaction to drive up to the site themselves, three bodies had been recovered from that wreck. Only the bodies of Chuk, James, and Josie had returned in the back of Kelechi's pickup. Sam wouldn't let me near them, patiently, solidly blocking my view of the tarpaulin-draped forms, though I screamed at him in the most frightful, disrespectful way. But what my eyes had not witnessed, my imagination filled in. And continued to fill in though I battled my mind's inexorable drift into the events of that day. Now out of the smoke of the confusion and shock that had smogged my brain for the past weeks, a thread of doubt dangled before my vision. What ghastly end had come to my Anya that not even a corpse was recovered?

Chapter 12

S ue pulled a few cookbooks off the shelf, sat down at the kitchen table, and began paging through them, resolved to concoct a supper worthy of the occasion—the whole family together for the first time in over four years. Yet the thought arrested her. It wouldn't be the whole family. And in fact, the whole family had never been together, since the African girls had never met their great-grandmothers, or uncles, aunts, and cousins. A wave of loss nearly capsized her determination and her shoulders slumped.

Ever since Lynnie, her first child was born, Sue had felt her children's every pain and anguish in almost a physical sense. More than once, she had had to set aside her own fears to avoid discouraging them from trying something new. Like the first time she drove them out to the mountains for skiing. Her sole experience on the slopes as a fourteen-year-old had been a demoralizing, painful failure, with ill-fitting boots that cut into her calves the whole day. Worse yet was being relegated to the beginner class on the bunny hill when her church youth group friends were whizzing down the advanced runs. Years later, taking her kids to that resort for ski lessons created all sorts of dread and guilt. But she'd reminded herself she'd felt the same about swimming lessons when they were much younger and that had turned out well for them.

This new experience, something she'd never dreamed could happen to their family, had brought her unspeakable pain. When that horrible phone call from Africa first came, her stomach had clenched in a spasm of terror. She knew her own feelings must be a mere fraction of what Lynnie was going through.

Sue had never experienced the death of anyone close to her. Her father had left when she was too young to remember him, and she hadn't known Glen's father very well by the time he died. And no Hardy child had ever died, not even through an early miscarriage. She only knew that pain vicariously through a friend who'd lost a baby. This catastrophic, gruesome death of her young granddaughters and son-in-law at the hands of terrorists was not just tragic but sickening in its brutality. Sue almost wished she could feel it physically, to somehow share Lynnie's burden of pain.

Taking the cookbook in hand again, she heaved a great sigh. Someone had to carry on. Someone had to keep the rest of the family living and loving one another. For sweet Lynnie there needed to be a place of refuge right now. Somewhere that she could catch her breath, drink deeply from God's living water, and keep from falling into despair. And she would need support far into the future, too. For Sue, the only source she knew was faith and family. There hadn't yet been time for her and Glen to discuss with Lynnie how she was coping in the faith department, but if there was one thing Sue knew how to do, it was family. She paged through the cookery manual, gleaning ideas. Something special, but unique, yet not unfamiliar. Comfort food was what was needed on this cool spring day. And for a centerpiece, she'd ask Grandma to bring over a pot of her ever-blooming African violets. Or would that be a triggering misstep?

Her gaze roamed the walls of the room, alert now to everything that might set off grief. Wedding pictures of the children, grandchildren's photos, and drawings on the fridge. But to remove them would not only be unnatural, it would also erase history.

She had to find some time with Lynnie alone to discuss these things, find out her take on everything and try to help her reach a place of peace.

I'd offered to help with the preparations when I found out Mom was planning a family dinner for the Saturday night after my return. She didn't object much, so I figured she was a bit stressed, maybe out of practice cooking for a crowd. "There'll be twelve of us altogether, right?" I asked her as I smoothed the tablecloth.

Mom straightened, mentally calculating. "Thirteen. Your brother said he'll be in town and can swing by for Nanny on the way home."

I found myself falling back into my accustomed role of sous chef, remembering without effort where things were, how Mom liked the carrots cut, grating the onion rather than chopping it for the sake of Grandma and Katie, who weren't onion fans, and locating the frozen bacon bits exactly where they always were, as though I had never been on my own or halfway around the world.

Mom stopped with her knife suspended in mid-air to tilt her head at me. "It's wonderful to have you home, Lynnie. I'd forgotten what it's like to have my right arm again." She smiled at me.

"Thanks." I smiled back, meaning it. I was thankful for home and the haven my parents had always made it. Where would I go, who would I be now without home to fall back on?

But Mom wasn't finished. "Are you going to be alright? I mean, reuniting with the whole family all at once like this?"

I gave a rueful smile. "Who would we uninvite? Maybe tell Grandma we scrapped the plan?"

Mom rolled her eyes. "Okay, then. Let's get these underway."

I stuffed the spinach and Swiss cheese into each chicken breast, and she breaded them, laying them in the pan.

True to form, Grandma arrived an hour and a half early, just as we slid the pan into the oven. She placed a securely wrapped parcel on the table and handed me a towel-covered tray, then slipped out of her boots and coat. I set the tray on the counter and was at her side in a second to hang her coat for her.

"Fresh buns," she announced.

"Oh, that'll be perfect with supper," Mom said, pouring rice into a pot.

Grandma reached for the small package on the table, peeling back multiple layers of plastic and newspaper. It was battened down like it was being sent to foreign parts, her distrust of the postal service being legendary. But she had only carried it the hundred yards from her own home. Out of the wrapping came a blooming mass of burgundy violets. She set the pot in the dish Mom had centred on the table for them. Then she grasped my arm and pointed to a chair. "You can sit now. I will help your mother."

Mom and I traded glances. I'd rather have been up and doing something, but I knew Grandma meant well. Immediately, she set to work slicing and buttering the buns, filling the breadbasket with them.

I smiled, watching her. "Butter them thinly, right to the edges, like you taught us kids."

Grandma peered wryly over the top of her glasses at me. "It's the proper way to do it."

I chuckled. "I think you made a perfectionist out of me, Grandma."

"The world could do with a lot more perfectionists," she replied.

Age didn't seem to have slowed her down. She worked at a speed none of us had ever been able to match, not a motion wasted.

The front door opened just then, with a gust of cold air and Katie bounced in, glowing with health and beauty in her red coat and white earmuffs. Letting the door slam behind her, she spread her arms and rushed at me.

I stood to hug her. "How have you gotten so tall and so gorgeous?" I said, my words muffled by the cool shoulder of her wool coat.

She didn't let go her tight squeeze for almost a minute, then pulled back, looked at me with soulful eyes, and embraced me again.

"Alright already!" I said, laughing.

But Katie wasn't laughing. Instead, her eyes were filled with tears, and I realized the sight of me made her see only my loss, not the big sister who had told her stories and played with her as a little girl. And if she was seeing me that way, how could I ever hope to have a normal life again? Would I forever be the black cloud at every gathering? Maleficent to every sunshine-and-roses fairy?

Miserable with that role, I turned the focus back to Katie. "So how's university?" Of all us kids who had taken early piano lessons, she was the only one who hadn't had to be reminded to practice.

"Great!" she said, the trouble clearing from her face at the thought. She hung her coat and moved toward the kitchen.

"I want to hear you play," I told her, gesturing toward the piano in the living room.

"Any time." She smiled and glanced at Mom. "But I'm trying to be a little less selfish and help in the kitchen more."

The door opened again and Lissa's two kids, Jade and Dylan, came through.

My mouth fell open. In the four years I'd been away, Jade had changed from a gap-toothed little kid to a young lady. She was only eleven. How was that possible? I folded them both into a group hug.

"Jade, Dylan, my pals. You've grown so much. I've missed you!"

Lissa came in next, bustling past me to the counter with a grocery bag. Still in her coat, she got busy pulling out bottles of salad dressing. She seemed to avoid my eyes.

"Do I get a hug, Sis?"

Finally, she came toward me, chewing her lip. She held me briefly, then pulled back to remove her coat. Mark entered and I embraced my quiet brother-in-law. Wordless, he patted my back. It was a touching gesture of helpless caring from my fellow introvert that for a moment made my eyes tear up.

I pulled out a couple of chairs for them and took one myself. "Sit, you two, and tell me everything that's been going on."

Mark sat in the chair offered, but Lissa sat farther from him, in the one next to me. This surprised me, given how glued to each other the two of them had been when they were first married. Was she trying to avoid looking me in the eye?

After a long silence, Mark mentioned they had bought a couple of horses so the kids could join 4-H. Uncharacteristically, Lissa said nothing. I had always relied on her chattiness to move the conversation along but now the awkwardness that settled on us left me floundering.

I sniffed the aroma from the oven. "Things are starting to smell good. I'll finish putting together the salad."

"No, no." Lissa jumped up from her chair. "I'll get that." She whisked off to the counter and busied herself with lettuce and bacon.

I couldn't help laughing at her eagerness. "Who's this Miss Homemaker and what has she done with my work-shirking sister?"

At least she made a face at me. That seemed more like old times.

Chapter 13

Can we find a friend so faithful,
Who will all our sorrows share?
Jesus knows our every weakness,
Take it to the Lord in prayer.
~What a Friend We Have in Jesus, by Joseph Scriven, 1819-1886

W e were seating ourselves at the table by the time Dad came in from feeding the cattle, settling into our old places like the folds of an old shirt. Even with all the changes in our family over the years we reverted to our old positions, kids on one end, adults on the other. The grandmothers sat next to each other, one short and round, one tall and skinny. The Ball and Bat, Lissa used to call them when we were kids and, ever since, I'd never been able to see them any other way. Come to think of it, Nanny, the Ball, was like a baseball in other ways besides physical. She had always been reactionary, flung here and there with every wind of doctrine but without any viewpoint of her own. By contrast, Grandma Hardy was the Bat. She stood alone—stiff and sturdy, unwavering—and if necessary could give you a good whack to get you moving in the right direction.

Dad bowed his head, and we did the same, joining hands. I'd missed this. Around the circle, we were united not just by the touch of our hands, but by our faith and our love for one another. At least, all of us except Nanny. But she never objected to our practice of prayer. Beside me, though, I sensed movement and squinted in time to notice Lissa yank her hand out of Mark's grasp. Something was amiss there, and it alarmed me. Hadn't there been enough loss and disruption in our lives without marriage problems? She should know how lucky she was to still have her husband.

When Dad finished, he raised his head and gave me his lopsided half-smile, then started passing the chicken. Everyone seemed eager to talk, telling details of their day, asking each other questions, until the plates were full and the chewing commenced. I noticed no one asked me anything other than about the food, and they were all quick to respond to anything I asked for.

"So Lance, tell me about little Blade," I said, cutting into my chicken. I wanted to take a genuine interest in my new nephew, but I also wanted to avoid making my situation the focal point. "He must be getting close to crawling by now."

Lance grinned like a schoolboy on a snow day. "Yeah, I can't wait for you to meet him. Crystal kept him home because he was so cranky today. But you should see him go. He does everything crazy fast."

"Like his papa," Mom said, passing the salad to her left.

"By the pictures online, I see you haven't kept your promise," I said.

"What's that?" Lance lifted an eyebrow in my direction.

"That if you ever had fat babies, you'd force them to exercise."

My family laughed.

"Ha, I guess I did say that once in my foolish youth. Trust you to hold it against me."

"Oh, there's lots we could hold against you, buddy," Katie said, her eyes sparkling with mischief. "Like the time you left me asleep in a grain bin and Dad locked the door, not knowing I was in there. Or on the rare occasions you did let me play with you, I had to be your dog and stay in the crate."

Lance and I burst out laughing.

"I seem to recall we named you Marlin," I said.

"And she had a fondness for the moldy mushroom yogurt we fed her," Lance added.

Katie rolled her eyes. "In captivity, one takes what one is given."

Grandma fixed us each in turn with a frown. "I sincerely hope no one was forced to eat anything moldy."

"No, no, Grandma. Just a kids' game of pretend," I assured her. With Grandma, there was no statute of limitations, and past sins could receive present censure.

At this point, Lissa jabbed an elbow into my ribs, bringing back all sorts of hilarity from our childhood. I stifled a giggle with difficulty, concentrating on gathering my remaining rice onto my fork. Suppressing the laughter made me choke and I went off into a coughing fit. From there, everyone showed the utmost concern, though I couldn't seem to gasp out that I was fine. At least the giggles were under control.

I was quite aware I was bordering on hysteria. Though it was wonderful to be home, everything that had happened to me simmered inside me and was barely skinned over by the ordinariness of life. Yet I so longed for a return to normal.

Mom brought out Black Forest chocolate cheesecake for dessert. When we each had a piece and she sat down, Lance turned to me. "So what's the next step for you, Lynnie?"

The tinkle of forks against china abruptly stopped. I could feel everyone's eyes on me. A flush of heat stole over my whole body and my tongue melted to the roof of my mouth. The silence stretched long. Then both grandmothers started to fill it.

"This cheesecake is delicious, Sue," Nanny chimed in. "I could keep on eating and eating if I weren't already so full after an excellent meal."

Grandma frowned at what she doubtless saw as gluttony, one of the seven deadly sins. Thankfully, she restrained herself this time.

"Lance, we must let the Lord lead your sister in his own way and in his own good timing." She set her fork down beside her plate that still held half her slice of cheesecake and taking her napkin, dabbed at her lips. "This is certainly a rich dessert."

Neither Nanny's attempt to change the subject nor Grandma's well-meant reproof of my brother helped to stave off the breaking of the skin of normalcy. The horror of the events of the past weeks— the loss, the pain, and the grief—erupted from inside me with a deep sob and a welling of tears. I grabbed my napkin and stood, letting my chair teeter backward behind me, then rushed out of the room. I stumbled up the stairs to my old bedroom and flung myself on the guest bed there.

Lance didn't mean to hurt me, I knew that. But the cumulative effect of the evening had exploded so violently that it had surprised even me. Now I muffled my sobs with a pillow allowing myself to feel everything I had stuffed down since I walked back into my childhood home. I had avoided looking at my wedding picture, displayed on the family photo gallery wall in the dining room, but I'd been conscious of it from the start. I'd turned away from the photos of Josie and Anya displayed on the sideboard. I had kept myself from thinking about Lissa's whole family being present while I was alone. And it had taken every bit of residual decency I could find to ask Lance about his baby boy. But to be asked the question that brought all of this to a volcanic head, the perplexing dilemma of what I was to do next had destroyed me. With all its attendant struggle about who I now was when my very life purpose had been snatched from me, it was the thing that most filled me with fear and despair.

A tentative tap sounded at the door. That would be Mom. How long had it been since she'd had to follow me up here after some teen-hormone-fuelled outburst?

"It's open," I said, wiping my face on my sleeve and closing my eyes again.

Her weight settled on the bed, slanting me towards her.

"Evelyn, my dear."

I looked up through blurred eyes. Not Mom, but Grandma. I made a move to sit up but her firm hand pressed on my shoulder, beginning a soothing circular stroking.

"It is very hard, isn't it?"

Did her voice just crack? I knew Grandma had suffered, though she rarely spoke of it. She had lost her first son as a toddler. Grandpa had let him ride on the fender of the tractor and he had fallen off and been crushed under the tire. Dad had told me Grandpa had struggled with depression ever after. So I knew she spoke from experience.

"There are sinkholes at every turn. The simplest things fan the flames at the most unexpected times." Her thin, cool hand smoothed the hair away from my face, then resumed the gentle massaging. "There is only one refuge, only one relief from the pain. And I know you know who that is." Her voice broke again so that the next words came out in rasps. "I want you to come talk to me as often as you need to. But more importantly, go to him, Evelyn. Every day and all day if necessary. Let Jesus be your comforter. He loves you like no other."

And then she began to pray, her words a humble pleading for help and strength for me, for answers to the confusion. Never in my childhood had she touched me like this, shown such deep emotion. Never had I heard her pray in this way, storming the gates of heaven on my behalf. It was a ragged song of praise to her God, full of trust in his good plans and his tender care for his own people.

My questions and demands for answers to the cruelty of it all clamoured to be heard, but her descriptions of the Lord's gentleness broke down my resistance. They shut my mouth and flooded my soul with a cool, soothing peace.

At length, I sat up, straightened my shirt, and reached for her. In the moonlight that silvered everything in the room, we held each other for a long time. Two women who had trusted God, endured unspeakable loss, and trusted him still.

Chapter 14

Ihsan's arms strained and cramped under the load he had transferred to his back for the long walk home from the burn site. The slight child clung to him so that at first shifting her to his back had provided relief from the burden. But now that she was asleep, she was a dead weight. He was thankful at least that her cries had subsided to whimpers and eventually to silence. Her head lolled against his neck, sticking to him by their mingled sweat, and her limbs, dangling and awkward, offered no help in clinging to him. However, the village was in sight ahead and offered the promise of rest.

But now, approaching home brought other matters to Ihsan's mind. How would Daniya react to this foundling? The longer he carried the child, the stronger was his belief that the event was a deliverance. Not only for the child, but also for his wife and even himself. He had lost his heart to the child on the spot, but would Daniya? He recalled other women he had known who had not taken kindly to the children of their husband's other wives. Would that kind of conflict and cruelty happen to him and this infant? These were not questions he had considered when he had made his fateful decision to bring the child home with him.

His steps slowed as he pondered the best way to break the news to his wife. But other concerns vied for his attention. What would the rest of the villagers say? For there could be no question of keeping the child hidden. If he and his wife were to raise the little girl, she would become part of the family and community. And village gossip was one thing, but would a visiting imam or Ihsan's Christian neighbours insist he search out her parents? The very thought brought a surge of turmoil to his gut. Stroking the small silky arm around his neck, he now knew he would do anything to keep from losing her.

The goats picked up their pace when they sensed familiar ground and eagerly surged up the dirt road into their pen behind his house. With one hand he supported his new daughter's bottom behind his back while with the other he filled the goats' trough with water, then plodded to the door of his home. In apprehension, he entered, pausing a moment to let his eyes adjust to the dim light. All was quiet. He lay the drowsy child on a mat on the floor, then searched for something he could eat. Uma must have come. There was an unopened bag of bread. He tore off a chunk and began munching. Then Ihsan moved aside the curtain to enter the room at the rear.

His wife still lay on the bed, as unmoving as he had left her. Her eyes opened when he crouched next to her. "Daniya," he murmured, stroking her cheek with his thumb.

Her eyes focused on him, but there was no joy in them.

"You must sit up. It is a great day. Yes, sit up now. I have brought something for you."

A spark of interest flickered in her eyes at his urgent tone.

"Come now. Sit up and straighten your clothes." He smiled at his wife who then raised herself on her elbows. Ihsan turned to retrieve the infant from the other room. The small child had wakened and now sat on the mat, rubbing her eyes with rounded fists. When she saw him, she reached up her arms to him, stirring his affection once again. He picked her up, took another deep breath and went in to Daniya.

His woman had obeyed and sat up but still stared despondently at the floor. Ihsan remained motionless, waiting, but Daniya paid him no mind.

"Daniya." Impatience tinged his tone, joined with excitement. This was a momentous day and he wanted her to feel what he felt at this amazing gift from Allah. Why couldn't she make an effort, just once?

At last, she raised her eyes, at first dully, then with a start of something he took to be surprise. It was a response. Heartened, Ihsan sank down next to the bed, setting the child beside his wife. "Look what I found today."

Daniya's silent gaze pulled away from the child, darting to him and back to her again.

"A baby, Daniya. Like you've always wanted." He took the small hand and placed it on Daniya's shoulder, the pale skin a marked contrast against his wife's dark skin. "I watched a terrible thing happen on the road today. Very bad. A car fire, set by Fulani. But out of the flames, something living came. I cannot understand it. It should not have been possible. A miracle! I found her there on the side of the road, without parents. She was all alone and crying."

His wife had not moved toward the child and the little one had pulled her hand back. Now he placed the girl on his wife's lap, waiting for some sign his wife would attach. It had not occurred to him that Daniya might resist. Surely, she would not reject the child. He would not allow it. Had she not longed for one? Yet her arms still hung limp at her sides and the girl turned her face toward him, reaching out for him.

"My wife, you must listen now. Allah has sent us a child," he announced in a firm voice, hoping an appeal to the Almighty would carry more weight with his despondent wife than a whim of his own.

But Daniya turned her face to the wall.

A spark of anger flared through Ihsan and he stood abruptly. He wanted to shake her. "Have I not been patient with you?" he hissed, stooping to place his face close to hers. "Have I not felt the loss of each one of our infants as much as you? Have I, too, not craved a son?" He squatted in front of her, his eyes boring into hers as though he could rouse her spirit by pure force of his will. "Now I have provided you with a child and you do nothing? You say nothing?" He gripped her shoulders, raising his voice. "Daniya. You will care for her. She must be thirsty. Give her milk and bathe her. She needs to be comforted. I say you will be her mother. Allah has willed it by letting me find her. And Allah has given this child to you."

Still Daniya made no response. The child began to whimper, perhaps because of his harsh tone. When his wife failed to embrace the girl, he steeled his heart against them both. He must leave them to it. Daniya would rise to the need. He insisted she should. He left the house to sit smoking in the shade on its east side. Should he consult with Uma? He thought of his visit with his sister that very morning when he had asked her to stop in on Daniya and comfort her. Whatever she had said appeared to have had no effect.

Yet so much had happened since then to change his own life. Now he was a father. He wiped sweat from his forehead. A father whose wife would not obey him and take care of his child. He pounded his fist on his knee, hating the feeling of helplessness at the *jinn* that had stolen his wife's good nature. Ihsan brooded on his family dilemma until the shadows of evening grew long and there was but a small slice of red sun on the horizon.

At length he became aware of his hunger again. He rose and plodded with heavy steps into the house, knowing there would be no meal waiting for him. Irritation swept through him again. He had been patient long enough. He stalked into the house to begin foraging for something more to fill his belly.

Inside, he stopped short. His wife was in the kitchen with the child on her lap. She looked at him without smiling but still, she held the sleeping child in her arms. Though the girl was as grimy as when he had brought her home, an empty cup with a dribble of milk running down its side sat on the table beside Daniya. She had fed the child.

Ihsan softened. This would work. In the simple tasks of caring for a child, Daniya's joy would return to her. And if it returned to her, it would fill the house as it once had. Then his own good humour, in short supply of recent months, would also return. He searched the shelf finding some leftover beans and more bread, then sat down to eat across from his wife. If only she would smile at him as she used to.

"The child must have a name," he said, jutting his chin at her. "Since it is a girl, you must name her."

Daniya looked from the infant in her arms to him and back again but said nothing.

No matter. Ihsan would wait. For tonight it was enough that his wife had fed the child and was holding her as she slept. A name would come in time.

He stood and took two steps toward the bedroom but stilled when he thought he heard Daniya speak. Leaning back, he caught sight of her and waited.

"Aminah. She is Aminah."

"Aminah?" he repeated. "Yes. A good name. Truly she is safe and protected." Ihsan smiled to himself as he prepared for bed. He had done a good thing today. He had obeyed the calling of God and Allah would bless him. He had made them a family at last.

Chapter 15

Be still, my soul, the Lord is on thy side!
Bear patiently the cross of grief or pain;
Leave to thy God to order and provide
In every change, He faithful will remain.
~ Be Still My Soul, by Katharina von Schlegel,
1697-1768

My face was swollen and blotchy the next morning, with dark circles under my eyes from my trouble getting to sleep. I did what I could with cold water to lessen the damage. I was grateful I could silently flee from my folks' place, and no one had to see me this way. I blessed my mom for having thought to provide this private refuge for me. After breakfast I called her to apologize for my meltdown and abrupt leaving the night before. She forgave me as I knew she and the rest of my family would.

I also had a question, one that was related to my growing, urgent inner drive. I needed to sift through the memories of my husband and children so that I could somehow—what? Finish grieving? Accept the upheaval of my life? Stop the pain? I didn't know but I felt compelled to do it.

"What became of that box James's mom sent out just before we left for Africa?" I asked Mom.

I had only met my mother-in-law, Lily Min, once— at our wedding. James said it was unheard of in his family for her to take three days off. Yet she made the trip from Toronto to attend her youngest son's wedding. Since emigrating from Korea and losing her husband shortly after, she had raised her boys alone while running the family store that was open every day, even Christmas. The box I was looking for was a collection of James's childhood keepsakes that we'd received from her a day or two before we were scheduled to leave for Africa and which I had asked my mother to place in storage.

"I put that inside a rubber tote in the storage shed with all your other belongings," Mom said. "I can help you find it if you give me about half an hour. Why? What's on your mind?"

I felt a little foolish speaking my plan aloud but told her anyway. "It's something my friend Damaris said she did after her son was murdered. She laid out all his belongings in order of his age, and picked them up and handled them, or read them or whatever. She told me she spent a long time just crying over the things, remembering, and praying. And she said when she finished, she was done the worst of her grieving. Before I left Jos, she told me to do this, that it would help."

Mom was quiet for half a beat, then said, "That sounds like a good idea. I'll meet you at the shed."

Even though I had bundled up in my mittens and parka, my teeth were chattering by the time I made it to my parents' gate. Mom unlocked the padlock of their packed metal storage shed and we stepped inside. She had all the totes neatly labeled and shelved so it wasn't hard to locate what I needed. I spied the "Lynnie's keepsakes" tote and asked Mom to carry that, too. My life and James's were interlocked, after all. We lugged the heavy containers to my cabin and set them on the floor.

"I've got to get back to work at home, but you take as long as you need at this, dear." Reaching for the door handle, she hesitated.

"Would you like me to bring your supper here? I know last night didn't go all that well and I'm sorry about that. I guess it was just too soon."

"It's okay, really. Nobody's fault. And it was a great meal and nice to see everyone. But you're right, maybe it was too soon. I didn't think I was that fragile." I nodded. "Yeah, if you would bring me supper, that would be nice."

"Will do. Have a great—I mean—I hope this will help." She gave me a quick squeeze and left me to it.

I sank to the floor between the containers, laying a hand on each lid. Would this help? Would it take away the constant ache? Somehow, I doubted it, but I had to try. It had helped Damaris. I still shivered and not only from the inner turmoil. The cone-shaped ceiling must have been pulling all the heat from the electric baseboard heaters upward, leaving a distinct chill on the floor where I knelt. How had I ever thought winter was fun, and enjoyed tobogganing or skiing?

I eyed the wood stove with distrust. Fire now scared me more than anything. I couldn't help associating it with the death of my loved ones. Would I always be crippled by that fear? But today was not the day to challenge my terrors. I bundled up and returned to my parents' shed for my box of winter clothes.

Back indoors and cozied into a wool sweater and socks, I stared at the totes of memorabilia with foreboding. The cabin's quiet accentuated the riot of voices in my memory. Was I up to facing them? Perhaps music would help. I found some of the tunes that had been our favourites and started them playing.

Within minutes I was reduced to a puddle of sentimental weeping. I had thought my outpouring of tears during the funeral had to do with my Nigerian sisters' songs of hope and comfort. But even pop songs overwhelmed me with emotion. I leapt up to shut off the music and grabbed a tissue to wipe my face. The silence was safer.

I lifted the lid of the box Lily had sent. She had placed items into neat files marked with each year of James's life until he left home. The year he was born held a birth announcement, hospital information, and congratulatory cards interspersed with photos and a calendar of "firsts." There was even a card labeled "umbilical cord." The tiny plastic bag attached contained a few dark dried crumbs. That was kind of gross. According to the stats, he was a pretty small baby, six pounds, compared to the nine I had weighed and the nearly eight pounds of each of our girls. But what a pelt the kid had. His newborn photo made me laugh aloud. He looked like a Muppet with his thick, spiky black hair fanning out from a wizened face. I pulled out my phone to compare this photo to Josie's newborn shot. No question, the resemblance was unmistakable though he won in the hair department.

"You were so cute," I whispered, swallowing the lump forming in my throat and pressing both pictures to my chest. Because clearly, I couldn't separate the strands of our lives that were so tightly woven together and feathered into the generations before and after us. Was this whole project misguided? Could I bear the flames of emotion licking at me like this again and again for hours or days?

I went on tabbing through the files. James held by his mom at the front the church for his baby dedication. His older brothers flanked her, dressed to the nines. James sitting up, crawling, learning to walk down the aisle of the convenience store using large pop bottles for support. There weren't a lot of pictures, no doubt due to Lily's busy life. All morning, I paged through childish animal drawings, and birthday cards, photos of the boy I loved pedaling a tricycle on the sidewalk in front of the store or playing with his brothers in their home above it. I clutched each item to my heart, doing my best to divert overwhelming feelings of loss into thanks to God for growing the man who was to become mine.

At noon, I scrounged in the fridge for some of last night's leftover chicken and one of Grandma's tender dinner rolls that Mom had packaged in a hurry to send home with me. When I turned back to the box, I found I had more than two-thirds of the contents still to go through and that didn't begin to cover his college years or our courtship. At this rate, it could take weeks.

"So what if it does? I have nothing better to do, no place to go, no one who needs me." That last bit choked me. My life for the past three years had been dominated by the urgent demands of babies who were utterly dependent on me. In these bereft weeks, I had been conscious of my arms, dangling empty and useless at my sides when they were accustomed to constant use. The cottage gave no answer but it encircled me in its quiet and light, granting permission to take as much time as I needed.

After eating, I sat on the floor surrounded by the boxes and piles of papers. I should do something with this history, document it somehow. Studying and handling everything here had brought the thought that Lily might now regret sending away these vestiges of her son. Her cry of anguish back when she heard the news still tore my heart. She hadn't seen James at all since our brief stopover on the flight out, and she had never met her granddaughters. Because of her schedule and low-level computer skills, online chats were impossible and, too often, my good intentions to send photos and letters hadn't materialized.

Do something for her.

A life journal began to take shape in my mind. I could compile these mementos and have it printed for her as well as for me. I pictured myself an old lady, sitting in my rocker, paging through this part of my life and my lost love. At thirty-one years of age, there could still be a lot of blank pages between now and then. This thought led to the troubling question that lurked always in the back of my mind. What would the intervening years contain? Was there to be only this short entry into my book of remembrance, followed by emptiness? Was there yet some purpose for me?

Chapter 16

Father-like, He tends and spares us,
Well our feeble frame He knows;
In His hands He gently bears us.
Rescues us from all our foes.
~Praise, My Soul, the King of Heaven, by Henry F. Lyte, 1793-1847

Immersed in my work in the weeks that followed, with a tangible goal I felt able to achieve, I was barely aware of the changes outside my panoramic windows. Each day I traced the life of my husband, establishing a timeline, writing details of memories he'd shared with me into the appropriate time slot as they came to mind, scanning photos. I was thankful to Lily for her meticulous labeling of pictures and the childhood drawings that became more realistic with each passing year. The school report cards showed an intelligent, inquisitive boy who excelled at both sports and studies, if on the over-talkative side. "James would do well to listen more than he talks" or some variation was the teacher's comment on every report.

Mom brought me my suppers most days, but one day Dad stopped in. He handed me the food containers, then surprised me by taking off his jacket and boots.

"How's my girl?" he asked, sauntering over to the couch, and taking a seat.

"Pretty good," I said, wondering what was on his mind.

Looking around and then at the wood stove, he rubbed his upper arms. "Why haven't you got a fire going?" When he met my gaze, he looked away. "Ah. I see." But instead of respecting my aversion, he crouched in front of the stove and began working with the kindling and wood that had lain ready but untouched since I moved in.

I forced myself not to cringe or back away, letting the heat at my back permeate my flesh. I told myself I would not react with emotion. I tried to relax in the comforting warmth as though it were the heat of the Nigerian sun. But as it grew stronger, I felt myself burning, my hair singeing and curling into ashy strands, my flesh falling off me in blackened flakes.

I lunged away, gasping. "Put it out, Dad! Please put it out," I sobbed.

He turned to me, grasping my arms. "No, Lynnie. You must take these thoughts captive. You can't let your imagination run free."

I leaned my cheek on his shoulder, shuddering.

He wrapped his arms around me. "I won't let you be crippled by this for the rest of your life. Fire is only a tool. Under control it does great good. God himself is a consuming fire, yet we know we can trust him. Don't let this grow in your mind into some kind of debilitating phobia, okay?"

I pulled back from him, nodding, and wiping my eyes. I made a deliberate choice to face the stove, praying for balance and control.

Dad returned to the couch, tilting forward, and resting his elbows on his knees. After a pause, he said, "The thing is, Lynnie, I'm somewhat worried about you. Your mom and I both are."

"What do you mean?"

"The way you're holing yourself up like this. And this business of your mom bringing you your meals and you never coming out of here. People at church and around town have been asking about you. We haven't known what to say." He scrubbed his jaw with his rough hand. "It isn't healthy." He waved at the view through the windows.

"You should be out in the fresh air and sunshine. Bet you don't even realize spring has sprung. Your mom's getting ready to plant the greenhouse. It'd be good for you to work in the soil with her, growing things. Therapy, like."

I loved my dad and could count on one hand the number of times he had disciplined me or had given me a talking-to. For him this was a long speech. Long and personal compared to his usual fare. He could talk farming, or if he got started on certain theological topics, he'd go for hours. But interpersonal relationships were not his forte. So I knew his concern about me was sincere.

I didn't know what to say. By now I was deep into my project of documenting the course of James's life, compelled almost by a sense of duty, to complete something permanent I could send to my mother-in-law and keep for myself. A monument, of sorts.

"It's something I've got to do, Dad. I can't explain why."

"But shouldn't you take a break once in a while? Get some fresh air?" His pleading tone got to me.

I had become so absorbed in my project chronicling James's story that it hadn't occurred to me how it might appear to my family. And I had shirked going to church, citing my unreadiness to face people. It hadn't occurred to me that this might worry them. Now that he said it, I was ashamed of expecting my family to serve me. "I guess I haven't been pulling my weight, have I?"

"Oh no, it's not that," he shook his head. "We only want the best for you." His eyes roamed around the room where I had James's drawings and photos of him and the girls propped or pinned everywhere. His gaze landed on the kitchen island where my laptop and printer were set up. It represented the last trip I had made to the shed to dig through my stored things and unpack essentials.

I made myself look past the window frames to the view I had been ignoring and tried to truly observe the outdoors. The pond was no longer covered in a sheet of white slush but reflected the blue of the giant prairie sky. Warming weather had brought back flocks of

Canada geese and they stretched out their broad feet to skid to a landing on the water's surface. Had I listened earlier to the racket they were making as I heard it now, even through the closed doors? And there was a distinct touch of spring green to the distant pasture that I hadn't noticed before.

"You're right Dad. I should get out a bit and help Mom. I'll do it tomorrow."

He stood up, smiling. "That's my girl." He reached to swing an arm around me as I also rose. "And do you think you could join us for suppers again and come to church with us, too? We've missed our Lynnie."

I nodded, touched by the affection in his voice. After he left, I opened one of the French doors and breathed deeply of the smell of the water, the old, dead smell of last year's rotting grasses, and whatever it was that gave the air a springtime tang. Sap was pushing out pussy willows on the nearby poplars, thickening the pencil lines of their bare branches. And the noise of chirruping frogs was loud when I stilled the narrative in my head long enough to listen. Best of all, the days were lengthening and the sun across the water had grown in power and strength. I felt myself relax. Dad was right. Tomorrow I'd go for a walk first thing in the morning, then stop in on Mom to see what I could do to help. And on Sunday, I would attend church with them.

Not to make excuses for taking advantage of my parents, but what had happened last month had left me in a weird state. Though I was a grown woman and had managed a home and family of my own for years, now I found myself returned to the role of a dependent child. Yet even a child has dreams for the future. I, on the other hand, didn't know where I fit or if I would ever fit somewhere again. But the adage about those who did not work should not eat came to mind. I could at least start with that.

The next morning, I stood on the deck of my cottage surveying what route my walk should take. I could follow the lane and take the gravel road past our farm, but it was flat and boring and would be equally flat and boring on the return trip. I scanned the circumference of the slough, wishing there was a path circling it.

Why not create one? If I walked the same way every day, by the end of the summer, the dead grasses would be worn down, creating a walkway. Animals did it all the time. I began picking my way around, skirting the pond. The untrod ground and thick old growth made walking tough and I worked up a sweat by the time I came around to my deck again. Tomorrow I would bring a rake and tug away some of the thickest tussocks to smooth the path.

My bit of physical exertion felt good. What also felt good was having another small goal. I could take a daily walk, help Mom with the garden, and eat supper with my parents once a week without distracting from my most important work—sifting through James's life and that of my girls. After grabbing a muffin and a slice of cheese for my breakfast, I crossed the yard to my parents' home.

The cinnamon smell of something baking wafted my way when I walked in the door. Mom was clearing up her baking dishes and looked up with a bright smile.

"You came out!"

I laughed. "The groundhog sees her shadow."

"Is there something you'd like to do today? Go shopping? Visit someone?"

"Nothing so ambitious. Dad mentioned you were itching to get started on the garden and I thought I could help."

Mom grimaced. "I hope he didn't pressure you into something you're not ready for."

"No, he was right. He said I needed a break sometimes and I took his advice and got outside for a walk today. It was great. And I think I'd like to work with you, making myself useful. You've done so much for me in the last few weeks, it's the least I can do."

"It was my pleasure." Her eyes filled and I knew she meant it. "I wish I knew how I could help."

I didn't want to go over with her the same ground that I plowed up every day as I went through my memories. "What can we work on today?"

She sighed. "Well, with all the uncertainty about the virus these days, Dad suggested I plant a big garden again. I had been downsizing it in the past few years with you kids away from home. But who knows what might happen?"

"What's this?" I had no idea what she was talking about. Lost in my own world in recent weeks and secluded in the cottage without Internet, I had been isolated from current events.

Mom opened her eyes wide at me. "There's a worldwide pandemic happening. I guess you haven't been out, but the store shelves have been empty of toilet paper and other basics for a few weeks now. Businesses and government have been on lockdown to try and stop the spread."

My stomach started churning. With this news, the conflagration in my life had spread to global proportions. Nothing seemed stable and I felt like my legs had been cut out from under me. I groped for a chair.

"Oh, honey! You're white as a sheet. I didn't mean to upset you." Mom hurried to my side and placed an arm around my shoulder.

Chapter 17

While all that borrows life from Thee
Is ever in Thy care,
And everywhere that man can be,
Thou, God, art present there.

~I Sing the Mighty Power of God, by Isaac Watts, 1674-1748

I t'll pass," Mom assured me, "don't worry. And we have hardly any cases here in central Alberta."

I sat down hard, feeling anxiety tighten its grip on me. Sickness and possible death of the only family that was left to me, forced shutdown of travel making my friends on the other side of the world seem that much farther away, panic regarding the economy... All these on top of the ashes of the other life I was mourning piled onto me in an overwhelming burden. "I don't see how I can take any more. It's too much."

"Sh, sh, sh..." she said, pulling my head against her soft middle.

I could hear the muffled sounds of her insides and pulled away slightly.

Mom drew out a chair and sat near me. "There's not a thing we can do about the rest of the world. You and I have to leave that to God. After all, we've both got enough of our own stuff to work through. Let's deal with what we can face right now, and that's getting a head start on the garden. Come with me." She pulled on my arm, and I rose to follow her. Stopping next to the stove, she found the timer was about to go off for the cinnamon twists and she fetched them out of the oven. The spicy aroma calmed me.

"We'll taste them when they've cooled. In the meantime, we plant." We entered the greenhouse Dad had made out of the unused back porch.

"Too bad you didn't have this when we kids were all at home." I looked around the small room, dazzling with today's sunlight, at the collected egg cartons, milk cartons and other containers we now began to fill with soil.

"It would have been nice. But somehow the kitchen windowsills did all right. Besides, we needed the space for all your coats and boots and skates and pets." Mom rolled her eyes and handed me a couple of packets of flower seeds, marigolds and pink lavatera. "I want you to take some of these over to the cabin with you to take care of. It'd be a shame to let all those wonderful south-facing windows go to waste."

I guessed that her motive was more than that. She and Grandma had always said gardening was good for the soul.

Mom went on methodically filling the seed flats and planting corn, cucumbers and tomatoes, plants that needed a head start indoors before the short growing season our region offered. We worked side by side, thinking our own thoughts, Mom humming a hymn softly. I listened, the words springing to mind from a lifetime of Sundays in church. *I sing the mighty power of God...*

As a family, we had often sung hymns while doing chores together, whether that was planting the garden, shelling peas, or butchering animals. Lissa and Lance had perfected the art of matching the song to the task at hand, like *Rescue the Perishing* while we were slaughtering chickens. The memory should have made me smile.

In a moment, Mom broke out singing the words.

I sing the goodness of the Lord

That filled the earth with food;
He formed the creatures with His word
And then pronounced them good...

I tried feebly to join in on the last stanza.

There's not a plant or flower below
But makes Thy glories known;
And clouds arise and tempests blow
By order from Thy throne

Oh, the cloud and tempest that had blown on me! My voice wobbled and cracked on those lines as I burst into tears and stopped singing. Mom eyed me with concern, finishing the hymn as though making sure I caught the words.

While all that borrows life from Thee
Is ever in Thy care,
And everywhere that man can be,
Thou, God, art present there.

I kept my hands busy, misting the planted seed flats to saturate the soil. Music had always had the power to stir my soul but now it raised a tide of emotion within me.

I focused on the work in front of me, my throat tight. It seemed as impossible for my life to arise from its bleak ashes as for life to arise from the dried seeds buried in the dead black dirt here. I pondered the song lyrics, all too aware that our lives were only borrowed, brief and fragile. Had my family been in God's care that fateful day? My head told me they had, but my heart feared and doubted. They had certainly been in harm's way in Nigeria's sometimes dangerous middle belt and that peril had overcome them. It seemed that evil had won. Yet the omnipresent God must have been present with them there. Present and waiting to receive them into his arms.

I swallowed. "Thanks Mom."

She nodded, wiping her eyes with the back of her hand. "We forget too often."

When we had finished the planting and had covered everything with plastic, Mom peeled off her gloves and crooked a finger at me. "Now how about one of those cinnamon twists?"

We sat at the kitchen table enjoying the first sugary bites of the fresh-baked treats. At length, she said, "Lynnie, I know this is a sensitive topic, but have you given any more thought to what your next step should be?"

I didn't answer. I wished we could have enjoyed our snack without ruining it by talk of the future. What future could I possibly have?

"Grandma has explained to us the importance of taking time to grieve and we've let you do that without interference. But you are young, too young to become a hermit. Dad and I would like to see you make a plan."

"I made a plan. I'm finishing documenting James's life and I've been thinking I should volunteer to babysit once in a while for Lance and Crystal."

Mom went quiet, then finally asked, "Are you sure you're up to it?"

I shrugged. "I remember what non-stop parenting was like. Besides that, I've decided I'm going to make a walking path around the slough."

Mom laughed. "A path? What a good idea! I'm glad you have something in the works." She paused. "But when I asked about plans, I was thinking more along vocational lines. Like pursuing what you might have done if you hadn't met James."

I brushed cinnamon and sugar off my lips with a napkin, trying to recall the Lynnie who enrolled in college with high hopes and ideals, if a low bank balance. It seemed a long time ago that I was picking courses that would be most in line with my ambition to be a wife and mother. Despite the teasing I'd received about it, even from Lissa, Dad had insisted mine was a high calling. He'd convinced me that I needed an education for whatever my life's work was to be, though for my goals it might need to be broader and more general. When you educate a boy, you educate a man, he had explained, but when you educate a girl, you educate a family. Now, the futility of my preparation to teach a family choked out words and I simply shrugged.

"You once mentioned social work." Mom tilted her head and lifted a brow.

I shrank from what seemed an insurmountable task of researching what might be required to pursue such a vocation. In fact, on principle I still resisted the idea of a career.

Yet I knew I had to face my altered future. "I guess since I'm not a wife or a mother anymore, I should think of something to do," I said, wringing my hands.

"I'm sorry, dear. I didn't intend to hurt you."

Sighing, I stacked my plate onto hers, "I know. And I didn't mean to sound like a martyr. I'm only facing the facts. It's true. That role in my life is over. I need to plan how to support myself and quit freeloading off you." I stood and pushed back my chair.

Mom rose and placed a hand on my arm. "Please don't think that's what we mean. You're free to take as long as you need. With the mission's insurance and all the money gifts that have been pouring in with sympathy cards you don't have to worry about money for quite a while. The thing is, we don't want you to get stuck. Fear can take over and paralyze a person that way." She drew me into a gentle embrace.

"I'll think about it," I said when she released me. I ambled to the front door for my coat and boots.

Mom delayed in the kitchen, shuffling through a drawer, then brought me a couple of the cinnamon twists wrapped in plastic. I took them, but she held on for a split second longer to get my attention. "You might want to go visit Grandma. She asks about you every time she's over here but she doesn't want to intrude on you. I think she's reliving some of her own grieving, thinking of you."

I stared at my mom, torn between two urges. I wanted to flee to my cabin and hide away from everyone and their sympathies and expectations forever. Yet I also felt an inner tug to find purpose and be of use to someone in this world. The two impulses had been fighting against each other since I had returned to Canada, although for the past two months, withdrawal had won out. Mom's suggestions now highlighted that other urge, the hunger for significance, for meaning. I needed to fill that void that used to be filled by nurturing and forming the characters of two innocent lives.

Could some sort of work with people offer me the same sense of meaning? If I gave myself another few weeks to chronicle Josie's and Anya's lives, would I experience the relief from grief I was hoping for and be strong enough to take on another project? Was I ready to face a new life?

Chapter 18

I was sinking deep in sin, far from the peaceful shore,
Very deeply stained within, sinking to rise no more;
But the Master of the sea heard my despairing cry,
From the waters lifted me, now safe am I!
~*Love Lifted Me, by James Rowe, 1865-1933*

A large envelope bearing the university logo sat propped on Mom's table when I entered the house on a hot mid-August afternoon. I snatched it up, eager for official word on how the new school year would be handled with the pandemic still underway. Since applying to the school of social work in spring, I had been nervous about acceptance. I had been out of school for so long. Then on being accepted, anxiety about the course load and my ability to keep pace filled my mind. Finally, the logistics of online schooling had been plaguing me in recent weeks. Dad teased me about my need to always keep the worry box full, no matter how small the concern. I didn't admit it to him, but I rather preferred these shallow, easy-to-solve problems to the embers of grief that smoldered beneath the surface.

Before I opened my package, Mom called from the back door. I hurried to help with her unwieldy armload of corn cobs and together we husked them. Like old times, we chatted as we worked. The smile in her eyes told me she was pleased to see the change in me. My body even felt stronger. Gardening and my walks around the slough had put back the natural blond highlights in my hair and energy in my stride.

"Finished the memory book today," I said plucking corn silk from the glossy kernels. "I hope to take it to town and get it bound sometime this week. Coil-bound, I think. It's going to be pretty thick."

"You'll show it to us sometime?"

"Of course." I plopped a fresh cob onto the counter. "You know, Damaris was right. Going through everything and all the pictures of James and the girls has been therapeutic. I feel like I've faced something that used to be vague and huge and terrifying where the least little thing could trigger me, and I've found it to be my friend."

"And how about those dreams you were having?

I hesitated. The dreams about Anya were the one disturbing thing about the grieving process that I hadn't been able to understand. I knew I was changed by the loss of my family, that I now carried with me a new reality of that loss. Visits with Grandma, listening to her experience with the grief she squelched for so many years had helped me see that. But I had no idea what to make of the dreams I had of my baby. They weren't horrifying anymore, but more...ordinary.

"They keep coming. Not every night, or even every week, but like this morning, I dreamed I was bathing her. She had been toddling around the yard and you know what the dust there is like. She was covered in it." I smiled. "Little gray baby. It felt so good to suds her up and get her clean. To comb her hair and see her eyelashes spiked together by the moisture." A catch in my throat made my voice quaver.

"Seems like those are the happy memories then. No more nightmares?"

"No, I haven't had one of those about the burning for a long time. The dreams about Anya are precious to me. I enjoy them, although waking from them is always painful."

"So do you think you're ready to tackle school?"

I shot a look at Mom. "Pretty sure, yeah."

We worked in tandem through the afternoon, Mom blanching the cobs and dropping them in cold water, me shaving slabs of golden kernels off the cobs until I had a large mound of them. Then I bagged the corn and sealed each package.

"We're taking supper to the field tonight?" I asked, after stacking the packages in the freezer.

"Yes. Dad's been over at Mark and Lissa's harvesting rye today." She paused in wiping the sticky counter and let out a long sigh. "I'm just so thankful those two have worked things out. Even the kids seem more relaxed now."

"What things? I thought I noticed something not quite right back in spring at that first family dinner, but no one's said a word to me any time since then. And when we see them in church everything looks fine."

Mom shook her head. "I shouldn't have mentioned it. It's not my story to tell, you know. And the family dinner table is hardly the time to discuss such a sensitive matter. Especially with Grandma present."

"I suppose. But even when Lissa has stopped by, she hasn't said anything about it to me."

"None of us wants to add to your load, dear."

"I'm not that fragile." I gathered the corn husks into a trash bag to take to the compost pile, thinking about the past few months. I had leaned hard on my family's good graces, their stability, their ever-ready support. Had I been self-absorbed, all take and no give? What if my preoccupation with myself had shut my sister away from the listening ear she needed? I somehow had to show her I cared.

The opportunity came three days later when Lissa called, asking me to help her make pies for another supper meal on the field.

"You should have invited Mom," I said. "Pie is her specialty."

"I already stopped by earlier to pick up the shells. I told her I wanted time alone with you. She seemed happy enough for that."

When I arrived, Lissa appeared to be in no hurry to get the baking done. She perched herself at one end of the long leather sofa and patted the other end with her bare foot. "Come sit."

I curled up on the cool leather facing her, breathing a prayer for wisdom. It had been a long time since Lissa had wanted to talk to me. "What's on your mind?"

My sister picked at her thumb cuticle for a minute before looking out the window at the ripening fields. "You must have heard by now. I left Mark in the spring."

This was startling news, and confusing too, since we were sitting in their home and Mark was out harvesting with our dad. "But you came back."

"Yeah." She fiddled with the short stray hair at the back of her neck that had escaped her messy bun, then looked me in the eye, almost defiantly I thought. "I had a crush on the dentist I worked for and moved to town so I could be closer," she said, all in a rush. She hurried on without waiting for a response from me, which was a good thing as I was shocked speechless.

Marriage trouble like communication difficulties or personality clashes I could understand. James and I had had our share of them, with his extreme extroversion and my introverted ways. But blatant planning for adultery was playing with fire. Still, it was Lissa's idea to confide in me and I was grateful, hoping I could be an encouragement to her in some way. I smoothed my expression so I didn't show my shock and reinforce her belief that I was a goody two-shoes.

"Dr. Muncie is married, but he made me think we had a future together. And then God hits me up with this worldwide pandemic." She gave a bitter laugh. "So there I was, no new guy, no job, and all alone in a dismal apartment with nothing to do and no one to talk to." Her eyes bored into mine, but I couldn't read her expression.

"Here's the deal, Sis. All that time spent thinking brought me to a few conclusions. One of them was that I missed my kids terribly. The next was that Mark and I were meant for each other and that I'd done wrong to leave him, that I was lying to myself. Moving into town wasn't about not wanting to drive the winter roads anymore. I'd been plotting to do something really sinful." Here her voice squeaked, and she went on in a whisper. "Only God could have stopped me from doing it. And he did."

I slid over to put my arms around her and Lissa gripped me hard, burying her face in my shoulder.

"I almost ruined my marriage, my life, and Jade and Dylan's lives, too!" She pulled away, wiping wet eyes. "But now I don't think I'm going to be able to relax until I make something right with you." She gave a wrinkly-nosed smile. "You, my perfect sister, have probably never had anything on your conscience, so you wouldn't know. But there's nothing like a hearty case of conviction to make you break out in sweats and jitters until you repent."

"That's where you'd be wrong, Kiddo. I've had my share of things to repent of."

Lissa rolled her eyes. "Oh, spare me. What, you snuck a candy from Nanny's junk cart? But seriously, it's been bothering me for years and I hope you'll forgive me. See, I was awfully jealous when you and James got engaged."

"What do you mean? You were the one to get engaged first when I was just a lonely tearoom waitress."

"But your story was such a fairy tale. You didn't run off and get married like I did, or even just announce to Mom and Dad that you were engaged. No, you two went all godly and James asked them if he could get to know you. Then you were super careful and always had a chaperone. I mean, taking Grandma places with you. Wow!" Lissa rolled her eyes. "And not even kissing until your wedding day. It was all so pure. My story looked pretty cheap by comparison."

"We never meant—"

"Oh, I know you never meant to make anyone feel small. You weren't just pure, but you've always been humble, too. It's been a bit of a tough act to follow."

"I'm sorry."

Lissa put her finger to my lips. "Just don't. This is my apology, remember? I'm the one who's sorry. I never showed an interest in your life at college. I robbed you of the matron of honour you deserved. I was too proud and spiteful to be of any real help to you. Mom ended up doing everything I was supposed to do, if you recall. And I never wrote back to you while you were in Africa. I'm so, so sorry, Lynnie. Will you forgive me?"

"Of course," I said, hugging her to me again. I had come to accept that our relationship had cooled once Lissa married, but I had to admit, I remembered each of the things she mentioned. At the time, they had stung.

She pulled back, giving me that intense look again. Now I understood it to be sincere and determined. "And another thing. I want your advice on being a good wife. I admired the way you and James were with each other. Mark and I need all the help we can get."

Chapter 19

The thrum of September rain on the corrugated tin roof was so loud that Daniya almost missed the weak cry from the small pallet next to their bed where Aminah fidgeted in sleep. She reached across and picked her up, still warm and moist from slumber. Scooping the child up into the snug pocket created by the curve of her own body, she could easily imagine that she herself had carried the child within her. The little girl nestled in beside Daniya, soon falling back to sleep. She stroked the child's silken hair, so different from her own wiry locks, enjoying the slippery feel of it between her fingers. It had grown in the time Aminah had belonged to them.

"My baby," Daniya crooned. "Little one, you are mine, you have been given to me. I am your mama."

The child slept on as Daniya drank in the beauty of her pale skin and bluish eyelids with their sweep of long, dark lashes. The tilt of the girl's eyes made Daniya wonder if she might have Chinese blood. Without a doubt, she was *butare*, white, and therefore different from anyone else in the village. Daniya—herself, tall, gangly, and from the only Muslim household in her village—had not forgotten what it was like to be different. Children at play could detect the weakness of another child as unerringly and viciously as chickens could spot blood. Daniya vowed to protect Aminah forever. Allah had at last sent her a baby, a beautiful child for her own.

Ihsan reached a hand across her to stroke Aminah's arm, too. "You are happy now?" he murmured in her ear.

"Mm," she agreed.

He gave Daniya a pat on the rump. "Then up you get and make me some lunch to take with me."

Without looking at him, Daniya could hear the smile in his voice. What a great change had taken place in their home in the six months since this small girl had come to bless them. Daniya eased herself from under the child's head and smiled to find a tiny ear print on her upper arm. She placed a pillow at Aminah's back lest she fall out of the bed onto the hard-packed floor, then hurried to dress.

In the kitchen, she had wrapped the spicy goat *suya* leftover from last night's meal with a tomato and cucumber for Ihsan to take with him. She tucked in the last of the *puff-puff*, too. Ihsan loved the way she made the deep-fried snack. In the kitchen, she fried *kosai* for breakfast using the black-eyed peas she had prepared the night before. It was good to be up early in the morning again even on a rainy day such as this, to feel hope and energy for the day's tasks ahead of her.

Daniya rarely thought about the years before Aminah became their daughter, but when she did, the memories were dim, like stick drawings in the dust, soon washed away by the vibrancy of the life-giving rainy season. That grim time of sorrows, of her hopes for a child snuffed out again and again, had been erased in just such a way. There was a new purpose to her housekeeping. Gone was the futility of merely keeping her husband and herself alive when no matter how often they came together they could not spark a new life. At least, not one that would live beyond the first few months' gestation. These days, she had a young child to raise and teach.

Months ago, after only a few days with them, Aminah had lost her wide-eyed watchfulness. Quickly, she had become the curious and playful little girl that Daniya had come to love. The child had learned so much under Daniya's patient teaching. As though they were discovering the world together, each day was an adventure. Last month, Aminah had caught on to toileting, and every day she learned more words. She knew where her toys belonged and understood when Daniya told her to put them away. Aminah even tried to bring Papa his prayer rug when he needed it.

From the corner of Daniya's eye, a small white-clad form now appeared at the kitchen door, one side of her face rosied and creased from lying on the sheet.

"Come to Mama." Daniya held out her arms to the child whose slow, drowsy smile lit her face. Aminah tripped toward her on tiny white feet and Daniya swung her up onto her hip. It was now her habit to do everything together with Aminah, whether it was making the bed, or cooking, or washing clothes. By this method, the child would learn everything she needed to know for daily life as well as the colours and numbers and letters that Daniya also planned to teach her.

"Bring Papa's bowl and spoon," Daniya said, setting the child down. Aminah promptly went to the table, barely able to reach. At times, it was agonizing to watch her slow process in performing such chores, but Daniya repressed the temptation to do the job herself. What would a child learn from that? She had heard other mothers of older children complain that their teenagers were lazy and ungrateful. Before she had children herself, Daniya was shut out of that realm, her opinions on child-training scoffed at. Daniya knew better than to offer advice to those frustrated women, but she determined to prevent that problem with her own child.

"Smart girl," she murmured when Aminah brought her the dish.

Just the other day, her sister-in-law Uma had stopped by with her two youngest children when Aminah was helping with the laundry.

"Look, Auntie!" Aminah had cried as Daniya supervised her twisting a dripping shirt on the stick.

The surprise on Uma's face at such a tiny girl willing to do the simple work brought a proud smile to Daniya's face even now. She attributed the child's clever mind and good nature to the careful and constant teaching Daniya gave her every day. If the time ever came when she felt confident enough to take Aminah out in public, she would let the child's achievements speak for themselves.

Aminah had learned new words rapidly. Now she was a cheerful, chattering youngster, full of questions. And when the little girl was ready for school? That vexing question Daniya had not yet brought up with Ihsan. She was determined her daughter would not only go to school but also excel, as Daniya knew she could. Her hope was that Aminah would continue for the full ten years and maybe even enter higher learning.

Her personal longing for more education had been cut short when she had to leave school to care for her younger siblings at the death of her mother. Daniya now directed these dreams toward Aminah's future. She well knew that she was going against the widespread prejudice against female education. The name of the dreaded Boko Haram group itself meant Western education is a sin. But Daniya was determined her child would learn. She had been teaching her colours and numbers, names of plants and animals, and soon, letters. All this she kept to herself. What Ihsan would say about her dreams for the girl, she suspected, might be influenced by his sister Uma's opinions. She was often Ihsan's authority in child-rearing matters.

"What does a girl need to go to school for, hm?" Uma had scoffed when the subject came up. "My daughters will marry and have babies very well with what I can teach them. I went to school long enough to learn to read and figure numbers. I keep a good house and raise good Muslim children. What more do girls need?"

Today when Ihsan left to tend the goats and after they had eaten breakfast, Daniya planned to take Aminah to visit Uma and her children. She had begun going there only recently and was still cautious about exposing Aminah to the curious stares of the village. She and Ihsan had grown accustomed to their white-skinned child whose straight, brown hair was so different from anyone else they knew. But she did not trust her neighbours to be so welcoming.

"Go...out?" Aminah asked now when she noticed Daniya wrapping her *khimar* around her head and neck.

Daniya laughed. "You want to be covered, too?" She found a cloth and wrapped it around Aminah's head. "Such a tiny Ma you are," she said, kissing her soft cheek. Then she picked up her daughter and grabbed the plastic sheet she used as an umbrella. She stepped out the door with a cautious check in both directions. No one was out in the pouring rain, which was just as Daniya hoped. Under the rain-pelted plastic, she splashed her way down the muddy street to her sister-in-law's home.

They arrived damp and took off their shoes at the door. Daniya set Aminah down inside while she shook the plastic off outside the door and folded it. When she stepped back in, Uma's children had already snatched their little cousin up and taken her off to play in the other room.

"She is like a toy to them." Uma smiled and offered tea. They sat together at the long kitchen table, scrubbed smooth by Uma's efficient cleaning.

"What work has the little Ma been up to already this morning, hm?" Uma asked, quirking an eyebrow.

Daniya did not let Uma's amusement and condescension bother her. After all, Uma had been the one to sit with her so often in the months when she was under the dark cloud. "She spooned *kosai* onto her papa's plate and put his lunch into the satchel."

Uma patted her arm. "She is lucky to have a good mama like you."

They chatted about housekeeping matters, with a smattering of village *gist* thrown in, while the shrieks and giggles of the children rose and fell from the other room.

"Will you bring Aminah to grandfather's birthday celebration?" Uma asked.

Daniya hesitated. There would be many people present to honour Ihsan's grandfather next week. He was well respected in the village despite tensions of recent years between the Christians and Muslims. "Ihsan will have to decide. People may not want such a young one present, especially if she needs her nap and gets cranky."

Uma raised her eyebrows. "You cannot hide her away forever, Sister."

Daniya shrugged. "For now."

The pitch of play in the next room rose, followed by a loud bump and the sound of Aminah crying. Daniya leaped to her feet, running to her child. She collided with Uma's oldest daughter coming through the door.

"The boys stepped on Aminah's *khimar* when she was running and made her fall," the girl said in a plaintive voice.

Uma rose from her chair, calling, "Boys!"

Daniya rushed past her niece to find Aminah cowering on the floor with the other children surrounding her, each of them rubbing her hair between their fingers. "Like chicken feathers!"

They laughed and repeated, "Chicken feathers!" plucking at it until the little one cried out again.

A protective rage swelled Daniya's chest. She swooped into the middle of them, snatched up her child and raced to the door. Fumbling for the plastic sheet and Aminah's shoes, she thrust her own feet into her damp sandals and raced for home.

"Daniya!"

Daniya's pained heart kept her running.

"It was only small-small..." Uma called from behind her.

But it was not small-small to Daniya. It was a big hurt to her, as if her own hair had been yanked from its roots.

Later, when she had sobbed out the story to her husband, she had to accept Ihsan's explanation. The children had not intended malice against Aminah. They think a *butare* strange and were only curious.

That evening, after feeding her husband and child, Daniya gave Aminah a bath. Fingering the girl's wet hair, she made a sudden decision. She placed the child on a low stool, reached for the scissors and with tears trickling down her cheeks, she cut Aminah's fine hair short. When she was finished, Aminah's shorn head still did not look like Uma's daughters' close-cropped hair. But Daniya hoped it was similar enough that she would no longer seem foreign to the other children. She would not tolerate her daughter being a laughingstock in the village.

Chapter 20

Day by day and with each passing moment,
Strength I find to meet my trials here;
Trusting in my Father's wise bestowment,
I've no cause for worry or for fear.
~ Day by Day, by Lina Sandell Berg, 1832-1903

My insides fluttered the first Tuesday of September, as if it was my first day of school ever. Despite my not going anywhere but to the kitchen table in my cabin, I was nervous as the family cat meeting a new puppy. I plunked myself down in front of my laptop for the opening online meeting. Though I had no new school wardrobe and no new campus to navigate, I was as anxious about meeting new teachers, fellow students, and the looming workload as I had been as a college freshman more than ten years ago.

At least I was familiar with the necessary technology, having been dependent on it while in Nigeria for communication with family and friends. My brother Lance had hooked me up with Internet service out here, so I had everything I needed. Except a tech-savvy husband to fix the inevitable glitches for me. But I squashed that thought. I refused to play the grief card in this new venture. I would copy James by relegating my personal problems to a tiny lock box in my mind and hoping the tragedy in my life would never leak out.

I had already shed tears this morning after waking from another dream. This time, Josie was showing me how well she could go potty. It had seemed so real, though I didn't recognize the house. She finished, then reached for me to pick her up, her eyes shining with pride. But the face that turned up to me was not Josie's but Anya's. And when I reached for her, my arms came away empty. That was when I woke up, teardrops rolling down the sides of my face into my hair.

Staring at the ceiling, I frowned, remembering the dream. I hadn't yet begun toilet training Anya. She would have had her second birthday two months ago. To replace Josie with Anya in my memory disturbed me. Was I forgetting them? I was suddenly overcome by an intense longing to have one more day to spend with them, imprint their voices and faces on my mind, the feel and the smell of them in my arms.

But there was no time. Today was my first day of graduate studies. Thinking of Josie's never-to-be-experienced first day of school made my nose prickle again. I would have dressed her in a little plaid jumper like my mom had dressed me in, with pigtails in her hair.

I shut off my waterworks with effort. Everyone had problems. If I was to embark on a career to help people, I would have to keep my personal life out of it. Today would be good practice.

For days now, I had gone over the syllabus for each of my courses, as well as the instructions for connecting to classes. And I was confident there would be no unexpected power failure as so often occurred in Africa. Fifteen minutes before nine, I logged into my first class of the morning, Diversity and Oppression, with Dr. C. Trites as professor. There were to be only eleven students in the class, all women.

When Professor Trites appeared on the screen, her hair filled the frame in a cloud of dark curls. And when I looked closer, her face was strangely familiar. Likely it was the same phenomenon as when we first moved to Jos. I had seen the people of home in the faces of my new Nigerian friends and even mentally named them for their Canadian twin until I got to know them. Then I'd wondered how I could ever have confused the two. Still, while we waited for the rest of the students to show up, Dr. Trites' familiarity kept niggling at the back of my mind.

"Welcome everyone," she said, glancing down in front of her. "I think we're all here now."

As soon as she spoke, I placed her. It was Charlaine Hampton, the new girl who had come to my high school. I could scarcely believe the change. She'd gone from lumpy, lopsided braids, wrinkled clothes, and a gap-toothed furtive look to glamour, confidence, and a perfect smile.

When I had befriended her, she'd been eager to come with me to my church youth group and through it she had come to faith. Excited to find this point of connection today, I gave a small wave of recognition, but she must not have been looking my way. Still, I was eager to reconnect. How amazing that she had gone on to achieve a PhD and become a professor. A twinge of inferiority pinched me at the thought. Charlaine and I had vied for grades, and I had topped hers as often as she had mine. Yet she was a PhD now and I was ... who? Not even a wife and mother anymore. A scorched wasteland of futility expanded inside me.

"I'd like each of you to give a brief introduction," Charlaine continued, "so we can get to know each other. This mode of meeting isn't ideal, but it will have to do until we can meet in person." She began calling names in alphabetical order.

Anxious about what I would say when my turn came, I barely heard several of the first intros but it seemed I had something in common with a couple of the other students. A young woman from Cameroon now seemed to me almost a next-door neighbour since her country bordered Nigeria to the southeast. And my antenna for fellow believers went up when a rural Alberta woman named Fiona introduced herself as a pastor's wife. A couple of others stood out; a

Muslim woman in a pale blue hijab framing her fine-featured face, followed by a middle-aged woman with oddly short bangs and purple glasses who wore an air of confidence that I envied.

During the summer I had worked out how to best avoid the topic of my losses with the people at church or in the community. But I had yet to face strangers, and the prospect turned my hands clammy.

When Charlaine looked up at me after reading my name from her class list, she started in astonished recognition.

I wiped my hands on my jeans and opened my mouth to speak. "I...I'm Lynnie Min. Um, I grew up on a farm, the oldest of four kids. Got an arts degree with a major in languages, French and Spanish, because I hoped to work oversees. I met my husband at a summer linguistics school, and we spent the past four years in Nigeria. Just got back here in time for lockdown."

The other students nodded or grimaced at the mention of lockdown, and I hoped I had dodged further questions.

To my surprise, Charlaine made no comment. I was sure she had recognized me, yet she seemed to be ignoring our connection. She called the remaining students' names, then addressed the class. "I'm sure you've all had a chance to go over the syllabus and have seen that your entire grade for this class will be based on one project, a portfolio broken down into gradual postings throughout the next four months. Do any of you have any questions about this?"

A few brave students asked for clarification, and I listened carefully. We were to document an aspect of diversity and oppression in our personal lives and describe how that story differs from the dominant discourse in the culture. I immediately picked up on the code words "diversity" and "oppression." In recent family discussions over the supper table, we had discussed these concepts. My dad had been nervous about my embarking on higher education in a secular university because of such ideologies. He said they often masked a misunderstanding of the true state of mankind and the causes of conflict and oppression. But, of course, I had my own experiences to draw from, and I looked forward to the opportunity to offer my viewpoint. I hoped not in front of the whole class, though.

"That's all for now," Charlaine said. "If any of you have further questions, my contact information is at the top of your syllabus. And Lyn? Can you stay awhile after we end the meeting?"

"Sure," I said, as the others left the screen one by one.

"Well, isn't this old home week?" Charlaine said when we were alone. "Nice to see you here, Lyn. Remember when we were competitors for top marks in high school? But I guess we lost touch when I moved to Toronto for university. So, tell me what you've been up to since then."

Happy she had acknowledged me, I was disappointed she'd referred to me as her competitor. I had thought we were friends. Not only that, but I had planned to focus on my rural upbringing and downplay my life since college to avoid dangerous questions. Now I had to think fast, something I was poor at.

"It's great to see you, too. I go by Lynnie now, since my married name is Min."

"Lyn Min." Charlaine chuckled. "I can see why. I can't believe it's been—what—ten or twelve years? What brings you back to school now after all this time?"

How had I thought I would be able to avoid awkward questions? I decided a simple, straightforward approach would be best. "My husband passed away in February, and I came back shortly after. Then I had to figure out what my new life plan was. I see by your name change that you're married, too?"

"Not exactly. I took my father's name when I moved back east to live with him. But let me say, I'm sorry for your loss. That's quite recent. Do you think you're ready for academic life so soon?"

"I do. I'm back with my family and I have good supports in place. I'm looking forward to having something new to focus on."

"Well I wish you the best. If you're half the student you were when I knew you, we'll make a first-rate social worker out of you." Pausing, Charlaine's smile disappeared. "Just so we're clear, I can't let your bereavement, or our previous acquaintance, affect my grading of your work. So please don't be looking for any favours."

I stared in surprise. "I wouldn't expect it." It bothered me that she might think I would. She was distancing herself from me, first describing me as a mere competitor, and now offering this disclaimer. And she'd made no reference to our mutual faith. Had she left that part of her life behind?

Chapter 21

Dare to be a Daniel
Dare to stand alone
Dare to have a purpose firm
Dare to make it known.
~*Dare to be a Daniel, Philip P. Bliss, 1873*

Lissa's gaze followed her sister's agitated pacing back and forth in the dimly lit living room. The kids had each gone to their friends' homes after church and Mark was napping as he did every Sunday during harvest time, leaving Lissa at loose ends. She had called Lynnie to keep her company on this drizzling September afternoon.

Watching Lynnie, Lissa thought more about this person who had always been there for her, always a steady beacon in Lissa's life. *I've taken her for granted. I've even resented her for being so perfect.*

Where might Lissa be now without her sister's faithful example? What kind of a worse mess might she have made of her life if not for Lynnie's unseen but ever- resent restraining influence on her? Lissa swallowed the lump in her throat. She hated getting emotional and cleared her throat to expel the feelings.

She raised her eyebrows and smirked when Lynnie pulled out her phone for the fourth time in fifteen minutes, checking for her prof's message.

"It's the weekend," Lissa said, kicking her feet up onto the coffee table in front of the couch where she sat. "Relax already. You always did take school way too seriously and now you're doing it again."

Lynnie had described the theme she'd submitted to her prof for her Diversity and Oppression portfolio. Students were to trace their experience of oppression through their lives. What her sister had proposed sounded good to Lissa but, then, anything Lynnie wrote sounded convincing. Lissa had always prided herself that she could have gotten grades as good as her older sister's if she had studied that hard. But could she have? Now she had begun to doubt. She had a new recognition that Lynnie had something beyond mere intelligence. Had always had it. Determination? Check. Faithfulness? Yup. Initiative? Uh-huh. Self-discipline? In spades! But something more. Wisdom, perhaps? The ability to see life the way it really was and to choose the good, the right, the true, no matter what. Yeah, that had to be it.

"I'm on pins and needles over this," Lynnie told Lissa. "If my proposal doesn't get approved, I have no idea what else I can work on. I mean, have any of us ever been truly oppressed a day in our lives?"

Lissa giggled. "Well not you, that's for sure. You have big-sister privilege. I, on the other hand, know all about oppression by the powers-that-be. And by that, I mean you. I was the one who never had a room to myself, who endured hand-me-down pants with stretched-out knees, and who was always compared to Lynnie, the paragon of virtue."

Lynnie rolled her eyes and expelled an impatient breath. "Be serious. I totally put myself out there with this proposal. I mean, I believe that society doesn't admire women who want to work in the home, raising their families. But maybe oppressed was too strong a word? It's so counter-cultural I'm genuinely concerned I won't get approval." She rubbed her hands down the sides of her jeans in that way she had.

"Stop worrying. I can't imagine anything you did not getting approval. Especially knowing your old friend is your professor. You're a shoe-in."

"No. She made a point of asking me not to expect that."

"I guess not." Lissa shrugged, widening her eyes at a memory of Lynnie's friend. "Remember when you introduced Grandma to Charlaine?"

"Oh yeah." Lynnie nodded with a rueful smile.

Lissa gave a stiff parody of Grandma. "'How do you do?' And Charlaine says, 'Do you really want to know or are you just making conversation?' Ha! I always admired her nerve."

"Well, I'm the one wishing I had nerve now. Waiting for her answer is agonizing."

"I can't see why. Seriously. You've always put maximum effort into whatever you do." Lissa grinned, taking a sip from her hot chocolate. "I, on the other hand, have a good dose of Nanny in me. You know, *que sera, sera*. I never bothered about studying much. There were more important things on my mind in high school."

"Namely Mark." Lynnie winked. "But still, your grades were pretty good."

"Like I said, I'm of the Nanny work ethic. Why slave for top grades when you can do well enough to get by and have more time for fun?"

"But think how well you could have done if you had buckled down and studied."

"See, you're just like Grandma."

Lynnie winced.

Lissa clapped her hand to her mouth. "Oops, sorry." This wasn't the first time she had made the comparison. It had usually shot out of her mouth when she was most frustrated with her sister. She knew it had always bothered Lynnie. But Lissa wasn't angry or defensive now and she shouldn't have let it slip.

"I know, I know," Lynnie said. She sat on the end of the couch, tucking her feet beneath her and facing Lissa. "Who wants to be a dry old stick like Grandma when you could be jolly like Nanny?" She picked up her mug and took a sip. "The thing is, I think you're right. You and I are cut from different cloth and, whether we like it or not, each of us is more like our grandmothers than we are our own mom. What's weird is that I'm starting to not mind that comparison." She paused, flicking at the cuticle on her thumb. "Remember my big outburst at our family dinner after I got back last spring?"

Lissa nodded. "That was a first from you, for sure."

Lynnie grimaced. "I know. Not one of my better moments. But my point is, who was the one to follow me upstairs? Not Mom or Nanny or you. It was Grandma. And believe it or not, she stroked my back. I think the surprise jolted me out of myself more than anything."

Lissa chuckled. "I can imagine."

"She's crusty on the outside, no question. And if I'm like her, that's something I'm going to have to guard against. But I wonder if that crust is her way of trying to protect a tender heart."

"Well, it's a pretty thick crust. And it's abrasive on the outside." Lissa's tone echoed years of being rubbed raw by her grandmother's scoldings.

"I know. But we both know there were hurts in Grandma's past. I know what it's like to lose a child. I can't imagine what it must have been like to feel responsible for it all these years." Lynnie looked at her, a pleading in her eyes.

Her look stopped short the critical comment Lissa had been about to make. Which was unusual. Lissa had long ago acknowledged herself to be the insensitive sister. How many times had her mother admonished her to be discreet, think of others? But Lissa had neither understood her concerns nor cared. She'd prided herself on her bluntness. Come to think of it, maybe she was more like Grandma in that way than she'd thought. Was this new curb on her speech part of the change that had been taking place in her since spring? Was God at work on her? Or in her?

The pocket of Lynnie's hoodie lit up and tootled.

"Oh, here's the email I've been waiting for." She fished out her phone and concentrated on reading, the device lighting her face with a blue glow.

"Your lips are moving," Lissa teased, curious about the contents of the message.

"She says that full-time mothers are a traditionally privileged group." Lynnie mumbled something unintelligible, then continued reading. "'As such, there are few disadvantages they would experience in a world that favours and accommodates them.'" Lynnie looked up, frowning.

"What?" Lissa snorted. "She's never been one, I take it."

Lynnie lunged out of her seat and resumed pacing. "I mean, in what universe are full-time moms favoured and privileged?"

"She's got that wrong." Lissa shook her head. "When I used to do our taxes before I got my job, I figured out that we would have been better off tax-wise if we weren't married, and Mark just paid me as a live-in housekeeper. Besides, name one celebrity that stays at home to raise her kids. I'll wait." She rolled her eyes and drummed her fingers on the arm of the sofa.

Lynnie gave a wry smile. "Thanks Sis. In fact, if you don't mind, I might use that bit about the lack of prominent role models."

"It'll cost you." Lissa snickered. "So, no approval?"

"Not exactly, but kind of." Lynnie scrolled through to the end of the message. "At the end, she says, 'I'm curious to hear what you might come up with. So go ahead, convince me.'"

"That's good then, right? It sounds like a challenge," Lissa said.

"Sounds like a recipe for a tough grade if you ask me. But I can't think of anything else in my life that could qualify as being oppressed."

"So go for it! She's given you the okay. You can do this, girl."

Lynnie stopped in front of Lissa and dropped onto the coffee table. She searched Lissa's face. "Do you really think I can? I've never been persuasive or influential. Or for that matter, brave."

Lissa stared at her, incredulous. Lynnie had been her north star throughout childhood, holding her back from all her worst schemes, the voice of reason in her distress, her cheering section of generous encouragement. Whenever she'd been irritated by her sister-conscience and shut out its warnings, Lissa had come to regret her actions. Whether consciously or not, she had looked to Lynnie's example for how to navigate life. How was it possible that this sister of hers was unaware of the power of her influence?

"Are you kidding?" Lissa swung her legs off the coffee table so she was knee to knee with her sister. She had never been a touchy-feely person but now she grasped Lynnie's arms. She cleared her throat against the swelling growing there again. "Your voice is the one I heard last spring telling me to call home, to go home. You've always blazed the way for me." Her words ebbed to a croaky whisper. "And brave? I don't know how you're even going on as sane and cheerful and normal as you are after what you've been through. I've never known anyone braver."

Chapter 22

Are there no foes for me to face?
Must I not stem the flood?
Is this vile world a friend to grace,
To help me on to God?
~Am I a Soldier of the Cross? by Isaac Watts, 1674-1748

I kept thinking of my prof as Charlaine instead of Dr. Trites. I had to keep reminding myself not to use her familiar name in case I accidentally gave away our friendship. It had seemed important to her to remain strictly professional. Dr. Trites had promised a couple of guest speakers would join us this week. She first introduced Patricia Hainstock, a fiftyish woman whose full face and high cheek bones revealed her indigenous heritage. The surname rang a bell. Hadn't there been a family of Hainstocks in our area while I was growing up? Maybe some relation? A vague memory of a woman dying in a house fire drifted through my mind. I would ask Grandma at dinner that evening.

With thirty years' experience as a social worker, Ms. Hainstock had the sensible appearance of someone who had seen it all and was surprised by nothing. I looked forward to hearing her stories.

When Patricia Hainstock began to speak, the lilt of her deep voice created a hush. "I wish I had known years ago what I'm going to talk to you about today. When I graduated with my degree, I was full of dreams about righting the wrongs of the past, taking on a government system I thought was faulty, and transforming people's lives." She rolled her eyes and shook her head. "To give you an idea about how naive I was, I'll share a little story about the first client assigned to me, a single mom, very young, with two pretty wild little boys. I found out about a parenting class that I decided would be a big help to her, so I registered her, arranged childcare for the day, and even ordered a taxi for her.

"She never showed up. I was so disappointed. But I learned the consequences of not allowing a person to take the initiative in her own life. The class organizers were peeved because someone else could have taken that spot in the class. And I had to pay the daycare and the taxi for their wasted time out of the social services budget. Big lessons for me. Money and programs can't solve most problems of the human heart. If you assume someone is a helpless victim, she will act like one. People won't change unless they have a stake in their own betterment.

"But even though there have been lots of disappointments in my work, it's all worth it when I see a teenage mom super motivated to clean up her life so she can prove she's a fit mother and get her baby back. Or the young couple, third generation foster kids themselves, who are so determined their son won't grow up in the system that they quit drugs. The father takes a job working for their boy's foster dad, and they start going to church. Or the day I watch sheer joy light up the faces of a couple who have waited ten years for a child when I place an abandoned baby into their arms. These are the times that keep me going.

"I've learned that every human being has dignity, value and worth, but also, that we all have the capacity for doing what's wrong. And yet, no one is beyond hope.

"I'll close with a quote from one of my favourite authors, Alexander Solzhenitsyn. He wrote, 'The line between good and evil is not between classes of people. It is a line down the center of every human heart.' Our job as social workers is to help strengthen people to fight that evil, to choose the path of wisdom, and to become strong enough that some day they will be the ones counseling others."

Her words resonated with me. For the first time since I'd come home from Nigeria, I had a clear vision of something I might contribute to this world. With a few deft pictures, she'd given me purpose and an identity. Full hearted, I applauded with everything in me, and wrote down her contact information. I looked forward to getting in touch with her for more inspiring stories from the trenches.

But I happened to glance at the face of the second guest speaker, a petite younger woman with an on-trend haircut. I did a double take. A scowl had darkened her face while she listened to Patricia's presentation. I was shocked at the open animosity. I watched her while Patricia fielded a few questions from the class. Was this professional jealousy? Or was the smaller woman a racist?

After a few minutes, our prof cut off the student questions and introduced the other guest, Amy Knowles-Daggett, a program supervisor from the government's department of social services.

"Ms. Knowles-Daggett, why don't you let our students know what some top issues in social work are today."

The woman flashed a saccharine smile that dissolved like candy floss before leaning toward her microphone. "My department colleagues across Canada share a deep sadness at much of what is occurring in the world. For example, we're committed to fostering communities of therapists and workers where broader relations of power are acknowledged and addressed. But quite frankly, we haven't been doing enough to consider privilege and dominance in our work. These are difficult topics, and we are still finding our way in relation to them, but we encourage students in the classroom, as well as on your own, to have conversations about whiteness and oppression."

Had the woman heard anything that Patricia Hainstock had said? Nothing the older woman recounted had anything to do with privilege or oppression. Perhaps that explained the animosity? The two speakers came from opposing viewpoints.

Knowles-Daggett gave that fleeting smile again before continuing. "Some of us enjoy much greater privilege than others. We've got to guard against thinking our difficulties are equivalent to those faced by people living with considerably less privilege. The lived experience of oppressed people must be central in these discussions. But I don't want you to get the idea that conversation alone is ever going to be enough to address these matters. Experiential knowledge is the key when it comes to teaching about racial subordination, and we white people have to remove ourselves completely from the conversation."

At this point I was mystified. Another student voiced my questions by asking, "I understand the concept of making room in discussion for marginalized people. But first you've urged us to have these conversations about whiteness and oppression, and then you say that we must remove ourselves from the conversations. Which is it?"

The speaker swung her hair out of her face impatiently. "It's not about 'making room' for Indigenous, Black, or LGBTQ people. It's about becoming an ally. Don't assume you have a right to have an opinion."

I worked up the courage to raise my hand. "I don't get it," I said, after moistening my lips. "I mean, what's the point of a conversation if it's one-sided?"

She gave me a hard look and I could tell she was getting testy. "Colonialism has meant that Indigenous and other oppressed people groups have been ignored for a long time. Now it's our turn to be ignored." She crossed her arms and leaned back. "Look, we are social workers. The very profession we're part of has played a shameful role in the subjugation, dispossession, and marginalization of Indigenous peoples and people of colour. We don't have to dig very deep or look back very far to find racist assumptions in our policies. Our concepts of what it means to be 'human,' our concepts of intelligence and self-actualization—these are all bound up with our history of racism. As white social workers we need to look closely at the effects of applying these concepts to people of other cultures in our professional work."

I glanced at the non-white members of my small class, wondering how they would apply these concepts. Were they exempt from the cautions white social workers needed to exercise?

"My understanding is that social workers often have to make decisions in a crisis situation," the first student asked. "How are we supposed to know when, say, an intervention needs to happen to rescue a child in danger?"

"I'm glad you asked that," Knowles-Daggett said. "There are other ways of knowing. I personally recommend a mindfulness-based approach to self-reflection and therapy. Try yoga principles like emptying yourself when faced with decisions that will impact people's lives."

I happened to glance at Ms. Hainstock for her reaction to this mouthful of gobbledygook. A mocking smile played at one corner of her mouth. Cautiously, I raised my hand again. "Can I use 'spiritual knowing' to discern whether an intervention should take place?"

"No," Ms. Knowles-Daggett snapped. "There's no place for anything spiritual."

I struggled to make sense of her answer. Weren't yoga principles themselves spiritual? I looked to Charlaine but was disappointed to find no objection on her face, only a benign acceptance.

"I hope I've made myself clear," Knowles-Daggett concluded. "If you are white, you have no right to have an opinion. You haven't suffered."

The words seared my still-raw heart, tearing away the fragile layer of healing I had tried to build up over the past months. I was breathless with shock. Even in Nigeria, where tribal and class prejudices were blatant, I had never heard such glaring bigotry. But worse than that was the cruel statement that I had not suffered. Could she have any clue of the depth of my pain at losing the three people most dear to me? To have my loss belittled and dismissed left me trembling with hurt and rage. Somewhere in my head, an alert sounded, warning me to keep my ideas to myself. I would accomplish nothing by blurting out my personal pain. Blindly, I left the room to catch my breath.

When I returned a few moments later, I caught sight of Patricia Hainstock's frown and felt sure she did not share Ms. Knowles-Daggett's beliefs. After class, I sent Ms. Hainstock a message. I had a feeling we had some beliefs in common and I wanted to know more about her career and her approach to social work. On impulse, I told her my story. I had been cautious sharing it because I didn't want to come across as the attention-seeking victim. But now I needed to know if what I'd heard in class that day reflected the mindset of the field I was entering. If it did, I wanted no part of it.

Chapter 23

On this late November morning of the dry season, Uma had finally convinced Daniya to come to market with her. "I tell you Ma, you cannot keep Aminah hidden forever. People must see you with her like any other mother and child. You must let them get used to her."

Over the months, Daniya had been worn down by Uma's insistence. She had no more excuses, but her stomach churned with anxiety as she followed Uma and her girls with their baskets toward the crowded centre of the village. A motorcycle whizzed by carrying two enormous sacks of rice and leaving behind its acrid fumes to mingle in the hazy dust.

As usual, Daniya had covered Aminah's head with a miniature *khimar* against the sun. The child's fair skin burned to the bright red shade of a rose apple if exposed. Daniya had learned this the hard way at the beginning of the dry season when the tops of Aminah's feet had suffered so badly the skin had peeled. Daniya herself had almost physically felt the child's pain. There was no need for Ihsan to have scolded her for carelessness. She blamed herself every time she smeared aloe on the burnt skin. How was she fit to be a mother if she could overlook such a danger and cause her child such suffering?

But the feet had healed. Now in her cloth headwrap, Aminah clung to Daniya's side, chirping the names of her cousins ahead of them. Uma's eldest daughters offered to take Aminah to see the array of toys and treats under a bright orange umbrella nearby. Daniya set Aminah down and smiled as she toddled away, clutching the hands of each of the bigger girls. Keeping one eye on them, she set to work bargaining for okra, garlic, and guava. As she paid the vendor and began piling the produce into her basket, she sensed a commotion.

Laughter erupted from a ring of brightly clad women that had formed. Daniya left her basket with the vegetable vendor and hurried over, fearing Aminah and Uma's daughters were at the centre of it. Words were exchanged. She elbowed her way into the circle and snatched up her daughter. She jutted her chin in defiance and scanned the faces of the women. She knew most of them.

"You babysit this one?" one curious woman asked, her eyes slanted in suspicion.

Daniya resented the assumption. She pressed the child protectively to her. "She is my daughter."

Another scoffed. "You be a fool! That is crazy talk. I know you. Your husband herds goats with mine. You two could not make a white baby if you cooked it up with rice."

The others burst out laughing again.

Daniya could not trust herself to speak. Aminah must have sensed the tension. She hid her face in her mother's shoulder with a quiet whimper.

"Where did you get her?" They persisted in their taunting, closing the circle. "Did you steal her?"

"No!" Daniya rasped. "We adopted her."

The circle of women tightened. "Pah, adopt! Did you pay big bribes to the government?" they demanded. "Where did she come from? From Jos where *butare* people are?"

"White people would give a poor goat farmer a baby? I do not believe you," said a big-eyed woman named Fanique. "How can you raise a child like that here, among us?"

Daniya lifted her chin, her chest hammering. "God has given her to us. He must mean for us to raise her. We will do our best." She turned to find a way out of the centre.

"But who would marry that *butare*?" Fanique pointed at Aminah with a sneer.

Daniya felt the words like a dart to her heart. Every protective instinct within her stood at high alert like goosebumps. She swung around, thrusting Aminah into her niece's arms.

"Who would marry *you*, with a face like a moo-moo?" Daniya hissed, rushing forward at the woman, ready to claw her eyes out. To her very depths, she hated the smug expression behind the hurtful words. She leaped at the woman, but someone slammed into her from behind stopping her with a fleshy arm. Daniya flashed a rear glance.

"Let me go!" she muttered. But Uma held her tight.

Daniya bared her teeth at Fanique and spat. The woman jumped back, upsetting a child who stood behind her. Her sneer was replaced with alarm, Daniya saw with satisfaction. *Let that teach her to spew hatred at my precious Aminah.*

Uma hustled Daniya and the girls away from the gathering. Holding back tears, Daniya retrieved her basket. Though the quantity of produce seemed reduced, she did not care. She wrapped Aminah into the sling, set the basket on her head and made for home.

Despite the haze of Sahara dust in the air brought from the northeast by the harmattan winds, a pink jumper flashed bright in the distance. Arriving back in his village with his flock, Ihsan recognized it as Aminah's and his heart gave a leap. Home had become a beacon of hope since the little girl had changed everything there. When she ran to him, her bright smile made glittering crescents of her eyes. It was a sight that never wearied him but, after today's warning, he made a sharp glance around the vicinity lest anyone should see her. It being mealtime, most villagers were occupied and no one noticed the rose-clad child.

Ihsan swung her up onto his shoulders. Her small hands crept beneath his *kufi* cap and tangled in his hair. She clung to him and tonight of all nights, it was balm to his soul.

Aminah chattered non-stop as he watered the goats from the barrel behind the house and fastened the wattle fence gate. Her short, staccato-like speech came rapid-fire, running through their evening routine and usually ending with a question.

"Mama goats?"

"Yes, child, these are the mamas."

"Fuzzy ears?"

"Yes, they are fuzzy. You want to touch them?" He swooped his daughter downward so her small hand could brush the soft fur behind the ear of the nearest doe. Aminah's wispy hair fluttered in the breeze of the cooling evening. She swirled her fingers in the whorl of goat hair and squealed with delight, sending the animal skittering out of reach. He propped her back up on his shoulders

"Babies soon?"

"Soon, my girl. Soon the mama goats will have little ones."

"Milk?"

"Yes. There will be more milk for you then, Aminah."

"Mm, good." Smack, smack.

For such a young child, she had an amusing flare for acting. Ihsan chuckled, the tensions of his day draining from him. To confidently give answers and to have them trustingly received was a welcome change. A far cry from what had happened that morning.

He grimaced as he made his way toward the house. Instead of entering, he lowered himself onto the rickety bench on the side of the house protected from the worst of the dusty air. He kept Aminah on his shoulders, where she went on chattering and playing her hands through his hair, while he dug in his pouch for the makings of a cigarette. As he meted out the tobacco and rolled and sealed it, the bitter memory of his day returned in full force. Ihsan struck a match and lit the cigarette, drawing in a deep lungful, willing the soothing smoke to calm his racing thoughts.

They had taken their flocks to pasture south of the village as usual. Ever since the fateful day they had witnessed the Fulani attack on Aminah's people, there had been an unspoken understanding among the villagers that they would not venture north again. It was this undercurrent of wariness that caused what took place this morning, he was sure of it.

One of them, Debare Garba, had kicked at the sparse grass where they intended to graze their flocks. A puff of dust emerged, then settled on his rubber sandal. "What is this crap? How can our animals get what they need out of such pitiful feed?" he grumped. "Tomorrow we go to the northwest." Garba, the son of a village Big Man shot a hard glance Ihsan's way. There were a few murmurs of agreement from some of the others before they separated to tend to their flocks.

Ihsan had kept quiet. It seemed to him they scrutinized him with a growing suspicion and distrust. Uma's husband, the other fellow Muslim in the group, did not meet his eyes, but Ihsan knew he felt the tension too. He was relieved when one of the other men said, "It will be even drier up there. We can try farther to the west tomorrow."

But that had not been the worst of it. When they had gathered under the sweeping canopy of a locust bean tree for the noon meal, the Christian farmers formed a circle, turning their backs on Ihsan and his brother-in-law. Where there had once been easy camaraderie, news of more frequent Fulani attacks in recent years had increased the friction in the village.

The two Muslims ate in an uncomfortable silence. Soon, Garba and another man from the circle ambled toward them. On instinct, Ihsan rose.

Garba approached close enough for Ihsan to feel his hot breath. "We know you have a *butare* child in your home. Where did you get her?"

A pulse throbbed in Ihsan's throat. "She is sent to us by the Almighty."

"It is a Christian child," Garba said, giving Ihsan a threatening look.

"You saw the wreck that day. The child was in danger, and no one did anything to rescue her. Her father is dead, and I have adopted her. She is well provided for." He tried to inject authority into his words.

Garba and the other man appeared unmoved. "If the police should come looking..." They left the threat hanging like a smoke ring in the air.

As Ihsan finished his smoke that evening, he put the day's confrontation together with another recent exchange. He'd been milking goats in the goat shelter behind his home when Pastor Monday appeared on the other side of his fence, his yellow cap gleaming in the sun.

Ihsan had stood for the leader of the local Christian congregation. "*Sannu!*" he greeted the pastor.

Monday asked after Ihsan's flock and commiserated about the weather, but eventually he came to the reason for this unusual visit.

"There is *gist* that you have a *butare* child living here."

Ihsan drew himself up in defense. "Our daughter."

"The child does not belong to you."

Rage began to swell inside Ihsan at this insult to his daughter. With effort, he quelled it. There was enough tension in the village.

"She does. God has given her to us."

"Where is the proof? You have no papers. The child may have family looking for her. Have you even tried to seek them?"

"If I had not rescued the girl, she would have been killed by Fulani."

A fleeting emotion passed across Monday's face at the mention of the dreaded nomads. "Still, you should make it official. You cannot simply keep a child not your own."

"She is our own." Ihsan wished no further conversation. He turned to resume his milking.

For a moment, Monday's feet made shuffling sounds. Then, without a word, he walked on.

Twilight had fallen and Daniya had called him a third time for supper. Now she came and lifted a sleeping Aminah off Ihsan's shoulders. Cool evening air chilled the spot where the child had rested.

He and his wife shared a long look. Yesterday, Daniya had told him what had occurred among the women at the village market. He could not face telling her what he was hearing from a community that seemed to wish them the worst of all losses.

Chapter 24

Hast thou not seen
How thy desires e'er have been
Granted in what He ordaineth?
~Praise Ye the Lord, the Almighty, by Joachim Meander, 1650-1680

T he road, scarved in the tatters of a chiffon fog, lay frozen and
flat in the tunnel made by my headlights. I stared ahead,
shivering, and transferred my travel mug from one hand to the
other trying to warm them. The Christmas break had been a special
time with my family. I'd even received a card from James's brother.
On his mother's behalf, he wrote that she had appreciated the
memory book I had sent last summer but was too sad to write back.
She had, however, enclosed a generous cheque.

The holiday had also been a much-needed rest from studying.
But my enjoyment of the time off was dimmed by the public
speaking that loomed ahead of me. Today, in the first class of the
new semester, I was to present my final assignment from last term.
Charlaine had contacted me last week, asking if I would present my
work to the entire class. I was honoured. It was a huge affirmation,
considering the fits the project had given me for the past four
months. I had poured inordinate effort into this assignment,
wanting desperately to cover every angle.

My insides ignited at the prospect of opening the first in-person class. But this nervousness was nothing to the jitters I'd suffered prior to high school or college speaking assignments. All those engagements at dozens of churches to raise support for our mission a few years ago had changed me. Back then, James had always been beside me. Confident, funny, and at ease with any new situation, he'd been able to charm the socks off the stiffest of audiences.

Still, I surprised myself by anticipating today's presentation. That had a lot to do with the brief but sincere-sounding commendation Charlaine had written on my term assignment.

"Well-researched and cogently written. You make an interesting case for an unexplored victim group."

I disliked the whole victim identity. The last thing I wanted was to give the impression I was whining for special treatment or worse, government handouts. I had only meant to draw attention to the censure given to stay-at-home mothers. I made a mental note to highlight a couple of phrases in my conclusion that would emphasize the point.

Charlaine had made it clear the other students would be graded on their scrutiny of the presentation as much as I was in giving it. So there were bound to be questions. Maybe even hostile ones. Though classes had been conducted online during the fall term, it was a small group and we'd gotten to know each other better than I expected. Of the four most vocal students in the class, I was most drawn to Fiona, the wife of a small-town minister. I felt sure we must share a common love for Christ.

Sheera, too, the brilliant and studious Cameroonian girl, seemed to hold Christian beliefs. She was my chief competition for top grades. And then there was Lasna, a Muslim. Exquisite as a porcelain doll, Lasna was nevertheless outspoken in her opposition to injustice wherever she saw it. But I anticipated the most push-back from the feminist in the class. I already knew that Brynn saw oppression of women at the root of any issue, that she was outspoken in her pro-choice views, and that she was a staunch supporter of the rights of sex workers. No doubt she would raise the most challenging questions.

I pulled into the college parking lot and followed my map of the campus to the humanities wing. I'd allowed plenty of time to orient myself and the building was mainly empty. From the other end of a long hallway, I spotted Charlaine striding toward me, her long camel coat billowing out from her sides. We arrived at the locked door of the darkened classroom at the same time.

"And so we meet, face to face," Charlaine said. Her cloud of curls hid her face as she dug in her briefcase for a jingling ring of keys.

I curbed the impulse to hug my old friend. She made it clear that a reunion was not on her mind. I'd forgotten how much taller she was, especially wearing those elegant high-heeled boots.

Charlaine flicked on the lights and swept to the lectern at the front of the room to begin setting up her laptop. There would be no fraternizing with the student caste. "You've got data to present on the screen?"

"Yes," I said, holding up my device. She showed me where to plug it in. I then moved toward a desk near the front of the classroom. I wanted to avoid everyone's eyes on me making a long trek to the front when called on. I shed my jacket and hung it from the back of my chair, then pulled out my notes.

By nine, the room had filled up with the classmates that until today I had only met online. Charlaine marched to the door to close it, turning to welcome us to the new semester.

"You've each received your grades for your fall term project. I was impressed with the caliber of work. Due to time constraints, I've asked only one student to present. The others will be posted online and you'll each be graded on your critique of them. For today," she motioned toward me, "I give you Lynnie Min."

I tightened my grip on my paper to stop my hands trembling as I made my way to the lectern and laid out my notes.

Scanning the group in front of me, I calmed myself with a deep breath.

"Should any girl be hindered, scorned, or prevented from following her dreams?" I began. "In a nation where women have advanced to the highest offices in government, industry, business, academia, media, and the arts, is there any realm where today's women might still fear to enter? With advances in women's rights in Western nations, is there any profession that women are still discouraged from entering?

"Professor Trites and fellow students, my answer to these questions is a resounding, but perhaps surprising, yes!"

I paused for effect, noting a few raised eyebrows.

"From the time I was a little girl playing with dolls, I have wanted to be a mother." I let that statement hang in the air, knowing it might raise a reaction. As I expected, there was some shifting in seats, and a couple of quiet murmurs. There were smiles, too, but I couldn't determine if they were sympathetic or mocking.

"Sociologists insist this is mere conditioning. Brain research and experience tell us otherwise. My younger brother used to bite his toast into the shape of a gun even though it was a toy that was forbidden in our home. By contrast, when I, as a very small child, rode with my father in the tractor, I'm told I bundled the wrench he kept there into a rag and cuddled 'my baby' close. No matter how egalitarian my parents might have raised us, I was wired to nurture." I clicked to the data slide showing the brain differences between boys and girls.

Charlaine surveyed the gathered students, as though watching for reaction.

Writing the paper had been one thing, speaking such a politically incorrect message to an unknown audience was a different matter altogether. Wiping my sweating hands on my slacks, I forged on.

I described the negative response to my aspiration to motherhood that I'd received in school, then related that to cultural messaging in media, literature, and education. I knew I was swimming against the received wisdom that said girls are hindered from reaching the top levels of their vocations or from going into STEM fields of study. But I gave statistics that showed that the freer girls feel to pursue what they enjoy doing, the more likely they'll be to choose traditional, feminine vocations.

By this time, I was avoiding eye-contact with my audience. The more I sensed their objections, the more I determined to plow through the material. Aware that my face must be flushed a deep red, I went on to cover taxation legislation that penalized single-income families, and the societal expectation that women earn respect solely by having paid work.

I'm doing this, I exulted. *I'm actually doing this. And it's not so bad.*

I gave proposals for improvement and offered examples before concluding.

"The women's movement opened the way for girls to follow their dream into any field of work, the more non-stereotypical the better. But at the same time it closed a door that many women long to enter. C.S. Lewis said this about homemaking: 'All other careers exist for one purpose only—to support the ultimate career.' Full-time mothering shapes, nurtures and civilizes the next generation. Isn't it time to raise motherhood again to its rightful place of honour?"

The silent room seemed extra warm to me as my trembling fingers gathered my notes into a perfectly aligned pile. Finally, my classmates applauded. I looked up, braced for their questions.

"I'm sure you're aware," Brynn said, "of what the famous feminist, Simone de Beauvoir said about housework." She read from her phone. "'Few tasks are more like the torture of Sisyphus than housework, with its endless repetition: the clean becomes soiled, the soiled is made clean, over and over, day after day.' Are you saying that women want to do that, more than, say, designing airplanes?"

Several of the students nodded their approval at this.

"Aren't repetition and tedium the nature of any work?" I countered. James and I had often talked about my work in the home. I answered from my memory of what he used to tell me, grateful for his support of my role. "Don't you think an aeronautic engineer has boring moments and frustrations in her work, or has to redo aspects of it? And cleaning up messes isn't the sum total of mothering. There's plenty of creativity involved in teaching children and creating a nurturing environment for them." I paged through my project notes. "My time today was limited so I didn't get to another of de Beauvoir's quotes. She said, 'No woman should be authorized to stay at home to bring up her children...because if there is such a choice, too many women will make that one.'" I focused on Brynn. "You can see she knew that the desire for motherhood is embedded in the hearts of women. But she thought it should be squelched. I'm advocating for true vocational choice."

Brynn frowned but did not respond.

Lasna was the next to raise her hand. "How do you suggest we raise awareness of this injustice?"

I smiled. "The simplest and most effective way is to change our own attitudes. Stop asking women with kids if they work. Don't let your eyes glaze over when someone says she's a homemaker. Stop approving of government incentives that push women out of the home and into the paid workforce."

"Haven't you overlooked the many women who don't have the luxury of someone to support them and are forced to work outside the home?" Fiona asked.

I hesitated, startled by the challenge in her tone. As a minister's wife, she must know the high value the Bible placed on homemaking. I stammered something about having sympathy and respect for all women and their choices but was distracted by Charlaine gesturing to the time.

She rose from her seat and came toward me. I left the podium with relief. Back in my seat, it took a long time before my knees stopped their shaking.

Chapter 25

Will your anchor hold in the storms of life,
When the clouds unfold their wings of strife?
~We Have an Anchor, by Priscilla J. Owens, 1829 -1907

Charlaine kicked off her heels and padded through the kitchen of her condo, dropping her briefcase, coat, and keys in a trail behind her. Preston's car wasn't yet out front. Good. She needed time alone to process what had just happened without the distraction of her partner's latest obsession—getting married. And having children. That was the last thing she wanted to discuss after today.

With only a year left until tenure review as an assistant professor, her next step as associate prof was so close she could taste it. Working her way through the ranks, she now had two letters of recommendation and a nice collection of positive student reviews. The pandemic had all but kiboshed an interprovincial conference she had organized last spring, but in the nick of time she'd managed to switch everything to on-line participation. The stress had nearly given her ulcers, but it was worth it to receive that second academic recommend. For years, she had busted her butt as adviser to a couple of student committees, been careful to follow all the latest faculty protocols, taken recommended webinars, and co-published articles in a couple of academic journals.

And now this.

When Dean Marielle Hendry tapped at her office door at noon, Charlaine had welcomed her in with a momentary quiver in her gut. She calmed herself by deciding it must be some clerical matter, then cast a glance up and down the hallway to see if anyone noticed her visitor.

The older woman sat heavily in the guest armchair across the desk from Charlaine. As usual, Marielle Hendry's bright auburn hair had a mind of its own, but now a thick line of white marked the roots. She shifted in her seat, stretching her short legs straight out in front of her and giving a small sigh.

"Whew! What a week this has been," she said in her faint Quebecois accent.

"I thought new term admissions would have settled down by now."

"Oh it's not that. Just, you know, issues." She put her full weight on the word issues as if Charlaine should be aware of what those were.

Charlaine nodded though she was as bemused as before.

The dean sat up straighter and directed her gaze out the narrow second floor window. "And how are your classes going? Everything *parfait*, as they say?"

"So far, so good. Some of my shy students have begun to come out of their shells. And not just on-line. They're commenting in class too." Charlaine kept to herself the tension that had developed on-line in the past two weeks. At least she was getting good engagement from her students. She prided herself on her ability to draw them out.

"But of course. You are a good facilitator, yes?" Dean Hendry made a series of nods. "So then, no problems? No conflicts between students?"

That quiver flitted around Charlaine's insides again. She grew cautious. "Nothing to speak of, no. What makes you ask?"

The dean cleared her throat and averted her eyes. She pulled up the half-glasses that hung from a rhinestone chain around her neck, then unfolded a single page from the pocket of her jacket. "We have received a complaint of academic misconduct." She fixed Charlaine with a meaningful look to emphasize the significance, then resumed reading.

Academic misconduct! Her gut twisted inside her. Who would complain about her? And why? She pictured the few seats that comprised her classes. All of them were dedicated students who were there to learn. The class had good rapport. Or so she had thought. Then her mind stopped at the seat halfway down and to the right. She had to admit, one student stood out as potential trouble.

Lynnie Min.

When Lynnie had introduced herself in orientation last fall, Charlaine knew she looked familiar. But with a different surname and the young woman's hair so much longer, it had taken awhile for her to click in.

Lyn Hardy. Charlaine's high school rival for top grades. The girl who had pressured her into attending the school religious group meetings. Lyn had invited her to her home often on weekends, which meant Charlaine was expected to attend the Friday night church youth group as well as the Sunday morning service. Of course, she accepted. At the time, it had been better than staying home with her mother's black bout of depression for company. But now, looking back, she wondered how she could have stood it. The juvenile games or a winter hayride, followed by watered down sugar drinks and home-baked cookies. On Saturday, she would be roped into helping with farm chores, lured by the prospect of a fall wiener roast or family games night. Then on Sunday, the doddering music and a simplistic but interminable sermon, followed by a noon meal heavy with meat. Lyn's parents were nice enough, but the meal became heavier still with a grilling by Lyn's grim grandmother on the state of Charlaine's eternal soul. No wonder she had looked forward to getting back to school on Mondays. Come to think of it, why had she ever kept accepting the invitations?

They'd hung out for that one year before Charlaine located her dad and moved to Toronto to live with him. Life's tantalizing possibilities in the city had opened after that and she had easily shed all her insecurities. She'd been glad to forget her old life in backward rural Alberta.

When Lyn had shown up on her computer screen in that first online class last fall, Charlaine had had an uncomfortable moment. She'd been startled by an unexpected inner tugging to those old days, an intangible longing for something like the solidity and hope that she remembered finding in the Hardy home. What played through her mind were the contrasts. Her tiptoeing, tomblike existence with her mother against the happy chaos of Lyn's *Little House on the Prairie* family life.

It made no sense to think of that now and she shoved it aside with the reminder of all she had achieved since then. But that returned her to the present problem. Someone had made a complaint about her. This could ruin her career path. The tension was killing Charlaine. What possible offence could she have given? Had she said something that wouldn't jive with Lyn's Christian beliefs? A spark of anger kindled inside her. If Lyn was behind this...

"Charlaine?"

Charlaine cleared her throat, blinking to focus on the short, shabbily dressed Dean of Humanities across from her. "Sorry. You were saying?"

Marielle Hendry frowned. "The complaint relates to offensive and harmful comments in"—she adjusted her glasses to scan the document again—"your classes as well as the supplementary online forums. Students felt threatened by the topics you've approved for discussion."

"Threatened! Did they specify? Is there documentation that I can review?"

"I will read you the pertinent allegations." The dean read out select phrases, "...discriminated against single mothers... poisonous remarks...choosing to give a voice to bigoted, hateful information while shutting out dissenting views...fostering harassing comments on class forum."

The blood pounded in Charlaine's temples as she tried to take in the accusations. They were a punch to the solar plexus and left her gasping. Her cheeks burned as she tried to gain control. She forced out a shaky, desperate breath. "Are there any dates or specific references to the course outline? How am I supposed to defend myself if I don't know what the student is referring to?"

"We can go over all that when we have the advisory committee meeting." The older woman had boosted herself up with a push on the arms of the chair. "I thought you might appreciate a heads-up before then. You'll be meeting with one other faculty member, the college president, and me in the boardroom next Friday." When she reached the office door, she turned and gave a sympathetic smile. "Don't worry, Charlaine. The college is just as anxious to settle this before it gets to the Human Rights Commission as you are."

The Human Rights Commission? Don't worry? She hadn't thought this was even a firing offence, let alone a legal matter. Did she need a lawyer?

Charlaine's pulse thundered through her veins. She had heard a few stories of HRC cases, racists and homophobes and perverts who had gotten what they deserved. But she had barely paid attention to them, confident they had nothing to do with her. She was a woman of colour with a PhD. How could this nightmare be happening to her?

Think, Charlaine, think.

Charlaine had done nothing but think since the brief meeting with the dean. She'd gone through her two afternoon classes on autopilot, her mind replaying the damning words *discriminatory, hateful, poisonous* until a full-blown migraine had tightened its steel band around her head. Hendry had said students felt threatened by the topics Charlaine had approved for discussion, that she'd "chosen to give a voice to bigoted, hateful information." These must be referring to Lynnie's presentation earlier that month. Charlaine had seen it as a unique opportunity for discussion but now she regretted ever letting her present. Still, Lynnie wouldn't have been the one to complain about her own content. Then who?

Charlaine sprang from her couch and began a frenzied pacing. Did it matter who had made the complaint? The more she thought about it, the more certain she was that Lynnie's ridiculous talk about stay-at-home mothers accounted for the charge of "discrimination against single mothers." Charlaine hadn't noticed anyone in the class that day who seemed outraged. But that had to be what the complaint was referring to.

Unless...Unless there was a racial component to all this. Was the grievance, at its root, because she was a woman of colour? She tried to recall whether Lynnie or her family had ever shown prejudice. Other than Lynnie's little sister wanting to play with Charlaine's hair, nothing came to mind. Still, Charlaine wouldn't rule it out. Best to keep the possibility of underlying racism in her arsenal of defences.

She came to an abrupt stop in front of her desk, opened her laptop, and searched for human rights cases. Long after Preston had come home, Charlaine studied the cases. She scarcely noticed the dinner of vegetable paella he brought to her at the computer. Ignoring his attempts at conversation, she was relieved when he went to bed alone.

Charlaine discovered the origins of the Commission and the fears at the time that there would be nothing to prevent complainants from making wild and false charges. It was a relief to find several academic cases had been dismissed but other complainants had been less fortunate. She read of business owners and professors wasting thousands of dollars and hours fighting the charges only to have the case fizzle out, their finances and reputations in ruins. And what about the sleepless nights and emotional toll?

Charlaine sank back in her office chair. There was no way she was going down without a fight. Nor was she going down alone. She refused to have all she had worked so hard for reduced to ashes because of a naive and thoughtless chick like Lynnie Min. Little Ms. Min needed to suffer some of the anxiety that Charlaine was now feeling.

Chapter 26

Do thy friends despise, forsake thee?
Take it to the Lord in prayer;
In His arms He'll take and shield
thee—
Thou wilt find a solace there.
~What a Friend We Have in Jesus, by Joseph Scriven, 1819-1886

I accepted a couple of Cheezies from the small bag Sheera offered me. A few members of our class were eating lunch together in the college cafeteria, discussing the course workload among other things. It was one of those times when I convinced myself I belonged in this world. Just a simple student, untouched by the upheaval of tragedy and sudden loss. I liked immersing myself in my studies. They gave me purpose.

Today I welcomed that focus. I had awakened to another strange dream, this time another positive one about Anya. In some vague way I had the sense that all was well with her. That was the good part. The hard part was waking again to my empty arms. As usual, I turned to my assignments as a way to discipline my mind.

Someone tapped my shoulder.

"Can I have a word with you?" From behind my chair, Charlaine bent close to whisper to me, her hot breath in my ear.

I excused myself from the group and followed her out of the cafeteria. She led me in silence all the way to her office, where she waved a hand at the chair across from her desk. A small vee tugged at her smooth brown forehead.

From the beginning, she had been so scrupulous in avoiding personal interaction with me that I was confused by this invitation. Other than singling me out by having me present my fall term assignment a few weeks ago, she had not so much as hinted in class that we had anything but a teacher-student relationship. That assignment had earned me a good grade and had generated a lively on-line discussion with the entire class participating. Maybe this was about my misunderstanding the point of the last assignment I turned in? I rubbed my clammy palms down my pant legs.

"There has been a complaint," she finally said, her face a tight mask as she focused on a spot beyond my left shoulder. Her full lips tightened, and she inhaled deeply, but said no more.

"A complaint about what? From whom?" For her to bring me in to divulge this must mean it had something to do with me. But I couldn't imagine what.

Charlaine now fixed her gaze on me, her dark eyes flashing. "The dean received a written complaint about the content in some of my classes. From the nature of the allegations, I believe they were classes in which you either presented or contributed to the discussion in such a way that other students were offended." Hostility radiated from her.

My jaw dropped. I brought my hands up to my burning cheeks in bewilderment as my mind raced to make sense of the accusation. "May I see it?" I managed to whisper.

"I'm afraid not. The complainants wish their names to remain confidential."

"What?" Names listed? More than one person complaining? Above the clamour in my head, I heard my dad discoursing on justice. *The accused must be able to face the accuser.* I fought hysteria, struggling to keep my Nigerian-low voice. "How can I correct my mistakes, or even answer them, if I don't know what I did to offend someone?"

"I'm sorry. At least for now, I can't divulge the details."

"So what do I do?"

Charlaine tilted back in her chair, giving me a hard stare for a long moment. "I suppose you do exactly what I've been doing since I first received this news. Lie awake all night wondering if my career is about to be ruined by someone who couldn't exercise a bit of discretion." She stood abruptly. "If you'll excuse me, I have another meeting to attend."

I fumbled, gathering my lunch bag and purse, slinking out of her office as quietly as I could. Rounding the corner leading back to the cafeteria I ducked into the lavatory, rushing blindly into a cubicle. I stuffed my sleeve against my mouth to muffle the sobs of betrayal and fear that burst from me.

I thought we were friends. I understood that professionally, Charlaine couldn't acknowledge our friendship, but to be cut off in the curt way she had just done... I remembered the troubled girl who had thrown herself into my family, clinging to my mom in tears in a private time that I had only seen from the doorway, taking her urgent questions about God and life to my dad, telling me how much she envied me having a brother and sisters. What could have happened to a person to make her forget a bond like that?

I searched my memory for interactions I'd had with the class. What had I said that might have offended someone?

True, my presentation on full-time mothers was counter cultural. It had aroused controversy, particularly in the on-line forum. But I had been careful to answer the "what abouts" with statistics and facts and I had thought the women in the class had seemed satisfied. I had not detected any serious antagonism. Instead, it seemed they'd been genuinely interested and concerned. I wound up proud of having opened their eyes to a rarely recognized demographic.

How could I have so badly misread the women I thought were my friends? I was comfortable with my classmates. We had had differences of opinion but, still, there had been rapport. I had sensed no hostility from them. Only from Charlaine today. My mind whirled with shock and confusion, searching for the source of the complaint. I had never intended to hurt anyone, least of all my high school friend. I had grown so much through these months in college. I had felt relaxed enough to share my beliefs more freely than ever before, even when I knew those near me might disagree. In courage and confidence, I was now a woman, not the little girl I had still been as an undergrad. I had grown up. Wasn't that what higher education was meant to produce?

A groan escaped me. *Help me, James!* He had always been the one who could see situations objectively. My heart cried out for him to sort out this mess, but instead my empty arms wrapped themselves around me.

Oh God...show me the truth in all this.

Someone entered the washroom. I held still, stifling my snuffles until she left.

Finally, I crept out of the stall and approached the mirror. My face was a mottled, puffy mess. I ran the water until it was icy, splashed my face with it, and headed back to the classroom wing.

Sitting at the outside edge of the room, I watched my colleagues from the corner of my eye as they filed into class. Now I saw them all through a different lens. I reviewed my interactions with those I had begun to know, scrutinizing every comment or even the mildest remark.

Was I wrong to have asked Sheera where she was from? She had spoken fondly of Cameroon and we had found common ground. To my recollection, it had been a friendly conversation, reminiscing over the things we each missed about Africa.

I'd had less opportunity to speak privately with Lasna. But one thing she'd made clear, she did not condone Islamist extremism. I'd been careful to agree with her mildly, without sharing that my family had been the victims of such terrorism.

Unexpectedly, I had come to like Brynn, the feminist. I was no longer intimidated by her outspoken condemnation of whatever she felt strongly about on a given day. Her ire landed on her victims in equal measure, whether meat-eaters, the patriarchy, capitalists, or body-shamers. Two red spots of passion would appear on her cheeks whenever she got going like this, and her raised voice would attract attention to our cafeteria table. But the fervour would subside just as quickly, replaced by a schoolgirl giggle over dropping her water bottle or some such. My impression of her had been that she enjoyed a heated discussion but that she was not a grudge-holder.

Fiona I counted on as my ally. I knew her to be a Christian and to my mind, this eliminated her as one who would have complained.

There were others in the class, of course, but they tended to fall into the camps represented by these women: The immigrants, the feminists, and the ordinary women who simply wanted to get a job after graduation. I felt sure that all of them, like me, had a sincere desire to help those less fortunate. But had I been naive?

One of them must be my accuser. Which one? I hated the suspicion that now clouded my relations with them, but I felt burned and betrayed. My dealings with them would now be tainted with wariness and distrust.

The pre-class chatter died down when the prof entered the room. Willowy and regal in her red knit dress and boots, with a glossy statement necklace and large hoop earrings, Charlaine was a woman who commanded attention. Today, I thought I noticed a hard look in her eyes and a stiffness at the corners of her mouth. I thought back to her exact words in our meeting earlier.

"The dean received a formal written complaint about the content in some of my classes...they were classes in which you presented or contributed to the discussion."

I sat up straighter, giving this some thought. The complaint had been against Charlaine, not me. Was that why she was so angry? Was that what was behind her comment about worrying her career could be ruined? Then how could she know it had anything to do with me?

Chapter 27

The new year had improved nothing in relations between Ihsan and his neighbours. Daily, the village pressure on him grew heavier. Debare Garba glowered at him when they were out pasturing their flocks. Some of the men simply voiced their disapproval of his having a white child in his home at all. Pastor Monday stopped by regularly to urge him to reconsider. Others took up the campaign to convince Ihsan to return the child, darkly hinting about the trouble that could come to all of them if police were to descend on the village. It was a worrisome prospect. The powers police took on themselves too often left people impoverished or imprisoned unjustly. Nobody wanted to draw their attention.

It hardly seemed fair how they stoked the fire against him. There was no village imam to defend him and not even his brother-in-law would speak on his behalf. In fact, Uma herself had once gently asked him if it might be wise to seek out Aminah's family.

But how? Did they think he was rich, that he could easily afford a trip to Jos? Even if he got there, how was he to know where the child belonged? He had kept all this worry to himself, not wishing to disturb his wife. If Daniya knew what the men were saying, she would be incensed. She would insist Aminah belonged to them, and he agreed. But the villagers' opinions had raised doubts in his mind. Yet the mere thought of separating his wife and her child was unthinkable. He feared what the loss of Aminah would do to Daniya.

He wrestled constantly with what had seemed such a clear sign that the little girl had been dropped into his life by Allah. Now with the disapproval of his neighbours and more recently, even the doubts of family, Ihsan was grumpy and disturbed. By far the most distressing thing was his own sore heart, rubbed raw by the prospect of tearing his baby girl away from him. He loved her little arms around his neck when he carried her to her pallet at night. When she ran to him as he returned each evening, his heart swelled with joy. She had brought life to Daniya and to their home. The thought of resuming their previous dull existence filled him with dread. Why couldn't his neighbours accept her? She was as bright and lovable as any other village child. Daniya had asked only yesterday, with tears streaming down her cheeks, how they could hate a child simply because of her skin? He had murmured comfort, downplaying the heat of their neighbours' animosity.

But the next time Pastor Monday came around, Ihsan challenged him with that very question.

"Everybody in Nigeria hates everybody else," Monday said, laughing. "If you don't hate all other Nigerians, can you really be Nigerian?"

Ihsan frowned. It was a well-known truth, but he was puzzled by the Christian's ease with it. "I hear your Sunday songs about love."

The smile vanished from Monday's face. "Oh yes. I know. It's a sin-sick world, it surely is." He shook his head sorrowfully.

Silence swelled between them. Ihsan pondered the words *sin sick*. "We Hausa have always hated Igbo people because they are good at making money and that makes us look dumb." He searched the other man's face. "And since the war, Igbo hate us. Igbo people and Yoruba people used to get along, but Igbo started hating Yoruba when they didn't back Igbo people in the war against Hausa."

Ihsan began pacing, recounting the hostility of man against man. "Ijaw, Ibibio, and Efik people hate Igbo people because Igbo bully them. Fulani hate everyone and everyone hates the Fulani." He stopped and glared at the pastor, overwhelmed by the weighty burden of hatred. "Everyone in Nigeria hates someone."

"No one hates the child," the pastor protested. "Only that we think she belongs with her family,"

Ihsan approached Monday until they were nearly nose-to-nose. He could count the large pores of the other man's cheeks, feel his hot breath. "Why does anyone ever bring a child into this hateful world?" he demanded. "How can one small child be a problem when there is far greater wickedness in our world?" He turned abruptly from the Christian and stalked into the house.

Daniya put away the rice and unused vegetables and wiped the enamel countertop, then took up the broom to sweep her small kitchen area. She made a playful sweep across Aminah's bare toes which made the little one giggle. Daniya smiled with pleasure to watch the child scamper after the broom. Aminah did not have a sturdy frame like Uma's children, but she was energetic and clever despite her slight build. She had grown and learned so much that she could hardly be called a toddler anymore. As Daniya had often wondered, again she asked herself how old her daughter was.

After the family birthday party for Uma's second daughter yesterday, Daniya wished she knew exactly when Aminah's birthday was. Daniya wanted to celebrate her child. Perhaps they should simply decide on a date and declare it her birthday. Ihsan had brought her home near the end of last dry season, so she had been theirs for more than a year now. Though she had been a tiny child, and still was, she had quickly learned words. Perhaps she was close to two years old at that time?

Plans for a third birthday celebration began to take shape in Daniya's mind. Special food, and a gift, and games for the cousins. She would have to decide on a date soon, before Ramadan which was coming up in two months' time.

Abruptly, the broom stopped its rhythmic motion as she pondered. With the busyness of motherhood, she'd had little time to think of herself. Now she wondered how many weeks it had been since her last cycle. In the foggy gray of her past life, she had always known precisely. She crossed to the wall where the calendar hung. The events recorded there gave no hint of the last time she felt crampy and slow moving.

Like the morning sun creeping above the eastern plain, a gradual awareness dawned on her. Could it possibly be? Had she been so preoccupied with Aminah's care and growth that she had been unconscious of a change in her own body? She propped the broom in its corner.

"Mama?" Aminah chirped when the sweeping game stopped.

But for the first time ever, Daniya ignored her daughter's voice. She rushed to the bedroom mirror as new thoughts sped through her mind. Turning to the side and flattening her bright turquoise dress against her middle, it was hard to tell if there was any change. But previous pregnancies, even to the third month, had never made a noticeable difference to her belly. Yet this time, her breasts felt fuller. That was a hopeful difference.

Think, girl, think! When was her last monthly? Wasn't it when the Christians had been blaring their Christmas music from the loudspeaker of their church that she had begun to feel tired in mid-day and had lain down for an extra rest? December. Two months! She sat down on the bed, her stomach churning with emotion. There had been so many false alarms in the years of her marriage, and enough losses that Daniya knew better than to hope. Yet she could scarcely help it. She ran her hands over her body, then wrapped them around her throat in excitement. In an instant her life changed, their family changed, the years ahead taking on a new course.

How wonderful it would be for Aminah to have a little companion. The way the child mothered the stick doll Daniya had made for her there was no doubt Aminah would love a baby in the house. Daniya barely gave a thought to the prospect of the additional work of diapers and night-waking. She counted the months. If her estimate of Aminah's age was correct, she would be three and a half years old when the new baby came. Uma never seemed worried about having children close together in age. She said that every month made a big difference in the littlest one's independence and the older ones' ability to help.

Her thoughts soon turned to how Ihsan might take the news. From her earlier miscarriages, he had learned to be cautious. At first, when she would confide the news of a pregnancy, joy appeared on his face. But as a tragic pattern began to emerge, a new pregnancy would crease his face with worry. Surely this time would be different, wouldn't it? Hadn't Allah already blessed them with a child, sent to them in such a strange and miraculous way? Wasn't that a sign that their fortune had changed? They would yet find favour and be given another baby, would they not?

For reasons she could not pry out of him, Ihsan had been preoccupied and irritable lately. If men in the community had been attacking him about Aminah like the women at the market had her, she could understand his grumpiness. She dug her fingers into the flesh of her arms, furious still at the memory.

Wouldn't the hope of a new baby be exactly the sort of news to cheer him? He was an attentive father to Aminah. Another child would be a joy to him. Perhaps a son to carry on the family name? A fine son who would look like him, be like him? This would make him happy. Daniya made a circular motion on her belly, letting her imagination fill in the unknown future. Perhaps she would wait a few more weeks to be certain. But her growing excitement would be hard to contain.

Chapter 28

In seasons of distress and grief
My soul has often found relief,
And oft escaped the tempters snare
By thy return, sweet hour of prayer.
~Sweet Hour of Prayer, by William W. Walford, 1772-1850

I stopped by Nanny's place on the way home from school. I would have preferred the time alone to process what had taken place that day, but Mom had asked me to bring Nanny home for family dinner night.

She greeted me with a tight squeeze, then pulled out of the embrace to find her coat and mitts. "Now you toddle into the kitchen there and help yourself to something from the junk cart."

It was easier to go along with Nanny's suggestion than to object. I shoved a mini pack of red licorice in my coat pocket, then helped her out to the car. Once I got her settled in the passenger seat, she turned to me with a rosy grin. "Isn't this the bee's knees going on a drive together?"

"It sure is, Nanny," I said, trying to smile despite my dark mood.

She leaned toward me, twisting her head to scrutinize my face. "Now Lynnie dear. You look a bit peaked. Is it all that studying that's got you down?"

Reaching the main street running through town, I turned left, sighing over how to explain my dilemma.

"Come on now. 'Fess up. What's troubling you?"

"I got called into my professor's office today."

"I thought by the time you got to college you didn't get in trouble with the principal anymore." Nanny giggled at her own joke.

I felt a small, unfamiliar flash of annoyance at my grandmother. Couldn't she be serious, just once?

Nanny must have sensed she'd overstepped. She patted my arm. "Never mind me, dear. Carry on."

"I was told there's been a complaint to administration about some of the classes I'm in and that it has something to do with things I've said."

"What on earth?" Nanny snorted. "I'm sure there's some mistake." Suddenly, she squeezed my arm with one mittened hand and pointed with the other. "Turn here!"

I shot her a swift glance. "Pardon me?"

"Turn here," she commanded, pointing to the right.

I braked obediently and turned down the side street she'd indicated. Nanny directed me halfway down the block, where she asked me to park. "You just wait here. Be back in a tick."

She waddled up the sidewalk and stepped into a bakery.

Ah, so that was it. It was classic Nanny modus operandi. After a few minutes she emerged carrying a wide, white box to the car. I got out to help her place it in the back seat. The box contained at least two dozen assorted doughnuts.

She settled into her seat and faced me with a broad grin. "Now then, these are exactly what you need to perk you up. So much tastier than the ones from the chain stores. And there'll be plenty to share."

Nanny appeared to have forgotten about my troubles entirely, which was just as well. How had I never noticed before that she was bankrupt when it came to dealing with the trials of life? My mom had never mentioned it. But maybe this was why Mom had found a closer relationship with Grandma, for all her stern sobriety. Nanny's well-intended "buck up and bring on the sugar biscuits" brand of comfort fell a bit short.

"What if Mom has dessert planned already?" I asked her.

"All the merrier. You can never have too much dessert."

At my parents' home, Nanny and I trundled into the house, sniffing the roast beef aroma appreciatively. Lissa and Mom were spooning the steaming food onto serving dishes.

Mom peered over the top of her fogged glasses at us. "Wash up and get to the table. Everything's ready." She eyed the doughnut box, then me, with a questioning look. I gave a slight shake of my head and she nodded. We had an unspoken communication that came in handy at times like this. I knew she understood that it was Nanny's idea, and we would discuss it later.

Grandma was seated at the table with Dad and Mark and the kids. Lance and Crystal were installing baby Blade in the highchair between them.

"Where's Katie tonight?" I asked Mom.

"She won't be home until late. She's accompanying a girl who's doing her voice recital." Mom set the platter of roast and a large glass bowl of creamy mashed potatoes on the table, scanned it once more for all the essentials, then sat next to Dad. Lissa brought the vegetables and salad.

I wanted to avoid questions about my day, so after Dad asked the blessing, I made much of baby Blade, asked Lissa what projects she had going, and generally filled in silences. I could feel Dad's eyes on me and realized I was overdoing it.

When Mom rose to bring the rhubarb cobbler, Nanny bustled to the kitchen, proudly returning with her tray of doughnuts.

"One dessert would have been sufficient," Grandma said with a sour look.

I caught the saucy eyebrow-waggling that Nanny aimed at Lissa. The grandmothers were getting more audacious than they had been when we were kids.

It turned out that Dylan and Jade were happier with doughnuts than they would have been with Mom's cobbler, which pleased Nanny. The rest of us were glad to get more of Mom's crunchy, tart dessert. Soon the two young families rose to get their children home to bed.

"I can run you back to town if you like, Nanny," Lance suggested before he left.

Nanny smiled up at his tall form. "No, no. You go ahead. Your mom can drive me home when I'm ready."

Hearing this, I flashed a quick glance at Mom. Had Nanny always presumed so much on others for her own convenience? I was beginning to see both my grandmothers in a different light from when I was a child. Mom responded to me with a weak half-smile, which told me enough.

The young parents and children said their good-byes, leaving Mom and Dad and my grandmothers at the table with me.

Dad ran his rough hand around the handle of his coffee mug. "So Lynnie, it looks like something's bothering you. Anything you want to tell us?"

I never was able to hide anything from my folks. The family dinner table was my safe space, a refuge from the outside world. Intruding on it with the nastiness of conflict from that world seemed a shame. I outlined as simply as I could that day's interchange with my prof.

"Offend someone, my foot. I say there has to have been some mistake," Nanny chimed in. "Our Lynnie would never say anything offensive. What I think, Glen, is that it's time for you to go in there and punch some noses." She shone a gleeful grin around the table at us, then steamed on in this vein, venting her indignation.

Grandma's lip curled ever so slightly, but she listened without comment to the other grandmother. She was the soul of discretion, but I knew her sense of justice was too well honed to indulge in blind family loyalty. I could almost hear the gears turning in her head. *If you've done wrong, Evelyn, you must make it right.*

I was certainly willing to do that. The trouble was, I still didn't think anything I'd said or done warranted a formal accusation. And even as I had replayed today's conversation, I grew more convinced Charlaine was throwing me under the bus because she felt her own career was threatened in some way. But I was careful to keep that suspicion to myself. Tonight, I wanted to present only the bare facts so the family could draw their own conclusions. To me it was vital to determine the justice of the matter.

Dad swiped his face with one hand. "There's likely something about this in your college student manual. It would be good to check. Until you can determine what the charges are, and who has made them, there's nothing to be done."

"That's just it, though," I complained. "Dr. Trites didn't give me any hint about that. She said she couldn't give details."

We batted the issue around for a few minutes, me recounting anything I'd said in my presentation that I thought might have raised hackles, my family asking about the temperaments of my classmates.

Finally, Grandma folded her hands together on the table in front of her and cleared her throat in her authoritative way. All eyes turned to her. "It is quite possible that this is all an emotional overreaction, Evelyn. As your father said, there is little to be done until you receive concrete accusations. It was premature, and in my opinion, unprofessional for this Dr. Trites to have burdened a student with such vague allegations before she could offer any specifics. For the present, your task is to discipline your mind against a needless cycle of worry. The best way I know to do that is to lay the problem before the Lord."

We murmured agreement—well, all of us except Nanny. But she joined us willingly enough as we closed the circle. I held her soft plump hand on one side and Grandma's wiry firm hand on the other and listened in to one side of a conversation between Grandma and her God. It wasn't entirely one sided either, the way she sprinkled quotations from the Bible in between her petitions, like God was answering back. She asked Him to give wisdom and clarity and a speedy resolution to "our trouble" as she called it. The way she owned it, including everyone there in facing it together shifted the burden.

By the time we opened our eyes and raised our heads, nothing about the situation had changed, except me. Almost physically, I could sense a weight rise from my shoulders. I still had to face the uncertainty of the days ahead but as I looked around the table at the people who had loved and shaped me all my life, for the first time since that morning, I saw a glimmer of hope.

Chapter 29

Did we in our own strength confide
Our striving would be losing
~*A Mighty Fortress is Our God, by Martin Luther, 1483-1546*

C harlaine had only a couple hours' notice before the meeting
scheduled to discuss the academic complaint. She'd come to
think of it as the summons to be burned at the stake. Perhaps that
was over-dramatizing since she had not been called before the more
ominous ad hoc disciplinary committee, but it was how she felt. Her
insides clearly viewed it the same way. She'd eaten little in the past
few days. Her mouth was dry as she paused before the boardroom
door, trying to drum up courage.

Marielle Hendry gestured to a chair across the boardroom table
from her and the other two academics present. Charlaine took the
seat, nodding at the college president, Harlan Chambers. Somehow,
her chair was slightly lower than the committee on the other side of
the table, making her feel small and insignificant.

"Dr. Trites," Dean Hendry began, without meeting Charlaine's
eyes, "we've invited Fran Dorn to sit in today as a representative of
the Diversity and Equity committee. You may already be aware that
Dr. Dorn teaches English and Women's Studies here at the college."

Fran's greeting was cordial but cool.

Charlaine had hoped to start out her defense assertively. But faced with three unmoving judges, she faltered. Her gut churned distractingly so that her opening remark left her head entirely.

Dr. Hendry peered at her over her reading glasses. "As you know, I received an anonymous complaint last week about some of your classes." She glanced down at a paper in front of her.

The word anonymous brought back some of Charlaine's resolve. "You say anonymous. Would I be correct in surmising that this was not a formal report?"

Marielle paused for a second, then nodded. "That's right. It was not a formal report."

"Was it perhaps communicated to you by email?" Charlaine pressed, hoping to discredit the source. "And if so, it would represent the opinion of only one student, correct?"

Dr. Dorn raised one pointed eyebrow. "Dr. Trites, we have asked you to meet with us so that we can get to the bottom of these concerns. If you'll allow us to proceed?"

Charlaine sank back as though her knuckles had been rapped.

"Suppose you give us your account of how you came to allow a student to"—Dr. Chambers scanned his notes—"'disseminate hateful and misogynistic information to the class?'" He raised one shoulder with an apologetic smile.

"Misogynistic?" Charlaine was aghast. The charge came as a shock. "That's outrageous! I am proud to call myself a feminist. My students are predominantly women and, I assure you, I hold zero tolerance for any ideologies or opinions that are hateful to women. But without reading the actual complaint or any other specifics, I'm at an unfair disadvantage in addressing the concerns." Charlaine's fingers tightened on the handle of her briefcase.

"Those who suffered harm because of this information being disseminated"—he read from the paper—"'felt it invalidated single mothers.'"

This accusation confirmed Charlaine's suspicions. Without a doubt, Lynnie Min was at the root of this entire debacle. How Charlaine regretted ever giving the woman the floor. Now she was forced to defend a student whose position she only meant to highlight, not condone. Charlaine tried to hold her anger in check, using it to go on the offensive. "I have a hard time believing anyone suffered harm listening to a talk on stay-at-home mothers."

Dr. Dorn inhaled sharply through tightly pinched nostrils. "Let me remind you, Dr. Trites, that we are an institute of higher learning. The whole point is to prepare women to take leadership in society. As long as women with children put family first, the goal that fifty percent of women will hold top corporate and government positions right along with men will never be achieved. Teaching our students to hide from making a valid contribution to society sets the women's movement back by a century."

"Look," Charlaine said, not bothering now to soften her tone, "I'm completely on board with preparing my students to take leadership. But if you're referring to the presentation I think you are, let me explain. I allowed class time for a student who had done interesting work in a unique area of study to share her findings with the class. I fully intended and expected that the other students would challenge her conclusions, which they thoroughly did, both in class following the presentation and especially afterward in the on-line chat. I believe it led to a fruitful exchange of ideas and—"

"To merely present information neutrally," Dorn cut in, "is not acceptable in the kind of learning environment we want to create."

"I beg your pardon?" Charlaine asked. With trembling hands she pulled out her copy of the college's academic freedom policy and found the highlighted lines. "Let me quote from the college policy manual: 'Academic Freedom is fundamental to the mandate of higher education institutions to pursue and disseminate knowledge and educate students.' I've always understood my job to be educating my students and trusting them to evaluate and discern the information presented."

"You are entitled to your opinions," the president said, "as are your students. But to favour one student's view over the others is not the kind of culture of learning we want to cultivate. I would also quote the policy manual that academic freedom is to be balanced with the responsibility we have to ensure that students' human rights are respected."

"But I didn't favour her." To Charlaine's dismay, the words came out as a whine. *Get it together, woman!*

"Perhaps you have history with this student?" Dr. Dorn interjected, her eyes narrowed. "An instructor whose prior relationship with a student results in bias in favour of the student could be construed as academic misconduct."

Did they know of the high school friendship? And if they did, how? Charlaine strained to recall any slip-up she might have made in class indicating the connection. No, it was definitely Lynnie who must have mentioned it. Her frustration was followed by a rising sense of panic. She stared at each of her interrogators in turn, landing finally on Dean Hendry. Gazing into the older woman's eyes, she silently pleaded with the dean. Charlaine was beginning to feel desperate.

She moistened her lips. "Let me respond with another point from the academic freedom policy." She turned the page. "'Differences in opinion are valued because the expression of unpopular opinions and research advances attainment of knowledge. Prevailing opinion is sometimes neither exhaustive nor comprehensive.' That's why I offered a student the chance to present. She had an archaic perspective that my students might someday encounter. Even if we didn't agree with her conclusions, I thought it was a quaint viewpoint that deserved discussion." The pulse in her throat hammered wildly.

"You have to ask yourself," Fran Dorn said, "what kind of a teaching climate you are creating if you uncritically present bigoted views to impressionable students?"

Charlaine couldn't believe this charge. "Impressionable students? This is not a first-year course. Two of my students are in their forties."

"Most, however, are still young," Dr. Dorn shot back, glaring across the table.

"Must I shield students from ideas different from their own? Isn't the purpose of higher learning to expose students to a wide variety of ideas? I didn't think my job was to insulate and protect them." Charlaine's voice cracked embarrassingly in the last sentence. Why was this session degenerating into a three-against-one pile-on? It was like they wanted her head and were trying any and every avenue of attack to get it. Instinctively, one hand went to her throat.

Mercifully, Dean Hendry cut in. "I understand this is upsetting. You were careful, were you not, to introduce the topic with qualifications? And you gave ample warning that this was but one person's viewpoint?" She nodded encouragement.

Charlaine thought back to that first class after the winter break. She couldn't recall the exact words of her introduction of Lynnie. "Perhaps not specifically, in so many words. I was relying on the good sense of my students to think critically and to sift and evaluate what they were hearing." Her argument was faltering. It was time to present her final defence. "With systemic racism an underlying threat to people of colour like me, is it possible that racial prejudice lies behind this complaint?"

The expressions on the faces of her interrogators immediately switched to concern.

Charlaine breathed an inaudible sigh of satisfaction.

Chambers drew himself up and looked at his watch. "I think we've heard enough, Dr. Trites. Be advised that we at this college aim to foster an environment of learning in which students feel safe and protected, no matter their identity group. And that goes for faculty, too." He avoided eye contact with her and began gathering his papers.

She took a deep breath. "I believe I have created a safe environment in all the courses I teach so that no one would have reason to feel discriminated against."

Fran Dorn pounced on this. "To give preference to one perspective over another creates a toxic climate that violates the trust our students and the community put in us."

Chambers frowned at her, then faced Charlaine, focusing vaguely on the empty chair beside her. "I had hoped for a little more conciliatory response from you. Can I have your word that you will do three things?"

"What three things?" Every muscle in Charlaine's body tensed, waiting for sentence to be passed. She was certain this meant a great dark blot on her academic record, perhaps even a serious delay in her path to tenure. The sick feeling in her stomach returned.

"Because the complainant has asked that their name be withheld, I recommend a written apology from you for the emotional and social harm done. We can pass this on to the student on your behalf. Second, it would be wise to make a general disclaimer to the class as soon as possible that neither you nor the college are hostile toward single parents. And third, I suggest you facilitate a class discussion on the special challenges and achievements of such parents." He tapped his papers on the table to align them and inserted them in his briefcase, as though he couldn't leave soon enough. "Once I have your written response, I will personally suggest the student write an online review and we will consider the matter closed. Thank you, each one of you, for your attendance here today." He nodded at each of the women and strode out the door.

With shaky limbs, Charlaine gathered her papers into her briefcase and made her escape. It took everything in her to resist the urge to flee down the long empty hallway and out to the parking lot.

Chapter 30

May the peace of God, my Father,
Rule my life in everything,
That I may be calm to comfort
Sick and sorrowing.
~May the Mind of Christ, My Savior, by Kate B. Wilkinson, 1859-1928

The cold had begun to stiffen my fingers despite a deceptively bright sun and my double-mittened hands. I tried to pick up my pace on the home stretch of pathway around the pond. The glittering fresh snow was beautiful, but it made walking strenuous. I was grateful my cabin wasn't far ahead.

Today I had planned to make serious inroads on my major term assignment. As per Grandma's instructions, I had been doing my best to turn worry about school into prayer followed by action. The distrust of my classmates sparked by my recent session in Charlaine's office pushed me to do something and I chose to direct the energy into my studies. I knew some of my classmates noticed that I had pulled back socially in the weeks since that awful day, spending less time with them and more time in a library study carrel. But one of them resented me and I didn't know which one. Something like that made a person wary. Charlaine herself had been almost too obvious in avoiding eye-contact with me since then, rarely calling on me for input in class discussions. My assignments had been returned with terse critiques and grudging comments though my grades were still good.

I now spent all day Sundays with the family, and I'd taken to spending an evening each week at either Grandma's or Lissa's, too. These were my true and faithful friends. I had determined to draw my warmth and strength from them.

But when I got up in the morning and saw the date, for a moment the events of last year at this time came roaring back to mind. Which is why I bundled up to brave the cold and pray through my overheated memories.

Once I got inside, I pulled off my mitts and set to work building a fire. It no longer spooked me to do so, and I loved the cozy heat radiating from my cheerful wood stove. Crouched in front of it, watching the flames lick up the birch bark kindling, I shucked off my jacket and toque just as my phone rang.

"Sis, can you babysit Blade this afternoon?" The urgency in Lance's voice made me stand up, alert.

But still, I hesitated. After Dad spoke to me last summer about emerging from my self-imposed isolation and rejoining the land of the living, I had intended to offer to watch my nephew. I really had. Often when I saw what a handful the baby was, it had been on the tip of my tongue to suggest they drop him off at my place some afternoon if they needed a break. But my studies had consumed a lot of my energy and attention. And I knew Crystal had her own exacting ideas about childcare. Then there was the awkward dilemma of payment. Of course I would volunteer to do it for free, but what if they insisted on paying? Not that I couldn't use the money, but little Blade was family, and they shouldn't have to pay me to spend time with my own nephew.

Oh, Lynnie. You know very well those are dumb excuses. The elephant in the room loomed large and it had a name. Or perhaps a multitude of names. First there was fear. I had done my best at family dinners to show interest in the little guy, but not once had I held him. I was terrified that the feel of a sweet, soft infant would rekindle vivid memories. And that would make me face the second grim presence in my life, grief.

"Lynnie?" Lance raised his voice.

"Yeah, of course." I gulped down my misgivings. "What do you want to do? Bring him here or should I come over there?"

"Over here. Gotta get to town." Lance was doing some awfully fast talking.

"What's the matter? Did you run out of pickles?" I giggled. Lance had a reputation for never being without a good supply of his favourite dills.

"Seriously, Lynnie. We need you." When he didn't laugh, I knew something was up.

"Right now?"

"Now!"

"Okay. Be right there." I scattered the kindling I'd started and closed the stove's damper, then noticed my computer and the books I'd left open on the table and wondered if I should bring them along. But Lance's serious tone lit a fire under me. I tossed my phone into my purse, grabbed my jacket again, along with my keys, and rushed to my car.

When I arrived at their mobile home three miles away, Crystal was already in the pick-up that sat running in the driveway. Lance rushed out the door at my approach.

"He's asleep in his crib. Any questions, just message me," he yelled as he sprinted to the truck.

"When will you be back?"

"No idea." He jumped into the vehicle and spun out onto the road.

It had to be some medical emergency. And since Lance looked fit enough, I figured maybe Crystal was injured somehow. But why wouldn't Lance tell me that? Not that he'd taken the time. I began to suspect something more personal.

I tiptoed into the house, ashamed to realize that I had never visited Lance and Crystal in their home, though I had been back from Africa for almost a year. How did that feel to them? It was a good sign, I thought, to be considering my actions from someone else's point of view. I had seen them weekly at my parents' but never spent time with them in their own habitat. I barely knew Crystal, having missed their wedding while I was overseas.

Today, it was obvious they had left in a rush, a carton of milk was still on the table along with the remains of lunch.

I put away the milk and wandered down the hall. I peeked into the first bedroom and found baby Blade slumbering heavily in his spiffy new crib. His dewy lips were parted with chubby pink thumb at the ready. I placed my hand gently on his back, enjoying his living warmth.

The room was decorated in green and gray wildlife prints and had a sweet baby smell. The old favourite books of our childhood displayed on a rack on the wall made me smile. I would have loved to read those to my girls. The thought brought back the memory of the few books we had in Nigeria and how much Josie had loved story time. Anya would listen for a short time but usually ended up coasting back and forth from toy shelf to couch while I read. Closing my eyes, I could picture the two of them, feel Josie's silky hair under my chin, sense their tiny bodies tucked against mine. An ache began to throb from deep inside me, dragging down the corners of my mouth and flooding my eyes with hot tears. One spilled out onto little Blade's arm. It came to me that he was twenty months old, the exact age Anya was last year at this time when...

Gasping, I pulled my hand away and backed out of the room. I'd thought I was gradually improving, not thinking about my dear ones every moment of every day. But this one-year mark brought fresh spasms of pain. Grandma had warned me of this.

Swallowing hard, I returned to the kitchen looking for something useful to do as she'd advised. No sooner had I begun clearing the table, than I heard a few squeaks from the baby monitor on the counter. I waited to see if Blade was serious about waking. More squawks, then he settled into a running babble of various sounds. I hurried to put away food, loaded the dishwasher and wiped the table, then washed my hands and ventured back to the nursery.

"Hey there, little man," I said hoarsely as I tiptoed into his room.

He turned his great blue eyes toward me in surprise, then craned his neck, trying to see past me. Poor little guy. Must be a bit of a shock to find a virtual stranger coming in when he expected mom.

"Wanna play with Auntie Lynnie?" I reached down into the crib and held out my arms to him. He hoisted himself to a stand and willingly let himself be lifted out. A diaper change was in order. Blade regarded me with a watchful eye as I took care of his needs. But when I whacked his chubby foot with his own sock, he smiled. When I balled up the sock and chucked it at his tummy, he chortled, which made me giggle.

I can do this. It was still as satisfying as ever to clean up a mess and get a baby comfortable and sweet smelling again. I snapped his pants closed and carried him into the living room, setting him down on the floor next to me. He toddled to the toy bin and brought me every toy he owned. I read him a dozen books from his shelf, making all the sounds of vehicles and animals.

"What does a goose say, Blade?"

"Konk-konk." His perfect nasal tone made me laugh.

"I think it's more like adworka-adworka," I said. He rewarded me with a belly laugh. Which made me do it again and again.

We played finger games, recited rhymes, and sang songs I thought I had forgotten. I made his crackers and cheese snack into a funny face and showed him animal videos on my phone. I was falling in love with my brother's child, and it did not hurt much at all.

When I checked the time, I found that three hours had passed. "Young sir, I believe it's time to find you something to eat."

The way Blade's head jerked up at the word made me chuckle.

"You know that word, don't you?" I got up from the floor and made my way to the fridge to search for something we could heat up. My phone rang just as I was pulling out a dish that looked promising.

Lance's name popped up. "Everything okay there?"

I told him what fun Blade and I had been having. "How are things going with you two?"

A long pause. "We lost the baby." He spoke as though each word weighed more than his tongue could manage.

The news hit me hard. The fires of adversity had taken another baby from our family. Would the losses and grief never end? And then I had another question: Why hadn't they told me Crystal was pregnant? Was I still so consumed with my own sorrows that they had to tiptoe around me, unable to confide their happy news? Now my brother had to endure the same kind of pain I knew all too well. "I'm so sorry, Lance," I whispered.

"I'm going to stay with Crystal as long as I can," he continued. "Will you get Blade his supper and put him to bed by about seven?"

"Of course. Don't worry about him at all. Just comfort your wife."

Chapter 31

Daniya heard the maa-ing of goats before she noticed the dust cloud stirred up by the flocks and herders trudging up the road. The village men were on the way home. She covered the pot of *jollof* rice, took it off the heat, and went to prepare the table. For two weeks she had been bursting with the news of her pregnancy, more certain of it every day. How hard it was to keep quiet, but she congratulated herself on keeping the secret until now. So far, Ihsan had not seemed to notice her thickening waist or her frequent trips outdoors to relieve herself. She smiled. Men seemed asleep to so much in life. She so badly wanted to tell him, but until she felt the quickening, Daniya couldn't be sure this baby would live. When she sensed the first movement, it would be a sign that the time was right to share her secret.

Another reason the news pressed urgently was that Ihsan's irritability had continued to grow. Something was gnawing at him, causing her a vague anxiety. Normally, he never would have barked at Aminah as he'd done the evening before. The little one had only been chanting her cousins' names over and over, as girls do, but he had roughly ordered her to stop. Daniya had muttered a reproach at him, but he ignored her with a scowl. She longed to erase the worry on his face and replace it with the joy she was sure her secret would bring.

She caught Aminah up in her arms. "Your father will be in soon. Run and show him the small-small stew you made." Daniya set the child down and gave her a gentle push toward the tin can she had fashioned for her as a cooking pot. In it were the bits of greens, onion, and peppers that Aminah had stirred to mush while Daniya cooked their supper.

Aminah ran outside to the edge of the road, holding her stew out eagerly in front of her. When Ihsan appeared, she held up her offering to him.

Watching them, Daniya was relieved to see him smile and pick her up, even pretend to taste the concoction. Could it be a sign that his bad mood had lifted?

Daniya waited while he tended the flock, securing the animals in their enclosure and soaping his hands and neck outside the door. When he had dried himself and entered the house, he thumped onto his chair at the table. No, the evil *jinn* remained on him, darkening his face and making his shoulders slump.

They ate their meal with a silence between them. Disappointed, Daniya focused on cutting Aminah's food and answering her many questions.

Today Ihsan was silent so long that she became nervous, fidgeting with her hands. Several times she asked questions about the flock or about doings in the village, but his desultory answers cut off her hopes for conversation. Perhaps later, once Aminah was sleeping Daniya might have opportunity to find out what was troubling him.

While she cleared away meal, Aminah brought her dishes from the table. Daniya tried to catch her husband's eye to share her pride in the child's industriousness, but he rose from his chair and turned away.

Aminah scampered to the corner where his prayer rug was kept and lugged it to him. The child had a sense about his routine. He patted her head, but his mind seemed to be absent. When he finished his sunset prayers, he stepped out the door to sit under the eave as though he didn't want to be near either her or Aminah. He had taken to brooding like this most evenings, and soon tobacco smoke wafted through the open doorway. At one time, he used to hold Aminah on his lap out there, often until she fell asleep. Now the girl no longer asked to sit with him.

Daniya finished her work and sat for a time, watching Aminah at her feet. In an exact mime of her mother's actions, Aminah pretended to wash and dry her makeshift cooking pot, then lovingly tended to her stick doll. At last, Daniya rose, sighing. "Time to wash up, my child." She led the girl to the basin where she washed and dried her face and hands and feet, using the old pink towel. Then she laid her daughter down on her pallet next to their bed, arranged the mosquito net around her, closed the doorway curtain, and retreated to the kitchen.

Ihsan stayed so long outside the house that Daniya gave up waiting and prepared to go to bed alone. This unusual silence of his filled her with foreboding. What was he thinking or planning? Life had been good since Aminah came. Why now was he so miserable? She lay on top of the blanket in the heat of the night, fretful and worried, trying to imagine what might be bothering him. Was there disease in the goat herd? Had there been trouble from the village Christians over Fulani attacks? Or had the herd grown so that he now felt able to take another wife? The longer he lingered outside, the larger grew her unnamed fear.

Daniya had only begun to drowse when, finally, Ihsan came to bed. He moved quietly, perhaps mindful of the child whose even breathing was the only sound in the stifling room. Before turning his back to Daniya, he nudged her with his elbow.

"Mm?" she murmured.

"Tomorrow you must go to market and buy enough supplies to make a large pot of *jollof* rice and maybe *puff-puff*, too," he said gruffly. "Get Uma to help you cook it."

She sat up and stared hard at him as though to pierce the darkness and bore a hole through his skull. But his eyes were closed, and his breath soon became rhythmic in sleep. Angry now, she shook his shoulder. "What are you saying? What is this food for? And why so much? You do not show your face to us. Tell me what is so big in your head that you no longer reach for me in the night. Tell me now!"

Maybe it was the cover of darkness that emboldened him. Roused now, Ihsan turned to face her. "I go to Jos in three days' time." His eyes glittered in the momentary flickering light of someone's trash burning barrel. "I will take Aminah with me."

"What?" Dread seized her, clenching her insides, raising goosebumps despite the warm night. The *jinn* of vague suspicion she had suppressed for weeks now leapt out of its bottle, filling her mind with stark terror. She struggled to force it down. "Why must I cook food? What are you plotting against me?"

Ihsan gave no answer, but his silence shouted to Daniya louder than any words he could have spoken. With the sudden shock of knowing, her mouth dropped open. He was going to Jos where *butare* lived. She knew it with a quaking certainty. He meant to seek out Aminah's family. He would take her child from her!

In wordless frenzy, she clawed at his arms and pounded his chest. When he curled his body away from her to shield it, she hammered his back. To keep from screaming lest she wake Aminah, she bit into his shoulder.

Cursing, Ihsan yanked himself away from her, grabbing her arms and pinning her down on the bed. He bent to whisper in her ear, but Daniya flung her head from side to side in desperate rebellion.

"Keep still!" he hissed.

Daniya stiffened. She narrowed her eyes at him, straining to see in the blackened room. "Why?" she hissed back. "Why must you take her? Where are you taking her?" She felt him drop down against her, loosening his grip on her arms.

His voice seemed to come from a great distance. "This is what must be. We must return Aminah to her own people. Do you never think what could happen to us if someone told police? Besides, she cannot live here among people who would hate her."

"No!" Daniya began to weep. "You must not! We are her people. She belongs to us now and we love her. She loves us. How can you send her to strangers? We are all she knows!"

"It has become impossible for me. You know nothing of what I endure. Or of the danger we might be in." His words were flat, devoid of feeling.

Panic rose up Daniya's body. "But you brought her home. You forced her on me because she needed us. It was the will of God, remember? Somehow, he plucked her from the fire. You said it yourself, Allah sent her to us."

Ihsan's grip on her loosened. "That I do not understand." His voice held despair and confusion. "Perhaps he only meant us to rescue her and care for her for a short season. I do not know."

Daniya jerked upright, a wail rising behind her words. "Then you must not take her away. If you do not know for certain, you must not. Have mercy!"

"Hush, woman!" He rolled away from her, his tone harsh again. "I must do what I must do, and you must obey. Tomorrow you cook."

Daniya lay tormented and whimpering long into the night. Spent from crying, her body limp on the tangled bedding, at last her trembling subsided. And in the blackness of the darkest night she had ever known, a tiny stirring happened. She caught her breath. Waited. Another motion, slighter than a hair falling, softer than a tiny finger brushed against her skin. But deep inside, she felt the movement. Without a doubt, there was life. Faint and unnoticed by Ihsan, it was life, nonetheless.

And a new kind of tears rolled down the sides of Daniya's face.

Chapter 32

Let Your Spirit, gracious Lord,
Our souls with love inspire,
Strength and confidence afford,
And breathe celestial fire!
~ Full of Weakness and of Sin, by William Bathurst, 1796 - 1877

My stomach commenced churning at Charlaine's opening illustration. On the classroom screen behind her was a photo of a young child of colour in a wheelchair, next to a bright-painted adobe building, flanked by her parents and siblings.

"The Suruwahu are a tribe in Brazil," Charlaine began, "with revered cultural practices and spirituality stretching back for millennia. A few years ago, American Christian missionaries living with the tribe clashed with the Indigenous people's traditions in a case that found its way to Brazil's Federal Senate. Today I'd like you to consider this case that reveals the tension between Western civilization ideals and more ancient cultures. The Suruwahu people have long practiced child-killing as a form of population control. Suicide, too, is thought to be a desirable death and an essential part of their cultural and spiritual tradition."

Her words seared my mind. The thought of child-killing carried with it a fireball of emotions. But it wasn't only that. Mention of

Christian missionaries immediately put me on the defensive. I released a long breath, telling myself not to jump to conclusions.

"When Western evangelical missionaries arrived," Charlaine went on, "they protested the killing of a child born with muscular dystrophy. They helped the girl's parents move with their daughter, Kanhu to the capital city of Brazil where they raised a national media and lobbying campaign to crack down on child killing. Then a second case came up involving this tribe. The Suruwahu decided that two children who weren't developing properly should die. The children's parents committed suicide rather than kill them, so the tribe then buried the children alive, according to their custom. One of them, a girl name Hakani, survived the burial but was left to starve. Her older brother managed to keep her alive for a few years by bringing her scraps of food. Eventually, he brought her to the missionaries."

Someone behind me gave a relieved sigh at this. It showed me that despite the caricatures, social workers truly were motivated to help the mistreated. I shuddered at the thought of a child buried alive and then starving. Humanity's capacity for evil at times seemed unlimited. But I, too, relaxed, hearing the happy ending of the story.

Dr. Trites scanned the class. "I'm sure you can see the obvious dilemma. The question for our consideration today and into the future is: What right does the state have to interfere with the customs of minorities?"

The other students fidgeted as I did, left to ponder the implications of her question.

I raised a tentative hand.

Charlaine jutted her chin in my direction.

"Wouldn't the clearest guideline be upholding the value of human life?" I asked. "The cases you just mentioned in no way interfered with the tribal culture. They saved the lives of individuals who were slated for destruction."

Charlaine paced the front of the room in silence for a long moment. "That, class," she finally pronounced, "is an example of typical Eurocentric, colonial thinking. Anyone else have any ideas?"

A minute of hesitancy passed before a couple of my classmates offered vague thoughts on preserving the rights of unique cultures or negotiating terms with Indigenous leaders. Our prof's personal viewpoint was showing, and the others were cautious, hedging their bets.

Brynn ventured a suggestion. "The country could launch an education program—"

Before she could finish her thought, Charlaine pounced. "And who would educate whom? Who's to say our Western notions about life are superior to the Suruwahu's time-tested way of doing things?"

I stared around at my colleagues. Were we all cowed, willing to give a nod to infanticide? I tried to catch Fiona's eye. As the wife of a minister, didn't she have some objection to what was being offered here? But she was scribbling notes and seemed unperturbed by the discussion.

For a split second I paused, teetering on an unseen precipice, trembling at what I was about to do. I had sat silent in similar discussions before, hoping to slide under the radar of the politically correct without ruffling academic feathers. A faint warning sounded in my mind. I'd been content to keep my head down and turn in assignments in exchange for a grade, hoping that my earned credentials would someday allow me to make a difference in real people's lives. But Charlaine's stories of helpless babies cruelly thrown away had opened an old wound. A fire of remembrance now smouldered in my belly. The warning to keep my mouth shut became a jangling siren but I knew I had to say something, or I would forever regret it.

"It is inhumane and wrong, regardless of cultural beliefs, to take the life of a human being." My voice betrayed me with an embarrassing wobble.

Charlaine swung to face me. "According to whom? These Indigenous people hold their beliefs as fervently as you hold yours."

An unnatural quiet had descended on the room. I wiped my palms on the sides of my jeans. "According to the God who made the human race. His law says that the taking of innocent human life is murder."

Dr. Trites cocked a skeptical brow, boring into me with her eyes. "Such an answer would be meaningless to the hundreds of tribes living in isolation in the interior of Brazil. The Brazilian Association of Anthropology says their government's bill to stop this practice amounts to putting Indigenous peoples on trial as savages. Are you prepared to judge entire people groups according to your own narrow sensibilities, Ms. Min?"

Heat flooded my face at what I was about to say. I thought of the martyrs who made their stand in the face of the rack and the stake. And I remembered my childhood concern that I would not be able to withstand torture if it happened to me. Inhaling deeply, I took heart. This wasn't even a mosquito bite compared to that level of persecution. I determined not to chicken out.

"Not according to my ideas. It's God who makes universal rules. And on that basis, yes, I'm prepared to say certain practices are wrong. Every culture has its faults. But some cultures are superior to others if we measure them against what is pleasing to the Creator. And any culture that involves the death of innocent people has to be stopped."

Charlaine put her hand on her hip and opened her mouth to speak, but I pushed on.

"To turn our backs while children, the disabled, the elderly and ill are killed or left to die is a terrible thing. The world still holds the German people accountable for living their comfortable lives while millions were slaughtered in death camps just outside their villages. How can we, as social workers, have any ground to stand on in condemning the destruction of Indigenous children in our own country if we look away from these stories from around the world?

Our prof strolled over to her lectern and perched atop the stool nearby. She addressed the class, avoiding the side of the room where I sat. "These missionaries," she used the term as though it tasted bad, "interfered with a cultural practice filled with meaning, one that the Suruwahu had arrived at after facing the harsh realities of survival in their region for millennia. Westerners shattered the tribe's symbolic universe. By defying their solutions to these problems, missionaries did irreparable damage to the Indigenous peoples' way of life."

My cheeks burned and I'm sure I had a wild look in my eye, but I was past caring. I saw only an image of my Josie and my Anya, not burning to death this time but desperate, struggling, suffocating, their panicked cries smothered under the dark weight of damp earth.

"The children you told us about are not problems," I burst out. "They're not interesting case histories, like some butterfly specimens that we can examine and discuss in theory. They are real people with rights. How dare we use culture as an excuse for not rescuing these helpless, suffering children? We're human beings, not animals. We don't discard or abandon the weak, the old, and the sick. We have mercy on them. Of all people, our profession should know that. We care for them, no matter what it costs." Breathing heavily, I gripped the edge of my desk to steady my trembling body.

Now Charlaine fixed me with a blistering stare. "Are you quite finished preaching, Ms. Min? Perhaps you might pause long enough to let us hear from some of the other students?" She surveyed the class where several hands were raised and nodded first at Brynn.

"The patriarchal, racist attitude that these missionaries had is oppressive and insensitive." Brynn sure had picked up on our prof's leaning in the issue. "White males have dominated and subjugated

women and people of colour for too long. The Indigenous people
should be allowed to govern themselves how they see fit."

Lasna spoke next. "It was wrong of Westerners to impose their
religion on people who hadn't asked for it. Why can religious people
not live in peace with one another? There is too much imperialism
of this kind all over the world." She looked as if she wanted to say
more, then clamped her lips shut.

Staring at her, I couldn't believe these words coming from a
Muslim. Was she unaware of the history of her faith? But I made
myself let it go. No point adding fuel to the fire that had ignited
inside me.

I relaxed a bit when I saw Fiona made a move to speak. I was
grateful for at least one supportive friend in what was beginning to
feel like a pile-on.

"Let's not forget," she said, "that in our own country, it was
churches who carried out the government's mandate to tear children
away from their families to 'get the Indian out of the child.' Lots of
evil done by missionaries in the name of religion."

This was a betrayal that cut deep.

Charlaine nodded. "I've brought this case forward so you'll take a
close look at the complex layers of cultural understanding required
in approaching people of a variety of ethnicities. In making
decisions, we must try to balance historical injustices. Nothing is as
simplistic as it may seem. And those of us who haven't walked in
their shoes are in no position to impose our values on them, in
particular, white people who have never really suffered."

It was too much. I jumped to my feet. "Never suffered?
Seriously?"

Charlaine tried to cut in, but I shouted her down.

"I was a missionary. My husband James and I went to Nigeria at
the request of Nigerians. They wanted help translating the Bible
into local languages. We loved the people there and learned as much
from them as they did from us. But they would disagree with you

about racism. You haven't seen it until you've seen the bigotry of African against African." I clenched my hands to stop their shaking. "Or how about the classism I saw, where a person can slap a stranger across the face just because he is poor and without family connections? And sexism? My Nigerian friend Rose would laugh at your micro-aggressions. Her two daughters were kidnapped by Boko Haram for simply going to school."

I shot a glance around the room. "And do you seriously mean to tell me that a culture where it's acceptable to kill children is equal to one where human life is protected and murder is punishable by law?

"Listen to me! One year ago, I came home alone from Africa." My voice cracked. Tears of rage and frustration poured down my face. I blazed on, heedless of my running nose or the croaking of my words. "Alone! My husband and our two little girls were ambushed by Islamist terrorists. So much for the religion of peace. My girls were just babies. Burned alive! I hear their cries in my sleep. I smell the smoke of their roasting flesh! Don't tell me that because I'm white I've never suffered."

Panting after my tirade, I glared at each of my classmates in turn, then at Charlaine. I swept my laptop and books into my shoulder bag and stormed out of the room.

I had burned my bridges.

Chapter 33

Do the next thing.
Do it immediately, do it with prayer.
Do it reliably, casting all care.
Do it with reverence, tracing His hand,
Who placed it before thee with earnest command.
Stayed on Omnipotence, safe 'neath His wing
Leave all resulting, do the next thing.
~Author unknown, Old Saxon poem

I'm not sorry. I tried to impress on my mind some sort of regret
or shame but even a stiff dose of Grandma's scolding wouldn't
have been able to drum up any. *I've ruined my future, but I don't
care.*

I boiled down the hall in a mad frenzy, averting my dripping face
from the students staring at me. I fumbled in my bag for a tissue
and came up empty. Veering into a nearby washroom, I snatched a
wad of paper towels to mop my tears and blow my nose, grabbing
extra to take with me. My eruption in class had opened floodgates of
the deep that wouldn't abate any time soon. I hurried out toward
my locker to empty it of books, papers, and personal items, stuffing
them into my shoulder bag. My career was ending before it started.
Then, swinging my jacket on, I fled the building.

It wasn't that anything I'd said was false, or cruel, or hurtful to anyone. This pernicious ideology that white people were the oppressors and all others were victims had slowly permeated every aspect of my studies, particularly in Charlaine's classes. My dismay about it had simmered for months now. The illogic of it, the ironic injustice of it, had ground my gears at every instance. I had handled it by discussing it with the family and found my father's deep reasoning and Grandma's common sense a refuge of satisfying wisdom. In class, I kept quiet about it. Until today.

But I knew there was more. The molten grief that I'd been able to keep submerged for most of a year now, had been rising inside me in recent weeks. Was it because of the anniversary of my family's deaths? Or the galling accusation that because I was white, I had never suffered? Whatever the reason, it was that loss of control that now embarrassed and shamed me. What would Grandma say if she had witnessed it?

One thing was certain—I couldn't enter that classroom one more day. I cringed at the thought of facing any of my classmates again, let alone Dr. Trites, knowing what a hysterical shrew I had been.

When the door of the humanities wing swung shut behind me, a chill wind made me race blindly for my car. I headed for home, unable to get there fast enough. I needed Mom and Dad. And Grandma.

I pulled into traffic and sped through the city as quickly as I dared. My mind churned, rehashing the class I'd just left and fearing the future.

My social work career plans were shot. Of that I had no doubt. The course was a crucial one required for graduating and was dependent on interaction in class. Charlaine's attitude toward me in recent weeks and especially in today's class, assured me I would likely flunk. I still burned inside at the memory of how she had been gunning for me. As if she had known I had been a missionary and her case in point had been planned to target me.

I couldn't say I was sorry for any of the truth I had spoken. It was only my fiery delivery I regretted. But what on earth was I going to do with the rest of my life?

I had almost reached the turn off from the highway to the secondary road home when my steering wheel began to tug to the left. By instinct, I slowed down. In a moment a loud bumping sounded from the left rear wheel. *No-o!* I pulled to a stop on the side of the road. A flat tire was the last thing I needed. I zipped my jacket and opened the door to inspect the debacle. Middle of nowhere. Not a single vehicle in sight in either direction and no farm buildings in the immediate vicinity.

A sudden terror gripped me. In just such a bleak and lonesome environment, James and the girls had been ambushed by evil men and had met their deaths. I fought the north wind for a deep breath, forcing myself to exhale slowly. Unexpectedly, Grandma's voice sounded in my head.

Do the next thing.

What's the next thing, Grandma, when you're stranded on the side of the road on a chilly March day with a flat?

Get out the car jack, Dad would say. Years earlier, before we were allowed to get our driver's licences, Dad had insisted Lissa and I learn a few basics of car care. But it had been a long time. I approached the rear of the car and opened the hatch. There was the spare, along with the lug nut wrench and jack. I pulled them out, hoping some of Dad's instruction would return to me, then noticed a step-by-step tire-changing diagram glued to the jack.

Do it immediately, do it with prayer. The words to the old Saxon poem Grandma had made me memorize spurred me on. *Lord, help me!* I fitted the wrench onto the first nut and tried to turn it. Tears of frustration sprang immediately to my eyes. I couldn't budge the thing.

Do it reliably, casting all care. A spark of anger flared out of my disgruntlement. How was I supposed to do this? And why should I have to? Wasn't it enough that I'd suffered so much? And that I'd just spent the morning humiliated and scorned in class when all I wanted was to do the right thing and serve God? I slammed the wrench down on the ground and stormed off in fury. Fuming, I paced the length of the car and back, heedless of my chilling hands. *Lord, I've had enough!* Exhausted, I slumped to the ground in front of the wheel again, groping for the wrench in the crunchy snow.

Do it with reverence... Okay, sorry Lord. But you are going to have to give me super-human strength here 'cause I can't do this stupid "next thing."

I flung my wind-whipped hair out of my eyes and wedged the wrench against my shoulder, trying again. Well, what do you know? It moved. I made a few turns, then shifted to each of the others, loosening them a bit. Next, I shoved the jack through the filthy mix of snow and gravel, in front of the wheel.

Tracing His hand, who placed it before thee with earnest command. I cranked the jack. So even a flat tire comes from God's hand? Though rebellion at the thought flared up in me, I knew it was the truth. Couldn't I indulge myself in a temper tantrum without scripture, or a hymn, or a Christian poem flattening my fun? But even this thought came with the reminder that to vent my spleen of bitterness or anger or even the full measure of its grief would inevitably hurt whoever was near, not to mention my own soul.

I cranked the jack, watching the car rise off the ground with a growing sense of wonder. Could I really do this?

You go, girl! Lissa would be so impressed.

I had a fleeting wish that Brynn or Charlaine could see me now. I'd bet neither of them had ever accomplished such a thing. My hands were stiff with cold by now, but the success of getting the tire off the ground urged me on. I finished loosening the nuts and removed them, then tugged gingerly at the tire to get it off the wheel. I was afraid it would come shooting off into my arms and I'd be hugging the filthy thing to my cream-coloured jacket. I pulled a little harder. It wasn't as easy as Dad had made it look. Long live the male species! Part of me wished for one of them to swoop down and rescue me now. I half-smiled at the grim awareness that I was a bundle of contradictions, one moment exulting in my independence, the next, wanting to be taken care of by a man.

At the sound of an engine and the crunch of gravel, I looked to my rear. A rickety old truck in a patchwork of colours pulled up about a car-length behind mine. I caught sight of an empty gun rack fastened to its back window. Who used those anymore? Wasn't it illegal to carry firearms out in the open?

I yanked at my tire, frantic to finish the job and get safely away from there. Finally, it slid off, teetered briefly, and toppled onto the ground. As I struggled to stand it upright, I kept a wary eye on the newcomer. And grabbed hold of my good, stout wrench.

Stayed on Omnipotence, safe 'neath His wing
Leave all resulting, do the next thing.

Slowly, the driver opened his door and even more slowly stepped down. He walked stiff-legged toward me, his gnarled bare hands held out from his sides. As he drew near, I noticed tufts of stiff gray hair poking through the black knit cap he wore. How long does a person have to wear one of those for that to happen? He stared past me through small, pale blue eyes, a cigarette with a long, precarious tube of ash hanging from the corner of his mouth.

"Have a flat?" he muttered between closed lips.

No thanks, I just had one. The stress of the day was making me punchy. But I didn't dare voice it. He probably meant well, but I kept my grip on the wrench just in case.

Without waiting for an answer, he came toward me. He brushed my hand away from the tire I had rolled to the back of the car, and I caught a faint whiff of beer. An *oomph* escaped him as he bent to hoist the tire inside.

The way he moaned and grunted when he straightened caused me to relax. I could easily outrun an old codger who appeared to be in urgent need of a knee replacement. More sound effects ensued as he located the spare and rolled it around to the bare wheel. Staring at the task before him, he held out a hand for my wrench.

I hesitated for a tick, then passed it to him. His swollen knuckles looked painful, but he set the dummy tire in place and tightened the nuts deftly enough. Then he stood up, though he still didn't meet my eyes.

"Thank you so much," I offered, sidling toward my driver's door.

"Mm." Suddenly he pointed a crooked finger out into the open field. "Right about there somewheres is where the first old timer come here and built a sod hut. Only place for folks to stay when the country was opening for homesteading. 'Bout ten foot by twelve foot. He'd have eighteen, twenty men stay over. Said when the first couple guys fell asleep, he'd hang 'em on the wall t' make room for the next ones." He paused, still staring into the distance.

I didn't know whether to laugh or scream. I was hardly in the mood to listen to homesteading tales.

"Take it slow," he said, then abruptly turned and stumped back to his vehicle.

"Thank you," I called after him, then hurried to get inside and crank up the heat.

Thank you, Lord, for sending help. And thank you Grandma, for drilling into me the words of a faithful Christian from ancient times.

I had been given the strength to get half the job done and had been visited by the strangest of angelic messengers to finish the task. Those odd ten minutes had shifted my despairing view of a hopeless future to a new assurance that, whatever unfolded in the days and months ahead, God would go before me.

Chapter 34

Does Jesus care when I've tried and failed
To resist some temptation strong;
When for my deep grief There is no relief,
Though my tears flow all the night long?
~*Does Jesus Care? by Frank E. Graff, 1860-1919*

I stopped in at Mom and Dad's first, hoping to soak up from them some of the homey comfort I sorely needed. Bursting through the door, I found Dad and Grandma sitting at the kitchen table while Mom was busy at the counter. All three turned questioning eyes toward me when I entered.

I had thought I would pour out my heart to my parents and hadn't expected Grandma to be present in the middle of the afternoon. I slowly took off my coat, more than ever ashamed to confess my behavior today in class.

"You're earlier than usual." Mom scrutinized my face, then beckoned to me to join her at the table. "C'mon. 'Fess up. What have you done? The look on your face tells me you've either been throwing eggs at the barn, or you slid into the ditch and got stuck."

"No, nothing like that." I took a chair next to Grandma, not relishing looking her in the eye for this discussion. "Though I did have a flat tire on the way back today."

Dad slapped down his newspaper. "How'd you get home? Need me to go change it?"

"You taught me how, remember?"

My parents' eyes widened.

"You changed it?" Mom asked, her eyebrows raised.

Dad started to get up from his chair. "I'll go have a look."

"Dad. Wait a sec. That's not the problem." Crossing to the table to sit with them, I looked around at each one. "I...There was an issue in class today. You know what I've been saying about how this woke ideology is being pushed, how everything is the fault of colonizing white people, everything is racism."

Dad settled back into his chair. "And?"

"And I reacted. In fact, I let loose and lost it. A regular meltdown."

I recounted the story of the South American tribe and the missionaries who rescued a child. Tears flooded my eyes again at the thought of the helpless victims. Then I described the class discussion denouncing the missionaries' actions. "I can't help but feel Charlaine chose that story deliberately to goad me."

"You can't judge her motives, though," Mom put in. "All you can control is your own response."

"Controlling my response is the part that bothers me. I don't think I'll ever be welcome in that class again. And I'm not so sure I want to finish the degree after all. I mean, if this is how the training for social work goes, won't it be worse in practice?"

Grandma had been silent until now but spoke up when I said this. "We are the Hardys. We complete what we begin. If you've done wrong, you need to make it right. But having once put your shoulder to the plow, you would do well to persevere."

My father eyed her for a minute, then turned to me. "You're a grown woman, and you'll have to pray for guidance on this. Give it a few days and then decide. You're pretty close to the end of the semester now. I doubt they could take away your course work or credits at this late date."

I didn't answer. Dad hadn't seen the expression on my prof's face. Nor had he witnessed my shrill outburst. But at least he wasn't expecting me to march right back into that classroom tomorrow morning. Deep down, I must have hoped he would tell me to do that exact thing. Then I would have someone other than myself to be mad at. As it was, the ball was back in my court. At least they hadn't reminded me I had a living to make. I mean, what was I going to do, live with my parents forever, babysitting for local families?

So, I would take tomorrow and the weekend to consider. Three days to make sense of my life and seek God's direction.

With a heavy heart, I trudged to my cabin, collapsed on the couch, and wrapped myself in a fuzzy blanket. Restless, I pulled out my phone, taking a desultory scroll through social media's offerings —anything to escape the worry over what was happening at school. I found a range of posts, from smug family photos accompanied by typical mom complaints to social justice activists' outrage over the latest offences.

It was all so depressing. I was about to toss the phone aside when I heard it ping with a few notifications. One was an adjustment from Charlaine of an assignment due date. Obviously, she hadn't yet deleted me from the class list. I didn't want to think about it and switched to a brief message from Patricia Hainstock asking how my studies were going. I put off that painful topic until later because I saw the next message was from my pastor in Nigeria, Sam Likita. I settled in, eager to read news from my African friend.

Darling Lynnie;

Judith and I rejoice in our Lord Jesus Christ that you stay faithful to him, even in your grief. We thank God for you, our little Canadian friend, and trust that it is well with you and that you have joy and peace. Ebos reads the messages from you to us while we eat. It is hard to imagine what snow is like when here it is so hot and dry now.

Still no words from the police about the evil men who wronged you. You know the police here have no interest in justice for Christians. But vengeance is the Lord's, He will repay. The people of our church stay faithful. I received word that the translators that your James worked with are nearing completion of the New Testament at last. This is wonderful news for the people of that language group. James fought the good fight and finished the course. He can rest in peace.

Yesterday Judith and Ebos met with our church aunties for Bible study and prayer. You remember Rose who came to Jos about the same time as you and James? This time she brought a guest to the aunties' meeting. We were surprised beyond measure to see who it was, the answer to our prayers for more than six years now. Her daughter Chichima! You know that she was one of the 276 girls from Chibok school in Borno state kidnapped by Boko Haram six years ago. Not long ago, she escaped with two other girls. The terrorists had trained them to scatter into the forest when government planes flew overhead. When it happened, the girls did like they were taught, but this time they kept on running. For two days they ran. Then Christians took them in, brought them to their home village, and finally Chichima came back here to her mother. Only Chichima escaped that time, not Hosanna. She is thin, but not hurt in body. But in her heart and mind it may take long to heal. For now, we are rejoicing.

It is well with you, Ma.

Pastor Sam

Rose wants me to pass this message on to you. These are her words that I copied down.

My sweetheart Lynnie Min;

It is well, dear. My heart is heavy with thinking of you these months since you went away. Like Joshua and Hur hold up the arms of Moses, the other aunties in our church hold up my arms for all these years after my girls are stolen from me and I hold up your arms in prayer. I pray for you, that your faith will be strong. I pray you stand firm against the enemy who would make you cry because your dear ones are killed by wicked men. Do not give up the faith. Jesus is real and will never leave you. I know this because my sorrow went on for years, but God, He says, "Joy comes in the morning." Now morning has come to me. My sweet and precious Chichima comes back to me. Not yet Hosanna, but Jesus gives hope now.

I see this verse in Bible and Holy Spirit say, tell Mama Lynnie: "Our God whom we serve is able to deliver us from the burning fiery furnace... But if not, let it be known to you, O king, that we do not serve your gods, nor will we worship the gold image which you have set up." Dan. 3:17, 18.

Be comforted mama. It is well with you. Do not give up hope.

I kiss you and miss you very much.

Love to you,

Rose Okafor

I shut my eyes, letting myself soak up the warmth of the love I knew they were sending me from half a world away. God's people all over the world were the most amazing thing ever, a living body through which the life of Jesus pulsed and spread. I couldn't help but think of the *faux* attempts at inclusiveness and unity that were bandied about in my college and in the wider culture. They thought they could create justice and love by force and censure. They were a feeble, pale copy of what the worldwide church already was. Diverse, far-flung, vast, yet intimately sensitive to the suffering of its members. Over the past year, I had received hundreds of emails from around the world sympathizing with me in the deaths of my husband and children, assuring me of the prayers of other believers, reminding me I was not alone in my suffering.

I re-read Sam's letter, hearing his deep voice and Rose's honeyed one in the words. I missed these dear ones. Reading Rose's lines again I stopped to ponder the scripture verses she had chosen. She seemed to be hinting at something.

"Our God whom we serve is able to deliver us from the burning fiery furnace." Do not give up hope.

But it was too late for deliverance for my loved ones. Yet Rose wanted me to hope. For what? At this lower-than-low point in my life, I had nothing to hope for. My family was gone and, with them, my purpose. It had been utterly miraculous that I should find one man so stellar, so loving, so accomplished. My dreams of marriage and motherhood had died the day he and the girls died. And the second-best option, a career in social work, seemed equally dead. My dreams of making a difference to struggling people were now a bleak landscape of scorched earth.

That night, for the first time in months, I dreamed again of Anya. Behind a dim veil, I watched her lively play and happy chatter, yet I could see her every dear move. At one point, she came face-to-face with me, her words emphatic but silent and unintelligible, separated as we were by the filmy curtain. No matter how I clawed and tore at it, I could not get to her, though she kept speaking, gazing into my eyes as though she had a vital message for me.

My pillow was damp when I woke.

Chapter 35

In Daniya's resting moments, the child within her frolicked and paddled about like a dancing tadpole. It always spread the smile of a secret knowledge onto her face, making her stroke her belly in smug satisfaction. But the rest she seemed to need so often through the day inevitably brought moments of grief and rage. She had refused to go to market the day after Ihsan's announcement that he was about to steal her child from her. What mother could ever agree to such a thing, never mind helping it along?

When Ihsan returned from pasturing the flock that evening and asked where the food supplies were, she remained silent.

"You did not shop?" he asked with a low-voiced menace.

"I will not let her go."

Ihsan had been furious and smacked her rear so that it smarted. "You *will* buy the food and you will cook it all tomorrow. I leave the day after."

And that was how Daniya found herself at Uma's door early the next morning, leaving Aminah in her care and asking for help with the cooking later and for the loan of her large rice pot. When Uma asked why this cooking session was so urgent, Daniya replied only that Ihsan had commanded it.

The strain of carrying two heavy sacks with flour and vegetables and the plastic basin of rice on her head all the way home added to

Daniya's foul mood. When she returned to Uma's, she answered her sister-in-law's cheerful chatter in noncommittal grunts. Thankfully, Uma asked no uncomfortable questions but followed Daniya to her home to begin the project.

Uma set the *puff-puff* yeast mixture to rise while Daniya chopped onions and peppers. She brought the rice to a boil in its tomato broth, then covered the pot and pulled it partially off the heat of the fire to simmer and become smoky.

With Uma's experienced efficiency and the help of one of her daughters, the deep-fried snacks were soon piled on a plastic sheet on the table. Daniya insisted Uma take some *puff-puff* home to the family. "There is far more here than Ihsan needs."

Uma mopped her shining face and wiped her oily hands with the same rag. She looked Daniya in the eye and the smile slid off her face. "I know why Ihsan wants all this food. It is so he can *dash* police or military some rice or snacks if he is stopped on his way to Jos, yes?"

"Yes."

Uma held her gaze for a long, quiet moment. "It is for the best, but I know you are hurting, Ma." She folded Daniya into her comfortable embrace until Daniya sobbed on her shoulder.

For the best? Whose best? Too weary to discuss it further, Daniya straightened and wiped her tears with the edge of her *khimar*. She sniffed and turned to begin covering the snacks she intended to keep so that Uma could take home her plastic sheet.

"I'll send Aminah home right away. You will want to cuddle her close tonight," Uma promised, and she and her daughter hurried off.

Daniya choked at the words as she stood in the doorway watching them go. This would be her last day of listening to Aminah's chatter around the house, the last evening of bathing her creamy body and lulling her to sleep. The last tender hug and kiss from a loving child. She felt sick to her stomach at the thought.

When Uma's girl brought a joyful Aminah tripping toward home, the pain was almost too much.

That night, when Ihsan held Aminah on his lap at the evening meal, his lip trembled. When she brought him his prayer rug, his eyes filled with tears. He heaved a deep sigh when Daniya reached for the child to prepare her for bed.

Daniya washed the girl with care, smiling sadly as Aminah tried to catch a soap bubble. She pared the tiny fingernails and toenails and snipped away a stray sprig of longish hair behind Aminah's ear. Then she took the girl's small face in her hands and gazed deep into her eyes. She wanted to imprint these eyes, this face into her mind, to cherish it forever.

"I am your mama, Aminah," she whispered. "I have loved you for half your life. I am your mama and you must never forget me."

Aminah's liquid dark eyes widened as though she sensed the solemnity of her mother's words. "I never forget you. I love you." She reached up soap-fresh arms.

Daniya pressed the child to her even as her heart quaked in pieces. After clinging together a long time, the mother placed her daughter gently on her pallet, stroking her silky short air and holding her hand until she closed her eyes in sleep.

Ihsan had been tender with Daniya last night, holding her as she sobbed, mingling his tears with hers, so that she could almost forgive him for what he planned to do the next day. She had not yet told Ihsan of the child she carried within. He did not deserve to know.

Before the sun was up in the morning, he roused her. "It is time. Pastor Monday will be here soon."

Dully, Daniya rose to her grim duty. With limbs like lead she gathered the containers of rice and bundles of *puff-puff* that Ihsan was to take with him. She helped him carry them out and stow them in the car that Monday had borrowed. With two men seated in the front, the packaged food in the back left just enough room for a small child. Daniya squinted to press the tears out of her eyes. Suddenly, she wanted to escape what was to come, to get this dreaded parting over with.

Ihsan came out of the house with a sleepy Aminah draped over his shoulder.

Daniya rushed past him. "Go now," she muttered, and fled into the house.

But when she heard the car engine roar to life in the still morning, she sprang from her bed. "No! Don't take her!" Barefoot she tore after the car, her anguished cries interspersed with panting until the red taillights of the vehicle disappeared down the black roadway. Her beloved was gone.

Any gratitude Ihsan felt toward Pastor Monday for arranging the use of the car and his willingness to make the long drive to Jos was obliterated by the grief sitting like a rock in Ihsan's gut. In just such a way, the prophet Ibrahim, the father of Ismael, must have felt when he journeyed to offer his son as a burned sacrifice.

Ihsan's curt answers must have discouraged the conversation Monday tried to carry on. They settled into silence that was punctuated only by the grunts each of them uttered whenever they hit an unexpected pothole.

Traffic increased with the rising of the sun, and with it, the likelihood of being stopped. Sure enough when they reached Bauchi state there was a military checkpoint. Ihsan handed over a tub of *jollof* rice as well as a package of *puff-puff*. A short time later, he was obliged to do the same crossing into Plateau. Not only that, but with each passing kilometre, Ihsan's anxiety grew over what to do when they arrived in Jos. He had no knowledge of the city, and little idea of how to find Aminah's people. He was relying on Pastor

Monday's vague but confident mention of a contact from a church in Jos.

They came to a *go-slow* on the northern edge of Jos with more cars than Ihsan had seen together at any one time stretched in a river-like channel ahead and behind them. It was a perfect opportunity for the police to meander among the stopped vehicles with outstretched hand. A uniformed officer stopped at Monday's window.

"No money," Monday said, grinning, "but we have something better." He motioned for Ihsan to pass a tin of rice. When the policeman raised his eyebrows in expectation, the pastor gestured for *puff-puff* to be added to the bribe. Satisfied, the officer moved on to the next car. At this rate, Ihsan feared there might not be enough left to *dash* whoever they needed to help them make contact with Aminah's family.

"I want bready-bready too, Papa," Aminah piped from the back seat, sitting up and rubbing sleep from her eyes.

Her term for food amused Ihsan. He reached back and opened one of the packages of *puff-puff*. Handing her the sweet ball, he smiled into her small, trusting face, then offered one to Monday.

"Mm, good!" Monday nodded, downing the treat in two bites.

Ihsan bit into his and thought of Daniya, bereft and weeping at home. He felt like an evil man for what he had done. But the pressure had been relentless, and he had begun to fear the legal consequences if he kept the child. In the end he had had no choice.

The snack seemed to give Pastor Monday a burst of boldness. Smirking at Ihsan, he maneuvered the car through the gridlock, even bumping across the median to get around a traffic snarl. Finally, the highway ahead was clear. Monday consulted a small piece of paper, frowned, then shifted forward in his seat in concentration. Finding the Kabong police station was not difficult; working up the nerve to enter it was. No one trusted the police. The two men gazed at each other for a moment before Monday left the car.

When he returned, he looked at Ihsan with a shrug. "They say, go to Anglo police station."

After what seemed a maze of false starts and stops, backups and returns, they found the blue and yellow compound. This time, Ihsan took Aminah by the hand and paced the broken, wet concrete sidewalk in front while the pastor entered the building. At length, Monday beckoned to them.

"I think they know something. Bring some of the food."

Stepping inside the building was a relief from the rain. In pidgin, Pastor Monday explained the situation to a tall, thin officer with Akinde on his name tag. He looked them up and down and scowled with evident contempt for the poor. More than once he asked what seemed to be the same questions. Finally, he jutted his chin at a plastic chair against the wall.

"Leave her there. We will see what can be done."

When Ihsan understood the man was suggesting he abandon his child to these strangers, he was outraged. He stepped back from the desk to confer with Monday, insisting he must stay with the child until she was placed with someone trustworthy.

Pastor Monday shifted from foot to foot. At last, he snatched the bag of food from Ihsan and returned to the desk. "The child cannot be left alone," he declared, giving the officer a stony look. "You must contact Pastor Sam Likita of the Good Shepherd church,"

Assessing the situation, Akinde finally snorted, grabbed a dog-eared phone book and made a call.

Hours passed before Sam Likita burst through the station door. The large man embraced Monday then turned to Ihsan. But he ignored Ihsan. Instead, his mouth dropped in shock as he stared disbelieving into the wide eyes of the familiar child in Ihsan's arms.

Chapter 36

Rejoice, the Lord is King:
Your Lord and King adore!
Rejoice, give thanks and sing,
And triumph evermore.
~*Rejoice, the Lord is King, by Charles Wesley, 1744*

Startled out of a deep sleep by a jangling ring, Sue felt something cold prod her back and drop over her shoulder.

Beside her, Glen mumbled, "Phone."

"Huh?" Sue peered through the darkness at the red numbers on the bedside clock. Twenty-six minutes past two. "Why can't you get it?"

"'Cause it's always for you."

It rang a second time in her ear, sending a shot of adrenaline through her. She fumbled to pick it up. "Hello?"

Crackle. Then a stream of incomprehensible verbiage blared from the handset. She sat up, feeling a pang of nameless apprehension.

"Wait. Slow down. Who is this?" The mouth-to-ear delay fed her own voice back to her, hoarse and wary.

The man on the other end paused, then began again. Gradually, Sue distinguished a few words and caught on to the deep-voiced, rapid African accent. She groped for her robe with one hand and crept out of the room to let Glen sleep on.

"Is Lynnie there?" the man was asking. "I must speak to her. This is Pastor Sam Likita from Jos. I have something very important to tell her. Can you get her to the telephone? Very important."

The fear in her gut grew heavier. "Well, it's the middle of the night here and she's sleeping. Can you wait about ten minutes while I go over to her house and get her? Or would you like to call back then?"

"Yes, yes. I will call back. Hurry please."

What on earth? The last phone call from Africa had left a wake of devastation in their family. For a moment, Sue considered letting it wait until morning. Hadn't Lynnie been through enough? The past few days alone had left her daughter wafting ghost-like around here, listless and dull. Sue pressed her hands to her stomach to stop the churning. But the caller's insistence...No, it wasn't fair to Lynnie to keep something from her that Pastor Sam had said was important. She jumped into action.

Texting Lynnie wouldn't work. Her phone would likely be turned off for the night. Sue would have to go there in person. Hurrying to the porch, she slung a jacket over her robe and stuck her feet into the first pair of boots that presented themselves—Glen's. What a sight she would be if the night weren't as inky black as it was. Stepping out onto the flagstone patio, she wished she had brought a flashlight. Rather than waste time going back for one, she felt her way along the fence line until her eyes adjusted, and she soon arrived at Lynnie's granary cabin. Hating to disturb her, Sue rapped on the glass, feeling sorry for jolting her daughter out of a deep sleep. She prayed Lynnie wouldn't panic. Nothing. She knocked again, longer and harder.

At last, a disheveled Lynnie staggered to the door. "Mom?" she mouthed behind the glass, rubbing her eyes.

"Hurry up and get dressed," Sue said, stepping inside. "I've just had a call from Africa. It's Pastor Sam."

Lynnie tilted her head as though to let the news settle into her brain. Alarm registered on her face. "Okay, wait a sec." She scrambled into her jacket over pyjamas, slipped into shoes, and together they wended their way back to the house.

The phone jingled again as they were removing their coats. Lynnie met her eyes and in that look, Sue saw a world of anguish. To give her daughter a moment's preparation, Sue rushed to the kitchen counter and picked up the receiver to answer.

"Pastor Sam here. Is Lynnie Min there now?"

Sue raised her eyebrows at Lynnie. "Are you okay to take this?" she whispered, holding out the phone.

Lynnie nodded, blinking and reaching for it. "Hello?"

Sue watched her daughter with a close eye. Lynnie's eyebrows knit together in puzzlement.

"Slow down, Pastor," she said. Her eyes widened and her head lurched forward. "What?" Lynnie's voice rose, quavering on a high note with the word. "But how—? I don't understand!"

Sue could hear the indistinct voice on the other end nearly shouting now. Anxiety spread through her limbs and she found herself digging her fingers into the nubby cushion of the kitchen stool.

Lynnie, too, appeared to be trembling. Her grip on the phone seemed to be slipping.

Sue approached and placed a stool next to her.

The younger woman sat down hard, listening in silence. "Tell me again," she said, her voice raw with emotion.

What in the world was it all about? Sue stood next to her, wrapping a supportive arm around her.

Lynnie shook her head. "It can't be!" Her shoulders began to shake. "I can't believe it!"

Sue stared into the eyes that brimmed with tears. What new horrors were unfolding now? *Oh Lord, hasn't my girl suffered enough? What else does she have that You could take from her?*

"Oh, Pastor Sam!" Lynnie choked out. "Is she alright?...I can't believe it...Thank you for phoning. Thank you so much! Oh, thank you! I will call you soon." Lynnie replaced the phone in its cradle and turned a luminous face to her mother.

"What is it honey?"

"She's been found! Anya is alive!" Lynnie collapsed against Sue's middle in sobs.

"What?" Sue grasped Lynnie's face in her hands, searching it. "What are you talking about?"

Lynnie's sobs became ragged laughter even as the tears rolled down her cheeks. "They found her! Pastor Sam has her. My baby! She's in his house right now."

Sue gasped, staring at her daughter without comprehension.

"Someone in a village... found her," Lynnie went on jerkily, "after the...after what happened. I don't understand it. But they took her home with them and kept her. So yesterday, this man brought her to Jos. To a police station." She clasped her hands to her chest.

"How is that possible?" Sue was crying along with Lynnie. They hugged each other. "Incredible!"

"What's incredible?" Glen appeared in the kitchen doorway, squinting against the light, his thinning hair a riot.

Lynnie jumped to her feet in agitation. "I've got to book a flight. Right now. I'll paddle a canoe if I have to, but nothing is going to stop me from going there to get her." She began pacing.

"Going where? What's going on?" Glen folded his tall frame onto a seat at the counter.

Sue rushed at him. "That phone call you didn't want to take? That was Lynnie's pastor, Sam Likita from Nigeria, with the most amazing news. They have found Anya!"

Glen's mouth fell open and he rubbed his hand across his face. "The little one? But how? And Josie too?"

Lynnie dropped her gaze. "No, not Josie. We buried her, remember? Only Anya."

Sue tightened her arm around her daughter's shoulders, trying to signal to Glen with her eyes.

For once he seemed to catch on. He shook his head, staring at the two women. "A little girl like that. How could she ever have survived?"

"That's what I wanted to know, Dad," Lynnie said. "Sam didn't seem to have an answer to that himself. He just kept saying, 'It's a miracle from God.'" She hurried to the porch and reached for her jacket. "What I've got to do now is get on-line and look for the first available flight."

"Hold up a second, kiddo," Glen said. "C'mon back and sit down. Let's think this out."

Lynnie paused to look back at them both, her fingers drumming on the granite countertop.

"It's the middle of the night," he cautioned. "We're not thinking straight. Let's get some sleep and plan out what we'll do in the morning."

"Are you kidding? I'll never be able to fall asleep after this!" Lynnie spoke over her shoulder as she slipped her feet into boots.

Glen raised an eyebrow at Sue and they chuckled. "I guess not. But we're both coming with you this time. You'll need the help."

A bright smile lit Lynnie's face, something Sue hadn't seen on her for a very long time.

The young woman did that thing she used to do when she was excited about something, hands fisted against her chest, her whole body shuddering. "Tickets for three then!" She reached for the door, but paused and more slowly, turned back toward them. "Maybe we should keep the news to ourselves for a while? I mean, until I have her safely in my arms again? It just doesn't seem real."

"Of course," her parents chorused.

After the door closed behind Lynnie, Glen turned to his wife. "You don't think all this could be a scam, do you?"

"Glen! How could you even think such a thing? Nothing could be crueller."

"Just scared for my girl, is all. There are all those foreign rip-offs. I'd hate to see her hurt all over again."

"Lynnie knows Pastor Sam's voice. And I've met him. He's a man of deep faith and integrity."

"It'll be nice to meet him. After all your talk when you came back, I kind of had a hankering to see the place myself. Never been off the continent." He paused, musing. "Ha. No doubt my mother will be thrilled to know her prayers all these years have been answered. I'm finally off on a mission to foreign parts."

Sue laughed, giddy with tonight's news. "To bring the wanderer home."

Glen gave a wry smile, swiping his face with his hand. "But right now, I've got to get some sleep. It was a long day and we've got church in the morning."

Puttering in the kitchen once Glen went back to bed, Sue checked her calendar. Next week, she was scheduled to drive Nanny to the city for her one-year hip check-up, attend the school play granddaughter Jade had been rehearsing for months, and host a church bridal shower.

A thrill ran through her at the thought of another little one in the family. Then she got thinking about what would be needed to prepare for Anya's return. A crib, clothes, diapers, toys.

"There's no way I can go to Africa," she murmured, pondering her responsibilities. She picked up her phone to text Lynnie. "Better I stay here and plan a baby shower for my own granddaughter."

Chapter 37

There is sunshine in my soul today,
More glorious and bright
Than glows in any earthly sky
~Sunshine in My Soul, by Eliza E. Hewitt, 1851-1920

Stubbing my toes on the uneven ground did nothing to slow my headlong rush to the cabin. My full heart raced almost as quickly as my thoughts. The world was overturned. When I stumbled in through the glass doors, I flicked on the lights, flung my shoes and jacket aside, and twirled around the room in joy. There would be no more sleep tonight, not now that the bond with my baby was re-ignited. I paused for a moment while my computer fired up, closing my eyes to conjure up the feel and fragrance of her.

I wanted to scream in my excitement but only let out a guttural "Ah!" I hugged my arms tightly around myself, thumping down into the chair in front of my laptop. Blinking away the happy tears, I set to work booking our flights. I was grateful my parents wanted to come along. Nothing would have stopped me from making this trip, but it was better not to travel alone, particularly inside Nigeria. Even shopping in that country had gone better with a Nigerian friend to barter for me. James and I used to joke about the "white tax" of the double or triple prices we had to pay if we shopped alone. The market vendors could smell *butare* money a mile away.

Trying one airline after another, I had no luck finding seats for immediate departure. There were far fewer flights now than when James and I had gone to Africa over five years ago. I removed all possible criteria, willing to fly at any time of the day or night, leaving from any airport within a day's drive from home. Nothing this week. My heart sank. Like in last night's dream, Anya was so close to me, almost within kissing distance, and yet so far. I searched for available seats for the next week without success, then realized I was holding my breath, and made myself exhale long and slow. Some flight would come up. It had to.

Meanwhile, I checked if anything had changed regarding travel regulations. Nigeria was still on the "not recommended" advisory list. That rating hadn't stopped us before. Only now I understood the caution all too well. But again, I could let nothing stop me this time. This trip was essential travel by any standard.

With growing impatience, I checked available flights often in the next few hours. In between, I rifled through personal documents to find my passport. With it, was Anya's Nigerian passport. I paused to page through it and found the baby photo, recalling with a smile how the Embassy guy had asked six-month-old Anya in a solemn tone, "How old are you? Are these your parents?"

He'd shrugged at James and me. "We have to ask."

Looking at her chubby face in the picture, I wondered what her condition would be now. Had they taken good care of her? Fed her nutritious food? Kept her clean and healthy? Anxiety flooded my mind at the possibility of physical neglect and sexual abuse. Why had they kept her for so long only to turn her in a year later? Had they grown tired of her?

I had heard of the horror of female genital mutilation. Had they damaged her? The thought was unbearable to me. An overwhelming urgency to pull her into my protective arms came over me. I rushed back to the computer again in an even more desperate search for tickets.

Finally, I scored two, having received Mom's text saying she would stay behind. But when I read the fine print, I discovered there were strict rules about what constituted essential travel. None of them quite fit my situation. I determined I would figure it all out if I had to storm the office of the Prime Minister himself.

For now, the eastern horizon was edged in rose and gold, and I began yawning. My adrenaline was wearing off and I lay down for a short rest.

I woke to loud rapping on the French door. Disoriented as to what I was doing on the living room couch and what time of day it was, I sat up. On shaky legs, I rose to answer the door.

Dad, in dress shirt and pants, stepped into the cabin. "Hope you slept well. Your grandmother took a dim view of your missing church this morning."

"It's Sunday? I am so confused."

"I managed to put her off." He grinned, holding up a palm. "Don't worry, I didn't mention anything about Anya. But your mother is busting to tell everyone."

"I know, right? I have no idea how I'm going to keep it a secret so long. I want to shout it from the rooftops." I moved to the kitchen bar where my laptop sat. "But the best I could find was a flight from Calgary in three weeks. And there's a snag." I showed my dad the convoluted pandemic regulations that threatened to prohibit us from travelling.

He frowned. "Let me make a call to our member of Parliament. I used to sell hay to him when he was still ranching. He might be able to advise us on this."

This was an idea I hadn't thought of. "Thanks, Dad.

"And if all else fails," he added, "we can raise a ruckus in the media. Stories about lost babies are headline news."

I groaned but didn't rule it out.

"Mom's got lunch ready so why don't you get dressed and join us."

I ran a comb through my hair, found a simple dress, slipped into a coat and shoes, and hurried over.

"Hey," I said to my mom. "I just realized—"

"—you'll need a whole bunch of new clothes for Anya." She pivoted to face me. "Yes, I thought of that after you left last night. That's part of the reason I decided not to go with you. I can stay here and get things ready. Did you book a flight?"

"Yeah," I said, slumping my shoulders. "But it's three weeks away."

Mom paused in slicing the whole wheat bread. "Aw, I know that must be disappointing." She raised the hand holding the bread knife and wagged it at me. "But that gives us some time to get ready. You're going to need a lot of things. A crib, a car seat, clothes, shoes, toys, books, maybe diapers."

"Drop your weapon, woman," Dad quipped, coming through from the washroom.

Mom glanced at the knife in her hand, blinking. "Whoops, sorry. Just getting excited."

"I know. Me too," he said. "We could do with another little one around here. And you're right about a car seat. We'll have to bring it to the airport with us for when we come home."

"And I'll pack some clothes for her to take with me," I said. "Except we don't really know her size." Again, the worry about Anya's physical well-being nagged at me. Was she malnourished? Had they brushed her teeth? Used sunscreen? Kept up with the anti-malaria medication?

"We can guess at her size," Mom assured me. "Your girls were always slight for their age, so even if we buy stuff on the big side, she'll grow into it."

"I hadn't thought about diapers," I said, grating the cheese Mom set in front of me. "She's past three. I wonder if they would have potty-trained her. With the price of diapers, most Nigerian moms are in a hurry to get their kids out of them." I paused, thinking. "But then, I don't even know if there was a mom involved. Pastor Sam said it was a man who brought her to the police. I sure hope there was a mom." The idea of my little girl in the keeping of a man alone sent terror through me.

"But they told you she was in good condition, right?" Dad reminded me as he filled the water glasses.

"Yeah." I tried to picture what Anya would look like now, what she would be like, but I came up blank. In my mind, she was forever a toddler with wispy brown hair and rounded arms and legs, just starting to say a few words. A new thought occurred to me. "I wonder if she still speaks English. Or if she speaks at all? I've read that trauma can make kids go mute."

Mom turned off the stove and looked at me. "Let's not borrow trouble, as Grandma would say." She moved the pot off the heat and began ladling the thick potato soup into three bowls, sprinkling each with Cheddar.

We sat at the table and joined hands while Dad thanked God for the meal and prayed for a smooth trip to go bring home my daughter.

"What with the earth-shaking news we heard last night, I don't suppose you've given any thought to finishing your school year?" Dad's eyes were on the butter he was generously spreading on his bread.

School. It had utterly left my mind. "I can't believe that was only three days ago. Feels like years. Sam's phone call has changed everything for me. It's weird. All those problems about the course ideology, my huge meltdown, and all that angst over my future career? Poof! Faded into thin air." I spooned up some of Mom's delicious soup. "I know exactly what I'm supposed to do with my life now. I'm going to be a mom again, just like I always wanted."

Dad gave no answer but, watching him, I had the sense he didn't agree.

I set down my spoon. "What? You look like you want to argue."

He slowly finished chewing his bite of bread and butter. "Three weeks until we leave. That takes you neatly to the end of your semester, doesn't it?"

Shaking my head, I built up steam. "Oh no. No. I can't go back there. Definitely not. And besides, college seems like a different life now. All I can think about is Anya."

He shrugged, but Mom took up the thread. And tugged.

"Have you thought through your future? Only two more years and Anya will be in school. You could find work or go on for your master's then. But what a shame it would be to have to start over when you're so close to completing this year."

I sat and stared at my half-eaten soup, bucking their argument. "Whatever happened to your support of full-time mothering?" I muttered.

"We've never denied it. But you have a unique window of time right now..." Dad left the suggestion hanging, letting me stew.

Grudgingly, I could see their point. I couldn't be dependent on them or anyone else forever. I would have a child to support.

I couldn't deny that my biggest barrier to completing the semester was my pride. With everything in me, I resisted making an apology for my behavior. I had been set-up by my former friend, humiliated, scorned, and betrayed by my classmates. Most stinging of all though, was the callous dismissal of the greatest wound I had ever suffered. That anyone could ever suffer.

I sat there, struggling inside for what seemed a long time. Then in my mind, Grandma stuck in her oar. *We are the Hardys. We complete what we begin.*

But I wasn't a Hardy anymore. I was a Min. When I found myself trying to wiggle out of her admonition with that flimsy excuse, I knew I was losing my inner battle. Like the cooked potatoes in my bowl, I began softening to my parents' way of thinking.

"Okay. I'll do it. I'll apologize and see where it goes from there." I stirred my now-cool soup. "And I'll do it tomorrow."

Mom reached over and stroked my arm. "I'll be praying for you."

Chapter 38

Just as I am, tho tossed about
With many a conflict, many a doubt,
Fightings and fears within, without,
O Lamb of God, I come! I come!
~Just As I Am, by Charlotte Elliott, 1789-1871

D read filled me at having to face my colleagues the next
morning. Still, I slept well, exhausted from the previous
night's excitement. The next day, I dressed up for class, hoping
clothes might lend me added confidence. I was as tight inside as the
time my sister and brother and I had to confess why there'd been no
eggs for a full week. We hadn't felt like washing them, so we'd been
chucking them at the barn wall and lying about the chickens not
laying.

For today's apology, every imagined scenario I went through
carried with it some glitch. What if Charlaine refused me entrance
into the classroom? What if I couldn't get the class's attention? I
envisioned the other students' faces, shocked as they had been the
morning I'd erupted. What if they laid into me in return? My
courage evaporated.

But I forced myself to eat an orange and a piece of toast, then got
in my car and drove to the college. I had arrived early so I could
catch the prof in private ahead of the students. The halls were

empty and as I leaned against the wall near the locked classroom door, I prayed for calm and control.

The sound of heels approaching made me look up. When Charlaine caught sight of me, she stopped for a moment, then made a brisk aim for the door, avoiding my eyes.

I'd expected that hard look on her face. I pushed off the wall and took a deep breath while she found her key and opened the door.

"Dr. Trites," I said, following her inside. "I've had a few days to think over my behavior last time I was in class and I—"

She whirled on me, coming at me, her face now alive with hostility. "Your behavior? Your behavior was emotional, immature, insulting, and unprofessional. Social work requires practitioners to remove their personal feelings from their work. If you are unable to do this, I suggest you find another vocation." She turned her back, busy with opening her laptop and shuffling papers.

"You're right," I said, moving to where I could face her. "That's what I came here to tell you. Please hear me out. As I said, I've had some time to think, and I'm deeply ashamed of my immaturity, of my selfishness in making the class lecture all about me, and for disrupting the class with my lack of self-control." I took a step toward her so that we were face-to-face. "I'm sorry. Would you please forgive me?"

Under her unreadable gaze, the silence stretched. I grew uncomfortable.

"Okay. Whatever." She bent to retrieve a folder from her briefcase and began to read, ignoring me.

I shoved my hands into the pockets of my jacket, unsure what her response meant. "I would like the opportunity to make amends to the other students as well."

"Fine," she muttered, not looking up.

I shuffled my feet in uncertainty, then took my usual seat at the side of the classroom. A partial weight had lifted from my mind, making me eager to get the next apology behind me. However, I didn't take off my jacket in case Charlaine dismissed me from the class permanently. *Okay, Lord, I've done my part. Whether I'm expelled or not is up to you.*

When my classmates arrived and there was a lull in the buzz, Charlaine said, "I hope you all had a restful weekend. Ms. Min would like a word." She directed a curt nod at me.

I took a deep breath, stood, and repeated my confession and request for forgiveness.

After a moment's pause, Brynn surprised me by crossing the aisle to give me a side hug. "I'm so sorry for your loss," she whispered into my hair.

Others, too, murmured condolences. It wasn't the forgiveness I had asked for, but I took it as amnesty. A lightness buoyed me up. It was the last weight that had burdened me. Now I just wanted to get through the rest of my school year and get on with being mama to my baby.

Charlaine began her lecture, a discussion of strategies for kids aging out of the foster care system. Suddenly, she stopped mid-sentence and turned to me, one eyebrow raised. "Ms. Min. I can turn up the thermostat."

Feeling all eyes on me, I stared at her, confused.

"Are you planning to keep your jacket on for the entire class?"

I blushed, shaking my head and slipping off my coat. It appeared I was reinstated in the course.

Not another word was said about the event last week. At the end of class, Charlaine's instructions took in the whole group of us while giving her final assignment.

The following Sunday, for the first time since my return to Canada, I attended church with my family. Until then, if I went at all I had made a habit of arriving late enough to miss the greeting time at the beginning of the service. But today I was bubbling with joy, fit to burst with the news of my lost lamb found.

People I had avoided for a year now took the opportunity to hug me, express their sorrow for my loss, suggest books they'd found helpful in grief. A year's worth of sympathy stuffed into a few minutes between Sunday school and the worship service. A few perceptive ones marveled at how well I was coping. "You're an inspiration to us all, the way the Lord has given you joy in your suffering," our retired pastor told me, squeezing my shoulder. I had never been good at keeping secrets and felt guilty for not sharing the whole truth.

At dinner with the family later, I made the mistake of mentioning my distraction about my studies, barely able to hold back the reason why. I sensed Lissa's eyes on me, and when I glanced up at her, I could tell she knew something was up.

"You will simply have to buckle down and apply yourself," Grandma advised.

I stifled a sigh.

While everyone else helped clear the table and started the clean-up, my sister hustled me into the back porch and shut the door behind her.

"Okay, spill it."

"What?" I tried to keep my tone casual and my face bland.

Lissa rolled her eyes. "Oh, come on. You've got to do better than that if you think you're going to hide whatever it is you've got going on. Have you met someone?"

"Don't be ridiculous." I concentrated on the sprouting seed flats under the windowsill, then outside at the drift of light green, new growth that recent warm weather had begun to coax out of the trees.

"Out with it!" Lissa tapped her foot loudly.

"Okay, okay." I fixed my eyes on her face. "I got a phone call last week." Pulling my hands into fists in front of me, I vibrated with excitement. "You're not going to believe this, but Anya has been found."

Her eyes bugged out. "What?"

"It's true. I've booked a flight. Only fourteen sleeps until I'm going to get her. I can't wait!"

"She's alive?"

I nodded, grinning. "Somebody found her and turned her in to the police a week ago. My pastor phoned to tell me."

"How can that be? I don't get it."

"I don't either, but it's true."

"That's incredible!" she squealed. I clamped my hand over her mouth, worried the others might hear. She clasped me in a tight embrace, and we danced around in silent joy. Finally, she pulled away. "We've got to go shopping."

"I'm dying to, but I've got a whole bunch of assignments to finish before I leave, and I'm still nervous about proving to Nigerian customs that Anya is mine."

Someone knocked at the door. "You girls want dessert?" Mom called.

"Be right out," I answered.

We smoothed our clothes and came back to the kitchen.

Grandma was elbow deep in dishwater. "One would think young ladies your age would know better than to shirk the washing up." Her lips tightened in a grim line.

"Sorry." I looked around the tidied kitchen for something to do. Lissa caught my eye and sent a surreptitious sneer Grandma's way. She took plates of pie to the table while I counted out the necessary forks.

I found myself antsy in classes during the last weeks of my course. My ability to focus was shot to pieces. All I wanted to do was find Anya and clasp her tight. Even cutting through the sticky tangle of government red tape ahead of my trip to Africa made me feel like I was taking a step closer to my daughter. But college researching and writing now seemed an annoying and futile chore. What made it onto the page was not my best work, but I soldiered on.

Grandma took to calling me each evening, checking on my progress in completing assignments, reminding me to finish well. She even offered to proofread for me. I let her examine a short assignment, though it meant extra time to print it off and bring it to her, then sit with her as she went through it, line by line explaining her edits. I could tell she was thrilled to have a part in my education again.

Mom, Lissa, and I made a quick trip to the city one Saturday to shop for Anya.

"I only want to get enough stuff to bring her home in. Once she's here, we can decide what else she needs." But I lingered over the toddler outfits, dreaming of dressing my sweet baby in them.

"Let me buy at least one cute thing for her," Lissa said, grabbing an adorable pair of peach floral leggings and matching ruffled top.

"I don't know..." I bit my lip, thinking of the uncertainties ahead. "It's like I don't want to tempt fate."

She stopped and glared at me, hand on hip. "Don't be stupid. If God had mercy on her to save her from the fire, don't you think he can bring her safely home, too?"

Duly chastened, I nodded.

Beside me, Mom chuckled, stroking a hair out of my eyes. "She's absolutely right, you know. And it's so good to see her trying to do something for others. Good for you to accept gifts with a bit of advice thrown in, too." She tilted her head to look at me. "You can't quite accept this is really happening, can you?"

I shook my head. "Not until I have her in my arms. Or maybe until we lift off from the Lagos runway."

"I know, honey. I know." She pulled me to her with one arm. "I'll be praying you home every step of the way."

During the last week before departure, anxiety rose inside me to new heights. From Monday to Thursday, no Government of Canada envelope arrived. I was near tears on Friday, my last day of school, fearing the explanatory letter wouldn't come in time. I had to force myself to drive to the college and refrain from texting Mom every ten minutes asking about the mail. Finally, close to noon, she texted back.

Official letter is here!

I expelled a long sigh of relief.

That afternoon, when I received back my final paper from Charlaine's course, I flipped to the end, intensely curious about my grade. Despite my preoccupation with thoughts of Anya, I had worked hard on it. Would my outburst affect it? Was Charlaine a grudge-holder?

On the last page, in her firm black printing, was the following message: "My condolences on the loss of your family. It would be wise to inform people of your personal situation to help avoid future misunderstandings." She had given me an A.

Chapter 39

We share our mutual woes,
Our mutual burdens bear;
And often for each other flows,
The sympathizing tear.
~Blest Be the Tie That Binds, by John Fawcett, 1740-1817

Still brushing out my hair after undoing its ponytail, I answered the knock at the door. It was likely Mom with one last reminder to pack something, I figured. We already had the car seat installed and our bags stowed in the car. Only my carry-on awaited the final items.

Wearing my hair up all day had left my scalp tender in spots. I massaged it with my fingers as I swung open the door.

I froze in astonishment. The last person I expected stood before me. Rye Hainstock filled the doorway, bigger and more bearded than I remembered him. He was so tall I had to tip my head back to look him in the face.

I had known Ryan since grade one. Or rather, I had gone to school with him. I had never really known him, and finding him at my door today confused and surprised me. The confusion was due to my mind already having raced halfway around the world ahead of me on the journey to get my baby back. The surprise had to do with the opposite worlds this guy and I had occupied in high school.

With rodeo in summer and hockey in winter, he had run with a rough, hard-drinking crowd. He'd gotten his nickname Rye for good reason. I still remembered my embarrassment when Charlaine had to explain to me the connection to rye whiskey.

I stared up at him, stupidly silent. He seemed so tall. All at once a line from a long-ago sermon popped into my head. "David looked Goliath straight in the knee-cap and said..." A giggle escaped me. Lousy timing. "Hi," I said, eloquent as ever.

"Hey Lyn," he said in a voice different from the raucous, mouthy one I recalled. He fingered the brim of his black cowboy hat. "I saw you at church awhile back and I heard about your story."

Church? I almost blurted it out loud but stopped myself just in time. Rye and church were nouns that my mind had trouble linking. They somehow didn't belong together. Also, I didn't want to make him feel bad that I hadn't noticed his presence, even in our small congregation.

The chilly outdoor air was making me shiver. "Why don't you come in for a bit?"

"Thanks," he said, brushing past me as I opened the door wider for him. He laid his hat on the shelf at the door and stood, looking uncomfortable with his arms held away from his sides like a defenceman. He dwarfed my cabin with his larger-than-life presence.

"Have a seat," I said, pointing to the chair by the wood stove.

With apparent effort, he pulled off his cowboy boots and sock-footed his way in to sit down.

I sat across from him on the couch, marvelling at the strangeness of hosting *the* Rye Hainstock, talk of the girls' tables in the school cafeteria. I had been too proud to join in their fawning giggles over his good looks and fabulous body, but it wasn't as though I hadn't noticed. Waiting for Mr. Right didn't make a girl blind to all the Mr. Wrongs in the world.

His attention was fixed on the framed photos on the side table next to him. He gazed at my wedding picture for a few seconds, then took up the one of Josie and Anya and brought it close to his face. "So these are your little wee girls."

The way he called them "little wee" caught me off guard and made my eyes sting. I swallowed the sudden bulge in my throat. "That's right. That picture's from about a year and a half ago. Josie was almost three and Anya was eighteen months old." Now she was past three. I had been so anxious about the government letter and my school troubles that I'd barely let myself dream. A surge of excitement shot through me at the thought of seeing Anya soon. Should I tell him where I was going in the morning? But my parents and I had agreed we should wait until we had her secure in our arms before announcing anything.

Rye slowly pulled his gaze away from the photo. "They're beautiful." Were those tears in his eyes? It was hard to think of this tough jock as a sentimental lover of children. But a long-forgotten fact surfaced. Hadn't Rye's mom died sometime when we were in primary school?

After a pause, he said, "I guess you've seen me in church recently?"

I floundered, not wanting to lie. "Uh, I don't always make it on time."

One side of his mouth quirked up, showing an appealing dimple. "Pretty weird, eh? Me, going to church."

I smiled. "Well, it's not exactly how I remember you."

He raked his hand through his dark hair. "That's a polite way of putting it." He caught my eyes with his frank gaze. "But then, you always were such a nice girl."

I was shocked that he even had an opinion about a low-profile kid like me. I was about to thank him for the compliment when he returned to staring at the photo again.

"It sure seems tough that such a sweet person like you had something so bad happen to her."

I shrugged one shoulder, awkward as always with sympathy, yet touched by it as well. His soft tone made me want to tell him the truth about the latest developments. Instead, I settled for a different focus. "All my life I've read stories of people who lived through the worst that life could throw at them and how God got them through it. Whenever I read those books, I used to worry that if anything like that happened to me, I'd fall to pieces. But I can honestly say God has carried me through it all. People say that Christianity is a crutch, but I'd say it's a wheelchair."

He raised his eyes to mine. "My aunt told me what happened to you out there in Africa last year. It had a big impact on me. I've been wanting to come over and tell you myself how sorry I am about your loss. I always respected you for being a true Christian, and now I see you're an amazingly strong person."

The open admiration on his face embarrassed me. Besides, it was surreal having a personal conversation with one of the most popular guys in the community.

Stray tidbits of thought came together for me just then. "Hey, your aunt doesn't happen to be a social worker, does she?"

"Yeah. Auntie Patty. She married my dad's brother. After my mom died, she used to have my brothers and me up to her place on weekends a lot when we were kids. Why do you ask?"

"Patricia Hainstock. She spoke to my class at school and was a major encouragement to me. We've emailed back and forth a bit."

He nodded and paused a second, staring down at his thumbs tucked into his fists. He pounded his knees lightly with them and it occurred to me he was nervous. Rye Hainstock, big man on campus, was sitting in my living room, jittery about talking to me, the nerdy religious girl. Wonders never ceased.

His chest expanded with a deep breath. "I also wanted you to know that I'm sorry for giving you such a hard time in school about your faith. I'm a Christian now, too, so I know what that kind of hassling is like. I get it from my hockey buddies all the time."

I shook my head. "I can honestly say I don't remember you doing anything like that, so nothing to be sorry for. I thought I was invisible in high school."

He raised one eyebrow. "You, invisible? I don't think so." He shook his head with a half-smile. "But you did kind of bug me."

"Bug you?" I searched my memory and couldn't come up with a single, direct interaction between Rye and me, let alone one where I antagonized him.

One corner of his mouth pulled up again. "Yeah, whenever I saw you come into the coffee shop, I had to tone down my language, or hide my cigarette under the table, or quit coming onto the waitress or whatever."

Incredulous, I stammered, "But I never—"

"I know you didn't. You were too nice to ever say anything about stuff like that. But everyone knew what kind of a person you were. There was something about you that, I don't know...I guess who you were made me ashamed of who I was." His eyes widened and he shrugged. "Hey, it was a good thing. I get it now. So thanks for always being a reminder to me of what a real Christian is. And if there's anything you need, or if you ever just want to talk about your husband and daughters, I'd be happy to listen."

His tender words strengthened my urge to spill all the excitement about the trip I was embarking on, but all I said was, "That's so kind of you, thanks."

He stood and made for the door.

I was moved by his making the effort to come by. "Rye?"

He winced and said, "I go by Ryan now."

"Sorry about that," I said, grinning as I rose to follow him to the entry. "I've gone back to my childhood name of Lynnie, myself. I just wanted to let you know that I think it's amazing and thrilling the change that Jesus has already made in you.

"You think so?" he said, pausing in pulling on his boots to peer up at me. "That's good to hear. Most days it feels like I've got way too far to go."

"I'd like to hear your story sometime," I added.

He tipped his head to one side as though appraising me. Perhaps gauging whether I could be trusted with a tale that must include some sordid parts. "I'll have to tell you sometime." He turned to grab his hat, clapping it on his head. "Maybe I'll see you at church," he said, nodding, then stepped out the door and shut it behind him.

I moved back from the French door, watching him as he strode out to his high four-wheel-drive black pickup. I remembered that jaunty walk he had. Spring-loaded kneecaps, one of his buddies had once teased. As he hopped into the driver's seat, backed out my short driveway, and drove out the lane, I shook my head in amazement at the strangeness of his visit. Curiosity about how he had come to Christ grew in me, too. I looked forward to hearing his story.

But for now, I had a few last things to pack. Ryan's unexpected visit had thrown my concentration off. I shut down the odd and conflicting thoughts about Ryan and fixed my mind back on my trip to Nigeria. Excitement returned in full force. The bubbling hope that in a day or two I might be holding my daughter in my arms flooded me with a wild joy. Ho would I ever fall asleep?

Yet I had to. Tomorrow would be an early morning, allowing two hours for the trip to the airport and another two for flight check-in and boarding. And every stage in the long journey was one step closer to my baby.

Chapter 40

I once was lost, but now am found...
~Amazing Grace, by John Newton, 1725-1807

Lissa's words of a couple of days ago looped through my mind on the early drive to the airport the next morning. *If God had mercy on her to save her from the fire, don't you think he can bring her safely home, too?*

Somehow, God had not only delivered my Anya out of a deadly fire, but he had kept her alive in the year since then. What made me doubt he could overcome all the obstacles to bringing her home to me? It was embarrassing that the sister I had always mentored should be the one to remind me of so basic a truth.

For the past fourteen months I had thought I was trusting God throughout my grieving. Like the biographies I'd read of past martyrs and missionaries, I had accepted tragedy and loss without turning my back on God. Maybe I was even a little proud of my ability to endure suffering like a good soldier of Christ. But pain had affected my ability to believe miracles still happened. I had to admit that mistrust of God's goodness had coloured my outlook on life. Since tragedy had turned my world upside down, whenever I heard of someone who was sick or injured, my first assumption was that they would die. I had developed a mindset that whatever the situation, the worst was inevitable. Did my negative thoughts amount to calling God cruel?

Lord, I'm sorry. Help me to trust you.

As though I were releasing a breath I had held for a year, I felt myself unwind. A barrier had dropped, and I could look to the future without having to brace myself for every potential misery. A thrill raced through me. I peeked over my shoulder at the car seat waiting in the back. My body shivered in excitement.

Dad glanced over at me. "Pretty wound up, aren't you? Gonna be able to sleep on the flight?"

I grinned at him. "I'll try." Balling my jacket into a pillow, I snuggled down for the two-hour drive.

Daylight streamed onto my face when we reached the city and turned east toward the airport. My mind whirled with the steps ahead of us, checking in our baggage, passing through customs, locating the departure gate. I was grateful Dad was with me, but I noticed him chewing on a fingernail as we approached the terminal. It occurred to me that he was a less-experienced traveller than I was.

Things moved smoothly until we got to the customs wicket. The woman checked my documents, frowning. When she directed us out of the lineup to be interviewed elsewhere, my palms started sweating in earnest. Desperation seized me and I paced the small office she'd pointed to while we waited for the next agent.

"Sit here and calm down," Dad whispered, tapping the chair beside him. "You look nervous and they'll think we're up to no good."

I sat.

The grim woman who had first singled us out was replaced by a jovial, chubby fellow who breezed into the tiny office, barely glancing at my passport. He made a brief scan of my Member of Parliament's letter of explanation. "Bringing home baby, are you?" he grinned.

"That's right," I said, breathing easier.

He handed the documents back to me. "Looks like everything is in order. Have a great trip," he said, and left as quickly as he'd come.

Dad and I gawked at each other in surprise, laughed, and gathered our things to go wait for boarding.

I tried to sleep on the long, cramped trip, but adrenaline pumped wildly the closer we got to our destination. I knew we had a major hurdle ahead with Nigerian customs and then a long drive north to Jos, but I couldn't help myself. I was mere hours away from Anya, whom I had thought was lost to me forever.

Exiting the plane in Lagos at last, the thick darkness of the humid night hit like a solid wall.

"That's some heat," Dad said, wiping the back of his neck. He looked around in wonder at the crowded airport. "So this is what it's like to be in the minority. Makes me feel for immigrants to our country."

His mood soured with each bribe he was obligated to pay going through customs. He was outraged at the corruption but I urged him to keep his opinions to himself so we could speed things along. What a relief it was to see Pastor Sam's smiling face when we were finally free to go.

He enfolded me in a big hug, then did the same to my dad. I couldn't help giggling at the way Dad's eyes bugged out over Sam's shoulder. Canada, meet Nigeria.

"Sorry for making you drive all this way and stay up so late," I said.

"Not at all," Sam boomed. He picked up one of our suitcases and motioned us to follow him.

I peppered him with questions as we walked: Was Anya healthy? Was she talking? Where had she been living? What had he learned about the man who had brought her to them?

Sam rumbled his deep laugh as he directed us to his car. "Little Anya is fine. Fine. She keeps quiet, but she is good." Sam had only spent a brief time with the man who brought her to the Jos police station because he and the friend who drove him had left the same day. The police had offered few details and Sam would not have had the money to loosen their tongues even if the officer had known more.

Despite my eagerness to get to my daughter, the fitful sleep I'd had on the flight caught up with me. The last thing I remember was Dad asking Sam if there was always so much going on in the middle of the night in Lagos. Even jolting down the bumpy road beyond the city didn't keep me awake. Hours later when the sun was brightening the eastern skyline of Jos, we pulled into Sam and Judith's courtyard. Sam switched off the engine and turned to me expectantly.

Suddenly, I was wide awake. All that separated me from my baby were the plastered walls of the house next to me. I wrung my hands together, my knees trembling.

"Welcome to my home," Sam said, climbing from the vehicle and hefting out our bags.

Dad and I grabbed them and followed him into the house.

For me, it was like stepping back in time. Judith, in her orange robe and headwrap rushed toward me, greeting me with a warm embrace. A thousand memories, warm and tragic, flooded my mind at the sight of her. She kissed both my cheeks, then shook my dad's hand.

"You must be hungry," she said, taking me by the hand, "but first you will want to peek in on your little one."

She led me down the short hallway and stood before a closed door. "I must tell you, each night we lay her in her bed and when I check her before I retire, she is not in it. You will see." She gave me her loving smile. "Go on now, open it."

The moment I'd been anticipating now made my insides churn. I pulled in a deep breath, wiped my hands on my skirt and tiptoed into the darkened room. On the floor beside the bed lay a small child, her cheek upon the cool tile. Why was she on the floor, rather than in the bed prepared for her? I looked back at Judith who shrugged.

"Every night, she does this," she whispered, then closed the door with a gentle click, leaving me in the semi-darkness.

The urge to pick Anya up almost overwhelmed me, but it was still too early in the morning. I would wait. Yet after such a long separation, how could I leave her? In the dim light that slipped past the window blinds, I stared at my daughter, inspecting every inch of her. She seemed so long, and thinner. And what had they done to her hair? I stifled a gasp. It was cropped short in uneven shingles. Why would anyone do such a thing? Like a bedraggled gosling, she looked scrawny and unkempt.

I reached across her for the child-sized pillow on the bed and gingerly lifted her head to slide it under. She stirred for a moment, then settled. Grabbing the light blanket, I tucked it around her, soaking in every detail. She was clean and her fingernails were trimmed, but having been here a few weeks, that would have been Judith's doing.

Oh, my precious little one. Where have you been? What have you been through?

Unable to resist any longer, I lowered myself next to her and carefully drew closer, cupping my body around her. The feel of her warm skin under the thin nightgown and the rhythmic in and out of her breathing was pure heaven.

Silent sobs shook my body and tears dripped from the corners of my eyes as I held her, overcome with thanksgiving. *She's alive! Thank you, Lord!*

I woke to movement beside me and a sore hip. Opening my eyes, at first I couldn't place the unfamiliar room. Then I remembered. I jerked upright in a frantic search of the space beside me. Where was Anya? I spotted her hunched into a tiny lump beyond the corner of the bed frame, peering through the rails at me, wide-eyed.

I wanted to rush at her, but the wariness in her eyes stopped me. It was the last thing I'd expected. I'd had visions of a rapturous reunion. But how could I not have considered this possibility? In my studies, I had learned there was a limit to how many times a child can successfully bond. Fear twisted my insides. Was she damaged for good?

Please God, help me reach her.

I tried to see recent events through her eyes. Who knew how much of James and Josie's deaths she had witnessed? Then there was the unknown intervening time. And now, being abandoned by her caregiver was yet another trauma in her short life.

"Hey, Anya," I whispered, from my side of the bed. "Did you have a good sleep?" I gave her a bright smile, tilting my head onto my folded hands, closing my eyes with a loud snore. Through one eye, I peeked to see what effect this mime would have.

She stared at me, unsmiling.

My heart sank. I kept up a stream of chatter, keeping my distance so as not to spook her. What I needed were the toys and goodies in my carry-on bag.

"You wait here, honey," I told her. "I have a surprise for you."

I crept out of the room and down the hall to find Dad at the table with Sam and Judith, laughing over something and looking like they'd been friends all their lives.

"You slept?" Judith raised her eyebrows at me.

I looked at the clock on the stove. "I guess so."

"And?" Dad asked.

Disappointment tugged downward on the corners of my mouth. In all my dreams of reuniting with my baby, I had never pictured this.

"Ah, Mama Lynnie." Judith rose and put an arm around my shoulders. "The little one will know you soon enough. For now, I will dress her and bring her out for breakfast."

Chapter 41

Great is Thy faithfulness! Great is Thy faithfulness!
Morning by morning new mercies I see;
All I have needed Thy hand hath provided—
Great is Thy faithfulness, Lord, unto me!
~*Great is Thy Faithfulness, by Thomas O. Chisholm, 1866-1960*

That day, I plied Judith and Sam with more of the same questions. They gave patient answers, even when I repeated myself.

"Yes, I met the men who brought Anya to the police station," Sam told me. "They were Hausa. One was a Christian brother, Pastor Monday, the other, a Muslim named Ihsan. With language differences, we talked very little. They had a long drive to get home before dark." He shrugged. "I know little more than you do."

I turned to Judith. "How did she look when Sam brought her home? Was she clean? What was she wearing?"

"Yes, clean. Even her fingernails and toenails. She wore pink flip-flops and a little blue dress." She rose from her chair and left the room, returning with the garment over her arm. "Here. See?"

I took the dress, searching it for...what? A brand name? A clue to where it had been purchased or whether it was homemade? It spoke little to me, only that it was not home sewn and was well worn.

Pastor Sam raised a finger, as though remembering. "The Muslim, Ihsan. He embraced the child for a long time before he turned her over to me. He looked very sad."

My heart squeezed, picturing this. It meant Anya had been loved. For the first time it occurred to me that the person who had turned Anya in to the authorities had done so with a sense of loss. Perhaps even as a painful sacrifice. I swallowed hard. "Did she seem sad?"

He considered this for a moment. "She did not cry. But, like now, she says nothing."

"Did she have anything else with her?"

"No. Just some dirty old stick," Judith told me, then laughed. "She does not let go of it even when I give her a bath."

During the week, with every trick I recalled from my Early Childhood courses, I coaxed and cajoled Anya, hoping for some response. Dad and I had only allowed five days before we were scheduled to return to Canada. In my eagerness to bring her home, I had figured a brief stay to recover from jet lag would be enough before turning around and heading home. I hadn't given much thought to the reunion from her point of view.

I noticed the stick she always kept with her.

On the second day, I was able to get close enough to Anya to put my arm around her. While I read a book to her, I eyed the stick tucked under her arm. The bark had been peeled from it and it appeared to be wrapped in a discoloured piece of cloth. One bulbous end with termite squiggles all over it looked like a head.

"It's a doll!" I burst out, interrupting the flow of the story. I reached for the toy. "Can I look at your baby, Anya?"

She said nothing, so I took hold of the stick for a closer look. She kept a tight grip on the other end but let me examine the toy.

"Did you make this, Anya? Did you find the stick and dress it up?" I bent closer to inspect the other side of the head. No child would have been able to carve eye sockets so delicately. The doll had been well loved and the features worn smooth, but someone must have made this for her. And what I'd thought were termite squiggles weren't. They were deliberate grooves that were meant to be hair, carved there by design. It was even straight hair, like Anya's, not the tight curls whoever had made the doll likely had. Tears sprang to my eyes. This answered so many of my questions. Though whoever had kept Anya all this time may have been poor, they must have loved her. The care taken in the carving proved it.

I swallowed, keeping my voice soft and clear. "Who made Dolly for you, honey?" I patted the stick-doll.

She said nothing, but reached out her other hand to pat Dolly, too. She loosened her grip enough for me to check inside the doll's dress. It was gray with much use, but it was hand-stitched and there was even a fragment of lace down the front. It had to be a woman who had taken care of my daughter. I looked closer. Wait! Was that the same lace from the T-shirt I had dressed Anya in the morning they set off on their fateful trip? I couldn't remember for certain, but it seemed familiar. Grandma would approve. Loving, but also thrifty. Again, my heart went out to those kind people.

"You love Dolly, don't you?" I laid my cheek against the stick, patting it again.

Anya looked up at me with shining eyes and for a moment, I thought I was about to eke out a smile from her.

Just then, the door to our room opened and Judith bustled in.

"The aunties have come to see you," she announced with joy. "Come have tea with us."

I smoothed Dolly's dress and tucked her back into the crook of Anya's arm, then held out my hand. "Let's go meet the aunties, okay?" She hesitated a moment, then took my hand, a breakthrough that tugged at my heart and threatened to bring more tears. I treasured the trusting feel of her hand engulfed in my own. Together we followed Judith to the kitchen table and the chatter of women. My dear friend Ebos had arrived, along with Damaris and Rose.

One after another, the women embraced me, kissing both my cheeks, then stooping to kiss my child. Standing behind them, with an uneasy look on her face, was a girl I'd never met. Rose took her arm and brought her forward.

"My girl, Chichima!" Rose squeezed her with one arm. "Like your girl, God has brought her back to me."

"Hallelujah!" the others exclaimed. "Glory to God!"

I took Chichima's hand. Her wan smile was fleeting. As I had with Anya, I wondered what Chichima's years of captivity had done to her. Though I didn't want to squelch Rose's rejoicing, I hoped she would pay close attention to her daughter's emotional health after such an ordeal.

Amid the prattle, Anya at first stayed close to Judith. But Judith was busy serving the guests. Perhaps unnerved by the crowded kitchen, Anya moved to my side and stayed close. I was thrilled when she let me take her onto my lap.

It was wonderful to catch up with my friends, to once again be included in this close-knit community of women. In the evening, Judith welcomed other old friends, men and women with their children. I worried about overwhelming Anya, but how could I squelch Judith's open-hearted hospitality? She made sure I was congratulated and reunited with the entire church.

The stream of visitors continued each day. Dad met each new person, doing his best to put names to faces. I recognized the telltale crease between his eyebrows, showing he was concentrating hard to make out their accent. He was good-natured when they laughed at his misunderstandings. He tried hard to follow their political discussions and seemed to be holding his own when the talk turned to biblical matters.

I was grateful for his socializing because, although I loved my friends, I was distracted. My mind was on Anya and how to make the smoothest transition home for her that I could. Judith understood my insistence on taking over all of Anya's care. Her appetite seemed good, and I was astounded when after a meal, she carried her dish to the counter. Someone had taught her to work.

At night, I went to bed early, at the same time as Anya, so that I could sing to her and pray with her. I had made a pallet for the two of us on the floor so we could be close. Despite the humidity, I wanted to be touching her, never to part. She seemed to accept my presence, but I longed to know what her thoughts were. Did she have any recollection of me? I ached to see her smile as well. A smile, a spontaneous hug, these seemed the measure of her well-being, and the measure of her bond with me. Without that, fear of the damage in her mind and heart loomed large. A dozen times a day I reminded myself to be patient. Adjustments of this magnitude took time. But I wanted to smother her with kisses, tickle her to hear her laugh, see her as the wild and giggling toddler she used to be.

During the week, in a rare moment alone, I asked Dad about his trip that day with Pastor Sam and Damaris's husband, Kelechi. The men had offered to take us north to the site of the ambush. I couldn't bear the thought, but Dad agreed to go.

"Pretty grim. We found the site. The Jeep was still there but dragged off the road. All we found was a black, burned-out hull. It's just as well you didn't go with us. We couldn't find any evidence of how Anya might have escaped. The windows were all busted out and the doors were missing, so there's no telling when that happened." He pulled in a sharp breath. "Sam figured she must have been in the back seat, because when he found them—the bodies— James had been shielding Josie underneath him. Stopped to walk around a couple of villages in the area, but nobody knew anything about it. I even hinted at a reward for information. Nothing."

I paused, letting the weight of this sink in. "You had a good time with the men, though?"

"Well, yeah." He made a furtive glance around, then murmured, "But that business of holding hands with dudes? That was a bit much."

"Did you do it?"

"Yup. Felt weird, but I figured, when in Rome..." He shot me a mischievous grin. "I barely restrained myself from swinging arms. Just don't tell me, come Sunday, I'll have to do the holy kiss."

I laughed. "I make no guarantees. You're being a good sport. Thanks."

"How's it going with Anya?"

"I think I'm making headway, but she never says anything. Not one word, to Judith or to me. Not even to other kids. I've read about child attachment disorder and I'm worried about lasting damage."

"Evelyn, don't—" he began in Grandma's voice.

"—borrow trouble," I finished for him. "You're right. I know. And believe me, I'm praying about it. I wish I could be a little more like Rose. She doesn't seem at all worried about her daughter reintegrating into life here."

"Nigerians sure are a happy lot, aren't they? I think we could all learn a thing or two from them. Well, tomorrow's our last day so we'd better get some rest tonight. From what I hear, Sunday church services here are anything but restful." He quirked a wry smile at me.

"Just you wait," I said, grinning.

Chapter 42

"Father-like, He tends and spares us,
Well our feeble frame He knows;
In His hands He gently bears us,
Rescues us from all our foes."
~*Praise, My Soul, the King of Heaven, by Henry F. Lyte, 1793-1847*

I had forgotten what a contrast African worship was to Canadian services. The vibrancy of it seemed a fitting celebration of the joy inside me now. From over on the men's side, Dad raised his eyebrows at me, and I returned a grin. We both joined in the energetic singing, sensing the palpable bond of love we felt from believers there. We competed with the rain drumming on the tin roof as we belted out the songs we knew, loving our Nigerian friends in return. Despite my worries about Anya's emotional wellbeing, I was filled, heart and soul, with an overwhelming gratitude to God for his mercy in sparing the life of my child.

Pastor Sam's sermon on the purposes in life's suffering seemed like it was custom prepared for me. For over a year I had pondered the tragedy that had struck my family. James was thirty-one when he died. His life had flared brief and bright, then was snuffed out in one final blaze. Why did it happen? I had never wondered, Why me? So many of my friends in Nigeria had endured great suffering, I could merely ask, "Why not me?" But understanding that God had a purpose in everything that passed through my life, was a different thing than knowing what it meant. I still needed an answer to that.

Sam spoke of God's great power to use even the worst things in our lives for our good and his glory. He asked a few people in the congregation to read verses that assure us God is with us in our pain.

Beside me, Rose read from a psalm: "'You number my wanderings; Put my tears into Your bottle; Are they not in Your book?'" The poignancy of this woman standing beside me affirming these trusting words caught at my heart. She had lost, and recovered a loss, and still suffered. A droplet leaked out the corner of her closed eye, yet she hugged the Bible to her when she sat down.

Others read about how the prayers of God's people are incense, precious to God, stored and accumulated throughout the ages.

"It is our job to trust God with our suffering, even if he never tells us why," Sam resounded.

I felt like he was looking right at me when he said it.

It was not for us, Sam went on, to know what God's purpose was in our lifetime. He had a grand plan that spanned human history and beyond. Our brains were too puny to comprehend how everything would be woven together for our good and his glory. His assurance gave my heart a greater foothold to keep trusting.

Later we shared the noon meal with them. Dad was game to try even the hottest of their spicy dishes, though they sent him into predictable fits of coughing.

I did what I could to help with cleanup afterward, not wanting to let Anya far from my sight. She was adorable in the little peach floral outfit Lissa had bought her, even though it fit on the loose side. I swelled with pride as she concentrated on bringing one dish at a time to the women who were washing up. The aunties all made much of her, praising her good work, but still she did not smile in return.

As we opened our umbrellas to leave the church, Pastor Sam reminded me of the thing I'd been both dreading and longing to do.

"Would you like to visit the cemetery now?"

I nodded, choking up. We drove there in silence. When we arrived, I stalled, remembering the last time I had been here. My head had been in a fog of incomprehension and confusion that day and the haze rolled over me once again as Sam, Judith, and my dad got out of the car.

"Why don't you go ahead," I said, pointing at Anya, asleep with her head in my lap. "If she wakes up, I'll join you."

Dad poked his head back into the vehicle. "We've got this one last chance. I think you'll regret it if you don't come with us."

I teetered on what seemed like the edge of a chasm of grief ahead. "You're right." I eased Anya's damp head off my lap and slipped out of the car, closing the door with a soft click.

The way I remembered it my family's plot was at the far end of the treed space. But in more than a year since the burial, many other graves had been added. Ahead of Dad and me, our friends' yellow umbrella stopped. This was it. The headstone had not been placed until after I returned to Canada, but Sam had had it made to my exact specifications. I knelt in front of the grave marker with the name *James Dae-Jung Min* carved in unyielding, permanent stone. The finality of it made me shudder. Then I gasped. Beneath his name were the names of our daughters. *Josie Aera Min* and *Anya Jin-Ae Min*. Two names.

With a shaking finger, I traced Anya's etched name.

"We will have them grind that one away, Ma," Sam assured me, patting my back.

I lingered after the three of them wandered back to the car, feeling somehow that I should communicate with my loved ones here. But James and Josie were not here, where I felt nothing of them. My memories of them were all elsewhere, in the land of the living. And in some other dimension, I knew they were alive still. *He is not the God of the dead but of the living.* I rose, eager to get back to Anya, whom I now had with me in warm and living colour.

Despite the long pre-dawn ride from Jos to Lagos, Anya travelled well, holding my hand when we were in lineups in the terminal, waiting patiently while we checked our baggage and answered questions. But I almost wished she would raise a fuss like some of the other children around us. Her unnatural soberness caused me increasing worry.

I was thankful there were no holdups at customs, and we settled into our seats on the plane, already weary. I let Anya sit at the window so she could see the buildings and vehicles below us grow tinier as we ascended. She watched but said nothing, and soon fell asleep.

In Toronto airport, we walked the long corridors heading for customs. Part of me longed to take Anya to see her grandmother Min, but I'd already decided not on this trip. Relieved to be on Canadian soil again, I wouldn't be able to fully relax until we had Anya home. She clung to me now and it occurred to me that she might be finding the sight of so many white people strange.

We had just emerged from the restroom when I felt Anya's hand slip out of mine. My heart skipped a beat. In this crowd, I might never find her again.

"Anya!" I elbowed past the large couple ahead of me, murmuring an *excuse me.* "Dad, she's gone!"

Panic flooded my gut. *Why hadn't I carried her instead of making her walk?* We both searched the area frantically. Dad found a security guard to ask for help.

Only a couple of minutes later, Dad yelled, "Over there!" He pointed to a bistro on the left side of the wide corridor where two brightly clad African men drank coffee at a high table. Anya was clinging to the long leg of the thin man in blue even as he stood staring down at her in surprise, awkwardly patting her head.

We rushed in and I snatched my daughter from him.

"*Uba! Uba!*" she cried, reaching both arms out, not to me but to the man.

This cut me to the quick. When I lifted her and she noticed his face, she buried hers in my shoulder. But not before I glimpsed her expression of overwhelming confusion and distress. I stroked her back to reassure her, a cauldron of emotion boiling inside me, too.

"We're sorry to disturb you," Dad said to the man.

"Not at all. How does she know the Hausa word for Papa?" he asked with a smile, sliding back onto his chair. "Too bad I have no peppermints to give her. Maybe someday I will have a little girl like that, but not yet." His companion laughed.

On the last leg of the journey home I pondered this interchange. On one hand, I was thrilled to hear her voice again, and know that she could speak. On the other hand, it was not English she had spoken. Her mother tongue was now a Nigerian language. And what I couldn't get out of my mind was that Anya had mistaken a stranger for her papa. She'd reached for him desperately. It broke my heart realizing that to her, I was the stranger. For the first time, I wrestled with doubts about whether it was right for me to have taken her from a family with both a mother and a father.

"Do you think I'm doing the right thing bringing Anya home?" I asked my dad.

He must have dozed off because he gave a start. "Hm? What are you talking about?" He covered his face with both hands. "Of course you're doing the right thing. She's your daughter."

"But it seems obvious that she had a father and a mother with these people she was living with. A child needs both parents. All I can be to her is her mother." An image flashed through my mind of Ryan Hainstock holding the photo of my "little wee daughters", his eyes filling with tears. Why I should think of that now I had no idea.

"Stop with the guilt and self-doubt already, Lynnie. From what I've seen of your mother, you'll have to battle enough of it in the course of raising a child, without all this angst about getting her back." He shifted in his seat, trying for a less cramped position. "Have you forgotten it was the people that found her and kept her for a year who brought her to the police station? Don't you think it happened because God's hand was on them, prompting them to give her up? He can take care of what they're going through, too."

Chapter 43

For Ihsan, the road home from Jos was long and painful. His arms ached in their emptiness; the weight in his belly like a rock.

Pastor Monday's intermittent spurts of worthless conversation was even more unwelcome than it had been on the drive south.

When they had passed through the worst of the traffic and had driven the highway for an hour, his companion's running commentary made Ihsan snap.

"I do not care about the condition of the roads. The behavior of the police in Jos means nothing to me. I have lost my child, the light of my life. Let me grieve in peace."

This shut Monday's mouth. Many rutted, twilight miles passed in silence between them. Ihsan kept his eyes on the road in front of him. He dared not glance at the empty seat in the back. But not looking did not mean not thinking of Aminah. Images of the child paraded through his mind to torture him with longing. He saw the tears streaking through the black smudges on her face on the day he first found her, heard again her piteous cries. He felt her fragile but tenacious arms around his neck as he carried her home on his back, arms that later she would fling around him in joy when he returned home from pasturing the flock. Neither her prattled questions cast up to him nor her throaty giggles when he tossed her in the air would ever come again. How would he and Daniya bear the silence?

He turned his face to the darkening window to hide the moisture gathering in his eyes.

And what of Daniya herself? She would never forgive him for what he had done today. He had robbed a doting mother of her child, without warning or explanation. How could any woman forgive that? She would be frantic, perhaps even do herself harm. Would she revert to the miserable shell of the woman she had been before Aminah's coming? Of course she would. That would be his punishment.

Giving in to the village pressure and his own smothering fears and pangs of conscience had done nothing to shift the rock of anguish in his gut. He supposed he would bear the weight of it to his dying day.

The familiar outlines of the land showed they were nearing their village.

Monday turned to him, blurting out a sentence that must have wanted to escape his lips for a long time. "You will have the memories of her in here always." He pounded his chest with his fist.

Ihsan grunted. He knew the Christian was offering comfort, trying to understand. But to Ihsan, Monday was the face of all the villagers who had shown their disapproval and urged him to turn the child in. His anger had nowhere to land other than on the man next to him. A man who had always made mild suggestions, never pressured. Who not only had taken time and trouble to borrow a car and make the trip with Ihsan but had supported him in dealing with the police. And so, Ihsan said nothing.

In the semi-darkness, he sensed the pastor eying him.

"You can rest now. You know you did the right thing. That pastor knew the child."

Ihsan recalled the look of shock on Sam Likita's face when his gaze landed on Aminah. It was true. The recognition was unmistakable. This was the one thing that had kept Ihsan from backing out of his resolve. The inner prompting he had experienced these last two months had been proven correct by Likita's reaction to the child. Though Ihsan and Monday had not been able to comprehend all of the large man's words, there was no mistaking the joy that burst out of his mouth. Aminah belonged to someone he knew there in Jos. This knowledge alone kept Ihsan's regrets at bay.

"He thought the child was dead," Monday went on, raising his eyebrows at Ihsan.

And now the child is dead to me. Now Daniya and I are to be bereaved.

"Think what it will mean to the mother," the pastor said, smiling. "A loved one come back to life."

"But it is a death to us."

"And yet the mother has known that pain. More than the death of one child, she lost her husband and two children." Monday paused, his hands fidgeting on the steering wheel.

Was grief a game about who had suffered the most? If it was, there could be no winner. Ihsan wished the man would quit talking.

"There is someone else who knows the pain of the death of a child."

When he did not continue, Ihsan was forced to ask, "Who?"

"God."

Ihsan snorted. "What does Allah know of such pain?"

"God watched his only son die. Not just that, but he gave his beloved son to pay the price for my sin."

"Allah has no son."

"The God of the Bible does."

Ihsan had no answer to this. He simply wanted to sink down into the pain in his heart and hear no more. If some god had offered his son in place of sinners, it was not the Allah he knew. He was alone in his sorrow, and he had yet to face his wife.

Daniya had spent the day between jagged bouts of crying and furious rampages about the house. At first, she nursed the faint hope that Ihsan would return soon, perhaps saying he only meant to take Aminah for a ride with him. But as the day wore on, she knew he was doing the wicked deed. This set off another lengthy storm of weeping.

Uma came to the door, but Daniya kept to her bed, ignoring the knocking until her sister-in-law went away.

Lying in the dark, stifling bedroom, her throat raw from sobbing, Daniya felt the old veil of grayness settle on her. The weighty mantle of depression had covered her during the years before Aminah had come to fill their life with colour. Her insides twisted in despair, bringing on dry heaves. Daniya rushed out the door to vomit into the mud beyond the house. She had not eaten all day and only a foul-tasting liquid spilled out of her. Her hands shook as she wiped her mouth on the edge of her sleeve, then noticed a pair of wide feet standing next to her.

When she raised her eyes, she found a woman in a turquoise dress with matching *gele* wrapped around her head standing before her.

"I am Maryam, Pastor Monday's wife." She smiled and shifted the basket she carried from her head to one hip. "Come now, into the house." She placed a sturdy arm around Daniya's waist and guided her inside where she set the basket on the table. "You are sorrowful today, I know. Monday told me where they were going this morning."

Daniya shook her head, sitting on a kitchen chair before she collapsed from weakness.

"You have eaten nothing?"

"No."

"I have brought you some good, hot groundnut soup. We will get that into you, and you will feel much better." Maryam bustled into the kitchen, pulling containers and packages out of her basket and laying them on the table. She exuded efficiency and good cheer as she looked around for bowls and spoons and set them out. She paused to pray over the food, then nodded at Daniya. "First we eat. Then we can talk."

The aroma of the steaming soup woke Daniya's empty belly. She spooned up a thick, golden spoonful, savouring the tender beef and enjoying the sweet-spicy flavor. "It is very good."

Maryam nodded, her eyes twinkling in response as she swallowed. "I always say, keep stirring so that it does not burn. No one likes burnt soup." She laughed and went on eating.

When they finished, Maryam placed a hand on Daniya's arm. "*Oya*, tell me what your heart says."

Her gentle, motherly presence made Daniya cover her face with her hands. "He took my baby," she began, pouring out her heart to Maryam.

The pastor's wife scooted her chair next to Daniya, wrapping her arm around her and making comforting sounds.

When Daniya's tears were once again spent, she peered down at Maryam through blurred eyes. "I am pregnant."

The woman bounced happily with a wide smile. "But this is wonderful! Hallelujah! You will have a child after all. When?"

"In August, I think." Daniya felt a small surge of enthusiasm at the thought. Maryam was the first person she had shared the news with and it was gratifying to receive such a joyful reaction.

"Only four months." Maryam glanced at Daniya's rounding middle. "Now Ma, do you have any baby things? We have a few months to get you ready."

We? Was she saying the Christians would help?

Maryam sat with her for several hours, leaving briefly to visit an older lady who was ill. When she returned she found some vegetables and the few remaining *puff-puff* that Daniya had held back and they ate again. Maryam was easy to talk to and Daniya confided her many pregnancy losses to her.

"All this sadness you carried alone?" She shook her head, squeezing Daniya's arm. "Come to me any time. You know where we live, next to the church. I must go now but I will visit again. We will be praying for you. And when will you share the good news with your husband?"

Daniya clamped her lips together, bitterness rising inside her again. "When I am ready."

"Ah, Ma, do not hold a grudge. Do you think he wanted to give up his little girl? No, no. He is hurting too." Maryam leaned forward capturing Daniya's eyes with her intense gaze. "Tell him. Give him some hope in this sad-sad time."

When Maryam left, it was already dark and Ihsan had not yet arrived home.

Daniya felt keenly the absence of her usual nighttime routine with Aminah. It was a simple matter now to prepare for bed and, as she lay there waiting for Ihsan, she thought over Maryam's words. Part of her wanted to hold tight to her resentment, yet she couldn't escape the pastor's wife's sensible advice. And there was the new baby to think of. Did he or she not deserve to live in a home without strife? She sighed and as she did so, she heard the rumble of a vehicle outside their gate. She heard voices, heard Ihsan's stealthy movements as he came into the house. For the first time it occurred to her that he might dread facing her. It gave her a sense of power, making her wish he would suffer. Yet knowing he, too, grieved made it easier to let her anger fall away.

In the days that followed, several of the village Christians brought food or stopped for a sympathetic chat. Daniya's heart softened, too, as she saw plenty of evidence of Ihsan's grief. She noted it when he fingered his prayer rug that Aminah had always brought him, or in his wistful glance at the empty floor at the side of their bed. One day, after they had finished a meal brought to them by Fanique, of all people, the woman who had insulted Aminah in the marketplace, Daniya felt her husband's eyes on her. He was watching her middle, which by now was unmistakably rounded. She smiled at him and drew near, placing his hand on her belly.

The little one obliged with a tiny kick that made Ihsan snatch back his hand and stare at her in shock. He raised his eyebrows and a slow smile spread across his face.

"Yes." She grinned at him. "This one is strong. He will live."

Chapter 44

All the way, my Saviour leads me
What have I to ask beside?
Can I doubt His tender mercy,
Who through life has been my Guide?
~All the Way My Savior Leads Me, by Fanny J. Crosby, 1829-1915

Waking at home the next morning, I reached over to the right side of my bed, expecting to find Anya. My breath caught in my throat. Again, the spot was empty. I popped upright, adrenaline surging. There she was, on the floor next to the bed, curled in a ball on the sheepskin. I sagged in relief. Loss had left me with deep scars. Would every minor event from now on become a crisis? *Lord, help me find balance.*

She opened her big, dark eyes, blinking at me.

"C'mon, honey, let's see what we can find for breakfast." First I took her to the bathroom, aware once more that someone else had toilet-trained her and I knew nothing of it. I had missed a crucial chunk of her life. Once more, I prayed, asking that loss and regret be replaced with gratitude. I pried Dolly out of her hands, then laid her to the side while I washed Anya's hands. I brushed her short hair and handed her a washcloth. "Now you wash Dolly's face."

Anya stared at me, immobile.

I demonstrated scrubbing the wooden face with the cloth wrapped around my index finger. Anya kept a close watch but made no move to copy me.

Sighing, I led her out to show her the living area of the cabin.

"What do you think of your new home, Anya?" Grasping both her small hands, I danced to and fro, then picked her up and swung her around. "Look up! It's round."

I pointed and she looked up and around, then back at me with a question in her eyes.

"That's right. Round!" I circled again, spreading out my hand as we whirled, then set her down. "Round." How I longed for her to respond.

Mom had stocked the fridge with fruit, yogurt, and muffins, but Anya ate little. It had been this way at Judith's too, as well as on the flight. She had little appetite. I told myself to be patient, that this was to be expected after a major upheaval like she had experienced. My own stomach was often unsettled these days.

Not wanting to bombard Anya with all things strange and new, we stayed home for the day. I wanted to get to know her and understand her needs, whether for food or play or rest.

I named the objects around us, repeating the words slowly and clearly. I told myself to expect nothing. Like a baby learning language for the first time, it would be slow and gradual, but it would come. When I showed her our family photo and the one of her and Josie, she took them in her own hands. I held my breath. She pointed to me in the picture and looked up at me.

"That's right, honey. Mommy." I pointed to the picture and patted my chest. "Mommy. Can you say Mommy?"

Nothing. But a glimmer of hope sparked in me that at least her looking to me was communicating. She didn't seem to need a nap and I wished I'd bought some books and toys. I had little to entertain Anya with, so I dressed her in the jacket we had bought her, and we headed to my parents' house.

When the door opened, Katie's piano playing blossomed out to greet us. My parents looked up from where they sat at the table, anticipation in their eyes. No doubt Mom had spent the day squelching every instinct to rush over to my place and wrap Anya in her arms. But neither of them made any sudden moves. We were all, it seemed, feeling our way with her carefully.

Except Katie. The piano came to an abrupt stop and Katie came barreling through from the living room with arms outstretched toward her niece, squealing, "Hey, sugar biscuit! Come to Auntie!" Before I could object, Katie had taken Anya into her arms and carted her off to the living room.

I started after her, worried that Anya would be overwhelmed.

Dad reached out a hand to stop me. "Leave them be. Let's just see how it goes." He pulled out a chair at the table for me. "She's not made of glass, you know. Kids can adapt."

I held my breath, listening to Katie exclaiming over toys in Mom's toy basket. I knew the holdovers from our childhood in its contents well. Wooden letter blocks, a few well-worn Disney puzzles, dolls, a fleet of small cars, and farm implements.

Mom looked at me with a grin. "I can't resist anymore. C'mon, let's take a peek."

We tiptoed to the door, keeping out of sight and watching. Anya sat spellbound by Katie's vivacious puppet rendition of Tigger's bouncy, clowncy tail. Next my sister whisked Anya onto the piano bench beside her and commenced a rousing chorus of "Heart and Soul," encouraging Anya to plunk along. And she did it, tentatively at first, then with increasing vigour. I was thrilled to see her entering the fun, but a wee bit jealous, too.

"There's less at stake for Katie than there is for you," Mom whispered, intuiting my thoughts in her uncanny way.

"Can you see Anya's face? I'm waiting for a smile."

"No, I can't. But don't worry, it'll come."

Supper with my parents and Katie went so well that I let Mom persuade me to bring Anya to church the next day. I was apprehensive about it being too much too soon, but she seemed unfazed by meeting the family.

I suspected Mom must have cautioned people ahead of time about swarming us, because old friends and family offered happy waves from a distance, letting us find a seat in peace. I was amazed when Nanny came to sit in our pew and raised my eyebrows at Lance who had brought her. When was the last time she had joined us in church?

At the close of the service, the pastor announced a potluck in honour of Anya's homecoming. Afterward, the men worked on clean-up while the women gathered to sit in a circle around me.

The pastor's wife claimed their attention. "I know many of you need to get your kids home for naps, but Lynnie, we all wanted to take some time to celebrate with you and express our love to you and little Anya. If there's anyone who would like to say a few words to welcome Anya, feel free."

After a moment of silence, Nanny clapped her hands together and giggled. "Well now, you may not know me, but I'm Lynnie's nanny. Anyone can tell you that I'm not one for making speeches. But I want to say to Lynnie that I'm so proud of how you've coped with everything that's happened. You've sailed through beautifully.

"There are always the sad sacks who will want to bring you down." Her eyes strayed for a second toward where Grandma sat, then refocused on me. "But I hope I've been your best cheerleader, encouraging you to keep on the sunny side of life. And look what thinking positive has done. You've got your sweet little Anya back. Another great-grandchild for me to spoil!" The way she rubbed her hands in anticipation made the women laugh. "You be sure to bring her to Nanny's house anytime for treats from my junk cart."

Then Grandma stood and cleared her throat. In a second, quiet descended on the room.

Lissa elbowed me, whispering, "You think she learned that in teacher training?"

"Shh," I whispered, holding back a smile.

"Before Evelyn and James left for Africa," Grandma began, "I asked her if she was prepared for what they were getting into. She told me they were aware of the dangers, but having prayed about it, they were ready to face whatever the Lord had in store for them. Along with many of you, I prayed for them every day. Then last February, when I heard the terrible news from Nigeria, my heart broke for Evelyn. She has been called to suffer a painful loss, but I never imagined the possibility that one of the children might survive." A look of wistful wonder crossed her face, as though, braced for the worst life could offer, she couldn't conceive of God being able to surprise her with his goodness.

"The Bible tells us that God is a consuming fire, not to be trifled with. He spoke to Moses through a burning bush. And he has spoken to us through the Min family tragedy. But how are we to understand such a hard thing? We try in vain to unscrew the inscrutable ways of God.

"The prophet Malachi compared Him to a refiner and purifier of silver. In my reading, I learned that a silversmith has a special purpose in applying heat to a lump of ore. He hovers over it, watching that it never gets too hot, and that it never remains in the fire too long. His purpose is not to destroy or damage the ore. He stays with it, even suffering the heat himself, until at last he can see his own reflection in the precious metal."

Grandma turned to me, her eyes brimming. "We see this in you, Evelyn. Your unwavering faith and courage reflect the goodness and faithfulness of God, reminding us that we can trust him, even in the painful trials of our lives." She sat down to a reverent silence.

I gulped, barely able to maintain control. Her words were almost like the commendation of God himself. There was no question that God had been with me through the fire. I thought of my many moments of doubt and fear and despair, amazed and thankful that anyone could see beyond them, let alone be helped by me.

After a few moments, the pastor's wife spoke up again. "We're all so thrilled your daughter has come back to you that we wanted to offer you a few things we thought she might need." She beckoned toward the kitchen, and two grinning young girls strolled toward me pulling a tote full of gifts. They were followed by another pair and then two more. I was moved to tears by the heaps of presents before me and tried to hide my face behind Anya, asleep in my arms.

"Have at it," Lissa said, reaching for a pink glittery gift bag from the nearest pile. She helped me open them, one after another, lovely expressions of joy and support. There were clothes and shoes, even a swimsuit and towel, toys and books—everything Anya would need for at least the next couple of years. Later, as the crowd disbursed, stopping beside me to extend well-wishes and pat Anya's head, a deep joy settled into me. With this family of faith surrounding me, I would not face the future alone.

Chapter 45

Teach me some melodious sonnet
Sung by flaming tongues above
Praise the mount—I'm fixed upon it—
Mount of Thy redeeming love.
~Come, Thou Fount, by Robert Robinson, 1735-1790

I revelled in the vocation I was designed for, my role as a mom. I was glad to shelve my academics, secure in the knowledge I could pick up where I left off in a few years once Anya was in school.

Through the summer, I planned daily activities for Anya to develop her language skills. Over time, she began naming things. I was proud of her perfect enunciation of anything she did say. We read books and played games. I limited screen time so we could interact with real people, with nature, and with the merciful God who had brought us together.

Getting to know the young moms from my church, I easily and quickly became one of them. We went to playgrounds and took our kids riding the neighbours' ponies. A couple of times, Lissa and I spent the day with our kids, floating down the river in inflatable rafts. Anya, dwarfed by her life jacket, was ultra-cautious of the water but Jade and Dylan soon had her willing to jump in with them. She knew them now and her eyes lit up whenever she saw them, but still, no smile.

The day we visited the zoo and Anya repeated after me the word "elephant" was a red-letter day. I knew she understood far more than her limited language revealed, and gradually she was adding vocabulary. But still, she did not call me mommy. Nor did she reach for me or give me a spontaneous hug or kiss. Had her foster family not shown affection? The thought of a year in a small child's life without demonstrations of love ached inside me.

I introduced her to all the fun of growing up on a farm. Kittens delighted her and she handled them with tenderness. Jade and Dylan and I taught her how to climb the stacks of small hay bales. Dad took her for short jaunts on the tractor. When Mom and I took her raspberry picking, her small bucket remained empty, but her face and hands turned a deep crimson. She loved them and pointed to the fridge whenever I made toast for her, expecting the raspberry jam I had made with her help.

Occasionally, clues to her missing past would surface. One weekend, my family joined in on our church campout. Someone had set up a petting zoo on Saturday afternoon, featuring miniature donkeys, potbellied pigs, alpacas, and peacocks. I couldn't catch up to her when she spied a pen full of pygmy goats and raced toward it.

She stopped at the fence and reached through it, shouting, "*Awaki! Awaki!*" It was only the second time she had used an African word.

"*Awaki,*" I said, crouching beside her.

She turned her face to me with a grave expression.

"*Awaki.*" I said again. "Goat."

With a firm nod, she said, "*Awaki.*" But before she followed a couple of other children through the gate into the pen, I heard her say more quietly, "Goat."

As I watched her stroking the animals and offering feed pellets, a shadow blocked out the bright sunlight to my left. I turned to find Ryan Hainstock leaning against the fence beside me, watching the kids with a grin on his face.

"I didn't see you here yesterday when everyone pulled in," I said, straightening to join him at the fence. "Did you just get here?"

He gazed down at me for a moment before answering. "Yeah. My dad wanted me to finish baling the last forty acres." He smiled again, inclining his head toward Anya running in circles after the goats. "She's a natural with them, isn't she? Sure is amazing how she could have survived. And even more incredible that you got her back. I guess that's one of those things that only God could have done."

At that moment, Anya tripped and fell flat on her belly. Before I could move, Ryan vaulted the fence and raced toward her. He scooped her up and ran back to me with her. Her head was tipped back, and she opened her mouth wide, but no sound came out.

The pulse in my throat started thudding as I took her in my arms. "Breathe, honey, breathe!" For long seconds, fear flashed across her eyes as she struggled for air. Then I heard the whoosh as her chest filled and she let out a loud wail.

"She's going to be fine," Ryan murmured, stroking her little back. His large hand almost covered it crosswise.

I nodded, unable to speak past the lump in my throat. In moments, Anya wanted to be up and running with the other children. I swiped the dust off her face and clothes and forced myself to let her go.

"I want to hang on tight, protecting her from every possible danger," I mumbled, staring after her.

"I figured," Ryan said. "But you know she'd only grow to hate that, right?"

"Yeah."

"My dad never even let me light a candle on a birthday cake."

I glanced at him, curious. "Why not?"

He shook his head. "One night when I was six, our house burnt down. My mom died saving us boys."

So, I'd been right. His was the family where that had happened. I made a sympathetic sound.

My niece stepped up beside me. "Can Anya come with my friends and me to the playground? We're going to play grounders. Don't worry, we'll take good care of her."

"Okay." I smiled, acting like I was at ease with this.

Anya took Jade's hand and off they went.

"Good job." Ryan half-smiled.

"I didn't think I was that obvious."

"I read your face. Being open and honest is a good thing. Too many game players in this world."

I looked at him. "I take it you've met your share of them?"

He glanced around at the noisy kids and parents. "We could take a walk."

I hesitated, thinking of James, then scolded myself for over-thinking. It was just a walk. "Sure."

We followed the sandy path away from the petting zoo and through the towering evergreens toward the lake. I stuck my hands in the pockets of my shorts, relishing the pine fragrance.

"Game players?" I asked.

"Yeah." He went quiet. "You said you'd like to hear my story sometime. I figured now was as good a time as any."

We strolled past the playground where Jade was pushing Anya on a swing, teaching her to pump.

"I guess you remember that I was...a bit of a carouser and rabble rouser in high school."

"Mm-hm."

"Well, it went downhill from there when I got a job on the oil rigs. Worked there for twelve years. The money was great, but on my weeks off it was party time. All that time I made over six figures a year and nothing much to show for it."

"But you're not still working there. What made you quit?"

"I was getting to that. I quit to come farming with my dad when I realized it wasn't work on the rigs that was the problem, it was the time off. Things ended up getting real dicey last fall, in a fight over a woman. Let's just say, shots were fired."

"Whoa, that sounds pretty serious."

"Oh, not by me," he added when he saw my eyes bug out. "But it was a near miss, so close that it shook me up. I couldn't get out of my mind the fact that I'd escaped death by a hair. I knew I wasn't ready to die. Made me break out in a sweat every time I thought about it. My Auntie Patty used to teach me and my brothers about facing our Creator and it scared the... it scared me real bad. I knew my life was a mess. The other thing I couldn't get out of my mind was what she'd told me about you the last time I talked to her.

"Losing my mom pretty much turned my dad, my brothers and me into alcoholics. But here you were after losing your whole family, going to school so you could help other people. Made me ashamed of myself. That kind of faith spoke to me loud and clear." He stopped and sat down on a rock looking out over the lake.

I sat on the one next to his, pondering this. It felt strange to think people were talking about me. But even more strange was that the worst thing that had ever happened to me had lit a path to Jesus for someone I didn't know. Could the death of my loved ones ever equal the salvation of one soul? I choked on the math, recoiling. It couldn't be that simple. But was it up to me to do that kind of figuring? Wasn't God big enough to look after it all? I couldn't deny that he had proved himself trustworthy in my life every step of the way.

"So I called Auntie Patty again," Ryan went on, "blubbering away about how I needed whatever it was you two both had. She told me to get in touch with a pastor. So I did. Pastor Bowen explained what Jesus did to pay the price for my sin and it all finally clicked. It was an incredible relief to know that the filth inside me could be scrubbed clean and I could start fresh. I can't get over it and I hope I never do. These days, all I want to do is listen to sermon podcasts and live for Christ." He grinned at me. "That's something, eh?"

"It sure is. It's encouraging to hear and I'm really glad for you." I smiled at him.

"I just wanted you to know you've made a huge difference in my life. But you probably want to get back to check on your little wee girl, right?" He stood and started back on the path.

There. He called her my "little wee girl" again. I liked that.

As we walked, he described some of the ways his thinking was changing because of what he was learning from the Bible.

I liked his enthusiasm for the faith and was surprised at the depth of his understanding, for someone so new to it. He seemed to have an insatiable thirst for learning and, much like the way James used to do, he quoted verse after verse of scripture to me.

We had come out of the woods into the clearing where the playground stood. Some distance ahead of us, Jade and her friends must have given up on their game because they were now walking the path back to the group campsite, teasing and giggling. I smiled to see Anya lagging, distracted by a patch of nodding bluebells in the shade off the path. When she looked up, the older kids had disappeared around the bend. It wrung my heart to see her searching around in distress, thinking she was alone. Did it bring back the terror she must have felt when her daddy and sister were killed and she was left in a wasteland, alone? Was this the mercy that God felt when he watched me rampage through the Jos marketplace the day I got the terrible news?

I broke into a run, Ryan right behind me. He got to her first and picked her up, but when she caught sight of me over his shoulder, she struggled. Reaching out her arms to me, she cried out what I had been yearning to hear, the sweetest sound on earth.

"Mommy! Mommy!"

I couldn't take her into my arms fast enough. My heart did somersaults. Tears of joy and relief spurted from my eyes as I breathed comfort in her ear. Holding her close and swaying back and forth, I lifted my face to Heaven, sending up a flare of grateful praise.

For the first time since her homecoming, Anya wanted me, needed me. She was mine again. Anya was home at last.

Glossary

Assalamu alaikim – greeting in northern Nigerian language, Hausa

Awaki – goat (Hausa)

Dash –bribe

Gele - African woman's headwrap

Gist – gossip

Groundnuts – peanuts

Ibrahim – Abraham

Ismael – Abraham's son Ishmael, as told in the Quran

Jinn – evil spirit

Jollof Rice – a popular Nigerian rice dish cooked with spices and vegetables

Khimar – waist-length headcovering worn by African Muslim women

Kosai – fried black-eyed pea mash

Kufi – flat, brimless cap worn by African Muslim men

Musa – the prophet Moses

Oya - So; Now then

Puff-puff – fried dough made with yeast, like doughnuts

Ramadan – Muslim month of daytime fasting and feasting after sundown

STEM – Science, Technology, Engineering, Mathematics fields of study

Suya – spicy meat grilled on a skewer

Uba – Daddy (Hausa)

Wa-Alaikim Assalaam – response to greeting

Dear Reader

Even a brief reading of church history will be a bloody tale. More Christians were martyred for their faith in the twentieth century than in the previous nineteen centuries put together, and the twenty-first century is shaping up to match that dreadful record.

In 2014, the world was shaken by news that 276 schoolgirls, mostly Christian, had been abducted from Chibok school in northern Nigeria by Boko Haram. Some managed to escape only to be betrayed and returned to the kidnappers. More than 100 others were released through a government-negotiated trade. But 112 are still in captivity. And these abductions and forced marriages occur frequently in certain countries where Christians are in the minority. And thousands of Christians in Nigeria have been killed for their faith in recent years in what some call genocide.

It's difficult to read of the pain and loss of our precious Christian brothers and sisters around the world, but to do so is vital. As we pray for them in their suffering, they are encouraged to stand firm and God answers by meeting their needs. At the same time, by their stories we are strengthened in our faith and certainty that Jesus is worth it all.

It's also essential that we have a clear understanding of God's purposes in suffering, sometimes as discipline to form Christ's character in us, sometimes as a testing of our faith, and always for

His glory and our good. How would we know the truth of the gospel if the apostles had not died gruesome and terrible deaths rather than recant their belief in Christ? How do we know Christianity is not merely a convenient and pleasant social construct if we are unwilling to suffer for it? How can we know we are not merely God's fair-weather friends if our Christian life is always sunshine and roses?

I pray that Lynnie's story will encourage you to cling close to Jesus in your own suffering, pray for the persecuted church around the world, and trust His kind providence on whatever path He takes you.

Grace be with you,

Eleanor

Pray for the persecuted church:

https://www.opendoors.org/en-US/

Voice of the Martyrs - https://www.persecution.com/

Acknowledgments

My first thanksgiving goes to the Lord, who brought me to Himself at a young age and has allowed me to live in freedom and safety for so long.

I owe unceasing gratitude to the giants of the faith on whose shoulders I stand—martyrs, teachers, and obscure, faithful Christians, down through millennia, who walked with Jesus and passed the gospel on until it came to me.

Thank you to Sara Davison, Janice L. Dick, Deb Elkink, and Carol Harrison, all extraordinary writers, who took time to offer their invaluable help and encouragement on the manuscript. I am indebted to Ebosereme Nwamu for her first-hand knowledge of Nigerian life and culture. My thanks to Erin Leschert, for the resources and insight on current social work academia, to retired social worker, Gail Peterson, for her stories and helpful encouragement, and to Janet Seever for sharing her knowledge of Bible translation work.

I'm especially grateful to belong to the Mosaic Collection of authors who teach and laugh and pray with me in this writing life.

Also by Eleanor Bertin

The Ties that Bind series:
Lifelines
Unbound
Tethered
Pall of Silence: My Journey from Tragedy to Trust
For more from this author, go to
www.eleanorbertinauthor.com
We hope you enjoyed reading *A Flame of Mercy*. If
you did, please consider leaving a short review on
Amazon, Goodreads, or BookBub.
Positive reviews and word-of-mouth recommendations count as
they honor an
author and help other readers to find quality Christian fiction to
read.
Thank you so much!
If you'd like to receive information on new releases and writing
news,
please subscribe to *Grace & Glory*,
Mosaic's monthly newsletter.

Next from Mosaic

Through the Lettered Veil

by Candace West-Posey

Not all wars are fought on a battlefield. Some are fought in the heart.

Aynsley O'Brien faces a choice—follow her deceased uncle's demands or fall prey to a ruthless band of brothers whose sights are set on Windy Hollow Farm. Without protection, she will lose it all.

Union Cavalry officer, Nolan Scottsdale arrives in the Ozarks to find his family ravaged by the war. Unwelcome at home, he turns to Windy Hollow needing work but finds Aynsley cornered. If he offers his hand in marriage, she may break his heart again.

The entire valley will be embroiled in yet another conflict if Nolan and Aynsley lose the farm. And it won't be the North and the South – It will be neighbor against neighbor. While dangers erupt on every front, another war rages in their hearts. If they win the peace, how will they mend the breach between their families? Between themselves?

The truth lies in three letters. If only Aynsley could read them.

pre-order: http://bit.ly/MosaicVeil